"How are you?"

"In shock. Can't imagine not seeing her again."

Her chest felt tight. This couldn't be fixed. That acknowledgment devastated her all over again.

Marissa heard a creak outside her door and she tensed. Kit or Griffin might be checking on her. Or was Jack patrolling her town house for security issues? Several seconds of silence passed.

She heard another creak.

"I have to go. Talk soon." She sent the message and squeezed her eyes closed. The noises were the house settling. She was safe.

Marissa felt a hand on her arm. She opened her eyes and came face-to-face with a man she didn't recognize.

Before she could scream, he clamped his hand over her mouth, pushing her back into her pillow, pressing her hard into the mattress. Her heart thundered and she tried not to panic. Pushing at his hand, she couldn't get his weight off her. He would suffocate her!

* * *

Dear Reader,

Marissa Walker was introduced in *Delta Force Desire* (Harlequin Romantic Suspense, June 2016). Marissa is a supermodel, and while she is used to being judged on her appearance, she longs for someone to see there is more to her than photographs and fashion.

As an operative for the West Company, Jack Larson deals with difficult problems on a daily basis. Watching over Marissa as a favor to a colleague should be easy. Keeping Marissa safe from a killer means staying out of the limelight, but with a woman like Marissa, her well-known face and beauty are noticed everywhere they go. Even Jack finds himself falling under her spell.

Jack and Marissa discover their initial impressions of each other are wrong. There is much to learn when they look closer with open hearts and minds.

I hope you enjoy this adventure with the West Company!

Best,

C.J. Miller

www.cj-miller.com

ESCORTED BY THE RANGER

C.J. Miller

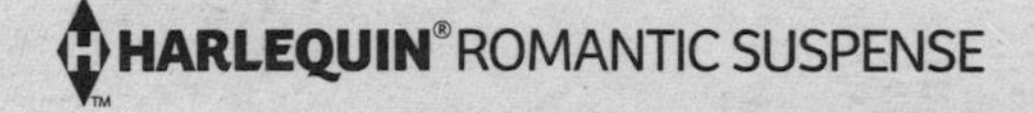

Recycling programs
for this product may
not exist in your area.

ISBN-13: 978-0-373-40215-1

Escorted by the Ranger

This edition published by arrangement with Harlequin Books S.A.

For questions and comments about the quality of this book, please contact us at CustomerService@Harlequin.com.

Printed in U.S.A.

C.J. Miller loves to hear from her readers and can be contacted through her website, www.cj-miller.com. She lives in Maryland with her husband and three children. C.J. believes in first loves, second chances and happily-ever-after.

Books by C.J. Miller

Harlequin Romantic Suspense

Hiding His Witness
Shielding the Suspect
Protecting His Princess
Traitorous Attraction
Under the Sheik's Protection
Taken by the Con
Capturing the Huntsman
Delta Force Desire
Special Forces Seduction
Escorted by the Ranger

The Coltons of Texas

Colton's Texas Stakeout

Conspiracy Against the Crown

The Secret King
Guarding His Royal Bride

The Coltons: Return to Wyoming

Colton Holiday Lockdown

Visit the Author Profile page at Harlequin.com, or www.cj-miller.com, for more titles.

To my husband, for his love and support of
every book and in everything.

Chapter 1

Glittering, colored lights lined the black shiny runway and music pulsed low through the air. The exceptional talent and star-studded audience were assembled for a fantastic show. Fashion designer Declan Ambrose's safari-themed fall and winter line was making its debut in New York and Marissa Walker was first on the runway.

Marissa checked her hair and makeup in the backstage lit mirror. She enjoyed the drama of the event and the clothing she'd be modeling. The anticipation around her was palpable. She had been modeling for fifteen years and this was the capstone to her runway career. Though she hadn't told anyone outside her agent, this was her last live show. She was one of the oldest models here and while many in the industry respected her professionalism and fashion sense, she wanted to retire at the top and with dignity, not be forced out by younger, thinner models. Her plans for the future were simple: travel and enjoy the sights, paint and relax, visit with family.

After working nearly every day for the last decade, she had earned a break.

Marissa recognized most of the people gathered backstage and in the audience and felt a pang of sentimentality. She'd miss this harried, busy world. Women and men she'd modeled with in the past, the cast and crew from popular television series and movies, Broadway actors and actresses, and investors and businessmen and women in couture outfits talking, networking and enjoying themselves.

Marissa caught a glimpse of her ex-boyfriend Rob in the mirror. She looked away, avoiding eye contact. After their drama-filled six-month-long relationship, she didn't want to see or talk to him. He could be sweet and attentive one day, dismissive and cold the next and who knew what she would get today. Sticking out the relationship with Rob even six months had been her attempt to prove she could make a long-term relationship work. The tabloids had been vicious about her recent dating history: a handful of dates with a series of men which hadn't turned into anything. Being seen out with a new man every few weeks had gotten embarrassing.

Rob was likely looking for Avery who was also modeling today. Let Rob and Avery have each other. Marissa couldn't revisit those emotions, especially not when Ambrose was counting on her to be fresh-faced and energetic for his show. Thinking of Rob and Avery exhausted her.

"Looking great, Marissa," Clarice said, slapping her high five with her right hand as she passed by, her left arm clutching a clipboard. Her straight blond hair fell down her back. The head-to-toe black she wore worked on her athletic figure.

Clarice was the backstage assistant for the show. She and Marissa had worked together before and Marissa admired her attention to detail. With Clarice working the show, every model would be wearing the right outfits and shoes, hair done to Ambrose's specifications, makeup perfect, and walking out at the right time.

Ambrose would be the talk of the city for the next few days. Marissa had looked at some of his designs and they were good. Great even. Ambrose deserved this. He had started in New York City selling tourists handmade hats on street corners and worked his way to fashion fame. Scoring a showroom this week was a huge boon. Ambrose already had several offers for his clothing line to be sold in high-end department stores. This was Ambrose's night. Marissa had consulted with him on some of the early designs and fabrics, but Ambrose had stepped up his game this season. They would celebrate after the show with champagne toasts at a private party he had organized at a nearby hotel.

Marissa strode past the gold tables of makeup and mirrors and the silver racks of clothing. Ambrose was probably in his office, reviewing the order of the designs to be presented. His obsession with perfection had launched him as one of the most sought-after designers.

Marissa stopped short when she heard Avery's

voice. She was speaking quickly the way she did when she was upset. Though Marissa was excited about today's event, the pressure could put other models, designers and staff on edge.

Avery was standing thirty yards away, hand on her hip, gesturing with her other hand at someone as if making an important point. She was wearing five inch heels; Marissa recognized them at this distance because hers were similar. Avery's long blond hair was in waves down her back and her lithe frame alluded to how much time she spent in the gym. A pang of sadness struck. If they were still friends, they would be hanging out today, enjoying the show and attending the after-party together. They would have critiqued the clothes and discussed which were their favorites. Avoiding Rob was easy; Marissa had washed her hands of him. But Marissa couldn't dismiss Avery. To rebuild the relationship, she needed to speak with her, but her sense of betrayal ran deep.

Marissa turned around, avoiding Avery. She wasn't ready to talk with her, much less interrupt her heated conversation to initiate an awkward one.

Thirty minutes later, Marissa's adrenaline was still pumping from her walk down the runway. The design was fabulous and her shoes were spectacular. The printed dress was a blend of greens, orange, yellow and tan, the fabric giving a bubble shape to the hemline of the dress; and her shoe design inspired by hiking boots without the chunkiness. Marissa could sense the excitement from the crowd over Ambrose's designs.

She was changing into her next outfit, giddy at the

idea of taking another stroll down the runway. On her next dress, the print was leopard on the sides, the front and back were black, giving the dress a svelte and sleek appearance. Though retirement and travel could provide a different set of excitements, it would be hard to top this.

"Avery!" Clarice was looking at her clipboard, tapping her pen against the metal top and speaking into her headset. Marissa glanced around and didn't see her. Avery was hard to miss. Even among other models, she was tall with naturally white-blond hair.

"Find her! She needs to be on deck!" Clarice said.

The staff was looking for her and some of the models appeared disdainful. No one wanted a mistake at the show and timing was important.

Ambrose was watching the show from the catwalk on the other side of the stage. Though Marissa couldn't see him over the bright lights, he'd be wearing a slim pressed gray suit, crisp white shirt and carrying his cane with the tiny bronze alligator head mounted at the top. On his feet, the alligator boots he swore were his good luck charms. He would freak if the event skipped a model or a design. Marissa pictured his slender, clean-shaven face morphing into disgust and his brown eyes narrowing in frustration.

Marissa heard a scream and whirled around, teetering in her heels.

Another model was backing away from a rack of clothes, hand over her mouth, pointing at the fabric. A collective gasp rolled through the air. Marissa walked toward the gathered group, straining to see what the commotion was about.

The pulse of the music seemed to disappear. The

voices around her faded. Her eyes zeroed in on a horrifying sight.

Avery was slumped between a red gown and an orange one, her body twisted in an unnatural way. Bile rose in Marissa's throat and she inhaled to keep from getting sick. She took another deep cleansing breath and looked again, moving forward to help.

No one else was touching Avery. Marissa set her fingers on her neck, looking for a pulse. "Someone help me." Nausea struck her. Avery's blood was soaking the clothes on the rack, turning them red.

Shock and sadness consumed her. The rest of the room fell away and it was just her and Avery. Her heart raced and the blood rushing through her ears was deafening. She shook Avery's shoulders. "Avery, wake up! Avery?"

No response.

Marissa looked at the crowd. Some were on their phones, maybe calling for help. Clarice stepped forward, setting a hand on Marissa's arm, trying to pull her away. Marissa shook her off. Was that Rob in the crowd? She glanced at Avery and when she looked up again, Rob was gone. Or he might not have been there at all.

Clarice touched her shoulder. "The paramedics are coming."

The stillness of Avery's body was disturbing. Marissa turned her head and took several gulps of air. All around her, more shouting and crying.

The sound of ambulances split the air, but Marissa knew it was too late. Avery was gone.

The police precinct was loud and busy. Desks were crowded together and the lighting was dark and depressing. The floor felt matted with grime and Marissa tried not to touch anything as she sat in the folding metal chair inside one of the closet-sized offices. Her sister had flown in on a private plane to help her and Marissa was grateful. Before Kit had arrived, Marissa had been waiting alone in the office for well over three hours. Three hours was a long time to think and panic and worry, especially after one of the detectives had asked her about Rob and Avery. The nature of his questions and the suspicion on his face led her to believe she was a suspect.

The office belonged to someone named "Captain Sparky," which sounded like a nickname. Captain Sparky's desk was piled high with papers stuffed messily into manila envelopes and his trash can was overflowing with tissues.

"Marissa, focus. You need to tell me everything you remember," Kit said.

Marissa looked at her sister. "I've told you everything. I didn't do this to Avery. I wasn't involved in this."

Kit's face flooded with sympathy, her brown eyes bright with concern. Her dark ponytail swung over her shoulder as she leaned forward. "Griffin and I believe you."

Marissa looked over at the tall, brawny man currently on his phone, standing outside the office. Her sister's fiancé was a force to be reckoned with, but this situation was out of their control. Kit claimed she worked for a car company in their import department, but Marissa knew there was more to the story. Kit's offer to help with a murder investigation proved that.

"Someone had to have seen something." An event

like Ambrose's show was milling with people. No one was alone and there was no privacy. Everyone dressed and prepped in a rush to make the timing on the runway.

Kit pressed her hands together. "According to Rob, you're the person who knows something."

Indignation rose inside her. Rob had pointed the finger at Marissa as an enemy of Avery's. Marissa had had to explain that she had dated Rob and he'd cheated on her with Avery. The police hadn't accepted her brief answers. They'd wanted details and dates and names and exactly what had happened between the three of them. "Rob is an idiot. I didn't do this. I was on the runway and there were dozens of cameras in my face."

Marissa hadn't even spoken to Ambrose yet. He must have been devastated. He had lost a friend, and the show he had worked so hard for had been cut short. The attention and circumstances could work in his favor or it could destroy his sales. Depended how it was spun in the news.

Marissa had gone over the events of the day beginning from the time she had arrived at work, trying to recall if she had missed something or could think of some small detail that would help. With so many questions and doubts swirling around her, Marissa wished she could go home and bury her head in a bottle of merlot.

"Did you talk to Avery at the show?" Kit asked again.

Marissa shook her head. When she had overheard Avery speaking in the hallway, she hadn't lingered around to hear who she was talking to or the topic of the conversation.

"When you saw Avery, are you sure you don't know who she was speaking with?" Kit asked again.

Marissa hid her irritation at her sister's attempts to help. Avery could have been speaking with Rob or Ambrose or anyone at the show—a security guard, a stylist, a photographer, another model.

Kit glanced over at the police detectives speaking together. "The police are looking at you for this and we need to give them a reason to look elsewhere."

Marissa scrubbed her hands over her face. Her makeup felt sticky and she was beyond exhausted, her eyes gritty with fatigue. "I didn't kill Avery."

"She stole your boyfriend," Kit said.

A fact everyone repeated to her as if she had forgotten the incident. "I've told you. I was more hurt about her stabbing me in the back than about losing Rob. At some point, she and I would have buried the hatchet and become friends again." At her and Avery's level, with years of experience in the industry and countless mutual connections and friends, their paths would cross. Their years of friendship meant something and after Avery dumped Rob, it would be that much easier to renew the friendship.

Was Avery killed by someone jealous of her? By another designer looking to ruin Ambrose? Someone had to have witnessed the tragic event. "When the police collect the footage from the show, they'll piece together it wasn't me." One advantage to being a model was that she was in photographs and they would be her alibi.

Kit frowned. "I'll do everything I can for you. What reason would someone have to kill Avery? You were close with her. Was she into drugs or gambling or was she in debt to anyone?"

Marissa couldn't imagine Avery getting in over her head with drugs or gambling. She drank recreationally but Avery was in control. "I don't think so. She didn't want compromising pictures of her splashed across the media. That would have impacted her career."

Kit and Griffin exchanged glances from across the room. Marissa felt a twinge of envy at their silent communication. When they were together, Marissa could feel their connection, like they shared an unbreakable bond. Two divorces had showed Marissa she didn't have what it took to be part of an indivisible team. Her relationships moved fast and she too easily got swept away in something that wasn't real.

"Tell me again. Close your eyes. Picture the scene," Kit said.

Marissa did as her sister asked. She shivered, thinking of a killer lurking, waiting to attack Avery. Marissa told the story again. She tried to focus only on Avery's voice and who she might have been speaking with. Marissa came up empty. She had been worried about talking to Avery about their fight and she had avoided her friend. If she hadn't, Marissa could have changed the course of events.

When she opened her eyes, a man with dark hair and gray eyes was studying her with a concerned expression. He needed a shave. His face had a hardness that made him look dangerous. Good bone structure though and a great mouth. Symmetrical face and a strong nose and jawline; he would photograph well. His jeans were worn and his black T-shirt fit around his broad shoulders just right. His forearms were covered in tattoos.

"Who are you?" Marissa asked. She shot a questioning look at Kit. Her stomach did a crazy flip when she again met his gaze. Every once in a while, a truly beautiful man, like the one standing in front of her, knocked her off her feet.

The man didn't smile or extend his hand in greeting. "Jack Larson. I work with Kit and Griffin."

"At the car company?" Marissa asked. She couldn't keep the sarcasm from her tone. Marissa didn't have the full picture of what Kit did, but it was coming more clearly into focus. Kit had been good with computers and Marissa had the impression Kit worked for an investigation firm, maybe hush-hush because of their clientele.

"Yes," he said. Nothing in his face gave away a lie.

Jack Larson was a good liar. Marissa knew the car company line was garbage and she was adept at catching men spewing crap at her. She'd dealt with it for years. Most men thought she was beautiful and therefore stupid. "What is it that you're here to do? Sell me a car?"

Jack cocked his head as if trying to figure her out. There was nothing to figure. Kit was cloak-and-dagger about her life and her job. Marissa was on public display every time she left the house.

Griffin crossed the room to join them, stepping into the tiny office and closing the door behind him.

Kit set her hand on Marissa's arm. "Jack will stay with you until we know what happened to Avery. He'll make sure you're safe."

Surprise wafted through her. "You think I'm in

danger? You think Avery being attacked means that I might be a target, too?" She hadn't considered it was an option. Nothing in what had happened indicated Marissa was in trouble.

Kit pressed her hands together in worry. "We can't know, but I want you to be safe. I'd stay with you, but Griffin and I have a project we're deeply involved with. You can trust Jack. Griffin has known him a long time and he's the best in the business."

"The car business?" Marissa asked. She wanted her sister to trust her enough to level with her. Their relationship had come leaps and bounds in the last few years, but she and Kit hadn't been close growing up. Marissa worked too much and now that she was retiring, spending time with family would be easier.

"Jack will make sure you are safe," Kit said, ignoring the question.

"I have bodyguards," Marissa said. Her bodyguards accompanied her to jobs and when she went out. Two were waiting for her call to pick her up. She hadn't thought she would need a bodyguard while at the police station.

"Jack isn't a bodyguard exactly," Kit said. She glanced at Jack and gestured for him to continue.

"Former army special forces," Jack said.

"An army ranger?" Marissa asked. She didn't need someone with super special skills to protect her. The size of her bodyguards intimidated people. Overly aggressive fans and photographers rarely approached and when they did, it wasn't a big deal for her bodyguards to let them know they had crossed a line.

Jack didn't answer.

"I know you have a home alarm system and a

great team of bodyguards, but Jack will stay with you around the clock, not just when you have an event or are going out," Kit said, plowing a hand through her hair.

Marissa's skin tingled. A handsome man like Jack staying with her all the time. With Jack close, Marissa would have a hard time maintaining professional boundaries. She liked her space. She lived alone and preferred it that way. Even when she had been in a serious relationship, she had liked traveling and being away from her significant other. Being alone meant time to collect her thoughts. Having a stranger with her would be draining. "I can hire Jack as a part of my team if that makes you feel better, but I'm not interested in twenty-four-hour protection."

"One day," Kit said. "Let him stay with you for one day and when the police know more, we can adjust."

Marissa was too tired to argue. She looked at Jack. He met her gaze evenly. No flicker of interest in his eyes. In fact, he appeared bored. He wasn't panting to get close to her or crowding her and that increased her interest in him. "One day," she agreed.

"I'll speak to the police and make sure you're free to go. The three of us will stay until we get this sorted out," Kit said.

Jack hadn't wanted to leave Springfield to fly to New York for this job, but he owed Griffin. Not sure what to expect, he hadn't anticipated being attracted to Marissa. She was knock-him-flat sexy. Long brown hair that fell like silky strands of ribbon and a body that was feminine and strong. She likely spent hours in the gym every day. Jack had seen her picture prior to today, but he hadn't anticipated how beautiful she'd be in person. Photographs could be edited. In Marissa's case, she was more breathtaking in person. Her eyes were expressive and warm. He had expected her to be whiny or completely rude and arrogant. She wasn't.

"I know Kit put you up to this, but I don't need anyone to protect me," Marissa said.

Jack felt a twinge in his knee, an injury from his last mission. Following his physical therapist's plan, in six months he planned to be back to full fighting strength. Working on his family farm in Springfield had been therapeutic in its own way. But Griffin had asked him to do this and Jack couldn't deny a friend. "Your sister feels you do."

Marissa shook her head and a few locks of shorter hair fell over her cheek. She brushed them away with graceful fingers. "She worries. I can't see what Avery's attack has to do with me."

He didn't either, but Kit believed there was a connection and Jack trusted her instincts. She worked for the same organization he did, the West Company. Though he wasn't privy to the specifics of her skills, everyone who worked for the super-secret spy organization was talented and smart. A pain shot down Jack's leg, reminding him that on his last op, he hadn't stayed sharp and he'd almost died because of it. His partner had betrayed him and it still stung that he had not seen it coming. Worse, he was expected to testify in detail what had happened. He was dreading it. "It's a wait-and-see situation. You'll be happy I'm around if something comes up."

Marissa studied his face with intelligent eyes. "I'd prefer my privacy."

"I can do my best to give you space, but I won't force my services on you. If you're planning to try to give me the slip or make this hard on me, forget it. I don't need that." He wanted to be clear about his boundaries. He was a world-class operative, currently on the sidelines with an injury. That didn't mean he was planning to involve himself in some ridiculous cat-and-mouse game.

Marissa inclined her head and folded her arms over her chest. "I wouldn't do that. I told my sister this was fine for a day."

Jack heard something in her tone akin to annoyance. "It's been my experience that these things take more than a day."

"The police will figure this out. My guess is that you'll be flying out of here tomorrow."

"There's nothing I'd like more." Springfield was home and he had fallen back into living as a farmer. The hard work and long hours were what he needed. If Marissa didn't need him, he'd get on with piecing together the twisted wreckage of his life.

Chapter 2

Marissa slept better knowing Kit and Griffin were in her guest bedroom, but Jack sleeping in her living room felt odd. He had insisted on being in a location between the front and back doors to keep an eye on the house and who came and went even though he would have been more comfortable in her other guest bedroom.

After checking the doors and windows on the main floor, Jack had sat on the couch. His laptop was open in front of him, but it seemed to interest him only slightly. He hadn't stared at her. He hadn't looked at her. Marissa simultaneously liked that and found it irritating. Men often paid attention to her and she was curious why Jack seemed uninterested.

Before she had gone to bed, she had offered him a drink. He had declined.

Marissa rolled over, adjusting her pillow to get more comfortable.

It wasn't just thoughts of Jack keeping her awake. Every time she closed her eyes, she thought of Avery, picturing the last words they had spoken to each other, wishing she could have talked to Avery about what had happened with Rob. Deep sadness and grief cut through her and regret followed close on its heels.

The police would find evidence at the scene and Avery's attacker would be found. Pictures taken backstage had to have captured something. Marissa flipped her pillow to the cooler side. She tried breathing exercises to slow her heart rate and induce a state of relaxation. Usually, she slept fantastically in her house. She traveled more than half the year and sleeping in her bed was a luxury. Tonight, sleep was elusive.

Her phone buzzed. She looked at the display. It was a message from Ambrose. You awake?

She typed a reply. Yes.

I am sorry about Avery. You were friends for a long time.

She and Avery had been close. Marissa should have worked harder to repair the relationship. Rob wasn't worth the loss of a friend. When they hadn't been on speaking terms, she had told herself she was fine. But it had hurt. Though Marissa had been through two heart-wrenching divorces, Avery's friendship had been the one solid relationship she'd had. How are you?

In shock. Can't imagine not seeing her again.

Her chest felt tight. This couldn't be fixed. That acknowledgment devastated her all over again.

Marissa heard a creak outside her door and she tensed. Kit or Griffin might be checking on her. Or was Jack patrolling her town house for security issues? Several seconds of silence passed.

She heard another creak.

I have to go. Talk soon. She sent the message and squeezed her eyes closed. The noises were the house settling. She was safe.

Marissa felt a hand on her arm. She opened her eyes and came face-to-face with a man she didn't recognize.

Before she could scream, he clamped his hand over her mouth, pushing her back into her pillow, pressing her hard into the mattress. Her heart thundered and she tried not to panic. Pushing at his hand, she couldn't get his weight off her. He would suffocate her!

The door to her bedroom slammed open, light from the hallway spearing inside, and Jack launched himself at her assailant. The relief of his heaviness being tossed from her consumed her.

Marissa scrambled to move away, her sheets tangling around her. She screamed out to Kit, a warning in the case the assailant wasn't working alone.

Griffin barreled into the room.

"One assailant. He's down," Jack said.

Griffin turned on the lights just as her sister appeared in the doorway.

On the floor at Jack's feet was her assailant, and he wasn't moving. Was this the man who had killed Avery? He had close-cropped black hair, a small nose and thin lips. He wore all black from his turtleneck to his sneakers. He didn't look familiar.

Marissa's heart was racing and she felt dizzy. "Is he dead?"

"No," Jack said. "Maybe he can tell us why he's here and what this has to do with Avery."

"Breathe slower or you'll pass out," Kit said, setting her hand on Marissa's back.

Marissa had been taking short puffs of air, but she finally inhaled deeply and focused again on the man on the floor in her bedroom. "I don't know him."

"An assassin?" Jack asked.

Griffin nodded once swiftly, agreeing with Jack.

Marissa looked between the three of them. "He was sent to kill me? How do you know?"

"Instinct," Jack said.

Kit's eyes were narrowed with concern. "It will be okay. I promise. We'll figure this out."

Marissa looked at Jack. "Guess you won't be booking a flight out."

Jack shook his head. "I'm settling in for the duration."

Jack didn't follow gossip columns, but he had read up on Marissa on the flight to New York. He wouldn't call watching over Marissa a mission. Though the intruder tonight had established Kit was correct in believing there was a real threat against Marissa, if Avery's killer was the same man who attacked Marissa in her home, they could wrap this up, get the answers they needed, and Jack could be home by morning.

Jack didn't know what to make of Marissa. Gorgeous, obviously, but she wasn't arrogant about it. She was confident. He didn't know how many women would be comfortable in a thin-strapped tank top and white silk pants while talking to strangers. The police had arrived at her home and had arrested her attacker. It was the second time in twenty-four hours that Marissa was making a statement to the police. The one upside to the assailant attempting to kill her was that she was no longer the prime suspect in Avery's murder.

Marissa was talking with one of the officers on the scene. She spoke with her hands, her movements and face expressive.

Marissa was every bit as beautiful in person as she was in photos and magazines. Hard not to picture her wearing a swimsuit or lingerie like she did in her ads. Those were hard to ignore. They emphasized her best features: her face, her long hair, her curvy, toned body.

Jack had expected for this project to involve drama, mostly that of her making, but that wasn't the case. The perpetrator had been arrested and they might be in the clear. A short assignment was fine with him. It had been a good distraction from the problems with Bianca and his last mission.

After the police left, Jack, Kit, Griffin and Marissa assembled in the kitchen. Kit had prepared tea. Marissa had a huge kitchen with white cabinets and black shiny countertops. Her dining room was expansive with vaulted ceilings, three of the sides lined with windows and the fourth open to the kitchen. Jack circled the room, closing the roman shades. No point in giving a marksman a clear shot of Marissa. She watched him but didn't question what he was doing.

Marissa sat at the head of the ten-person table. She had put on a short purple robe and wore light purple slippers on her feet. Her hands were shaking and Jack fought the urge to put his arm around her. If she knew him better, she would know she was safe. He had a sixth sense about his clients. When trouble lurked, he sensed it and reacted quickly.

"The police said they'll run his prints and try to get an ID. He wasn't talking," Kit said. "Reaffirms our suspicion that he was hired."

Marissa took a sip of the tea her sister had set in front of her. "I don't know why anyone would hire a man to kill me."

"We need to find the connection to Avery," Griffin said.

Jack agreed. He didn't know enough about either woman to guess the motive.

"Avery and I were friends," Marissa said. "But we hadn't talked much recently."

"Why's that?" Jack asked, sensing she was holding back information.

Marissa was tapping her heel against the floor. "Avery and my boyfriend slept together. Rob cheated on me. We fought about it. The friendship was over. I let the tabloids speculate and didn't talk to many people about it."

Love triangles and jealousy were fuel for anger. "Could this be career jealousy from someone in your field?" Jack asked.

Marissa shrugged. "Maybe. There's always someone who misses out on a product campaign or doesn't get a spot they want in a show."

"Or a stranger who became fixated on you and Avery," Jack said.

Marissa shivered. "Could be."

After tossing around a few more theories, Kit hugged her sister. "We have to pack for our flight. Unless you want me to reschedule?"

"Is it that late already? Or should I say that early? Don't reschedule. I'll be fine. I'll call you."

The sisters hugged and then Griffin and Kit left the room. Jack was alone with Marissa. She swirled the tea in her cup. Her eyes were dark with exhaustion.

"I should try and go back to sleep," Marissa said. She rose slowly, bracing her hands on the table as she stood.

"Let me check your bedroom and bathroom. Then I'll sweep the house again," Jack said. He followed Marissa up the stairs, looking away from her perfectly round rear end and her robe swishing around her legs as she climbed.

Her bedroom smelled faintly of spices. Jack couldn't have named which ones. With the exception of the unmade bed, the room was tidy and on the gray walls were black-and-white prints of famous architectural landmarks: the Taj Mahal in Agra, the Palace of Versailles and St. Peter's Basilica in Rome. Jack checked the windows, moving aside the semi-sheer curtains to ensure they were latched and locked.

"How did you know someone was in my room?" Marissa asked, sitting on her bed, legs over the side of the mattress.

"I heard the creaking of floorboards and suspected

you were either awake or someone had gotten inside," Jack said. He had wanted to check on her in either case.

The police had traced the location of the breach to a balcony on the second floor. The perpetrator had climbed to it and slipped inside a guest bedroom by forcing the nails from the outdated lock and opening the sliding glass door.

"You saved my life. Thank you," Marissa said. When she spoke her gratitude, it sounded almost sensual.

The back of his neck heated. "Glad I could be of service," Jack said. She must get tired of men staring at her, fantasizing about her, but it was easy to do. Her voice was gentle yet strong and her eyes were expressive.

Marissa rubbed her temples. "I can't believe this happened. I take precautions. I'm a private person." She laughed, the soft sound of bells. "I know that sounds crazy, because my picture is everywhere, but I feel like there's a public me and a private me. The tabloids dig around into my life and my relationships, but few people know me, the real me."

She didn't need to justify anything to him. He could understand the need to keep secrets, whether it was because the safety of the country required it or knowing it could harm someone. "Are you telling me there's something about the real you and Avery that could be bringing this on? Or something in your public life?"

Marissa stood from the bed and walked to her dresser. She fiddled with the photo frames on top of it. "I don't know. Hard to say."

"Tell me what the problem could be."

She threw her hands in the air. "Who have Avery and I angered enough that they'd want to kill me? I have two ex-husbands. I have money, but if I'm dead my brother and sister inherit it all, and I know they didn't do this. I've told the police I don't know who would want to hurt Avery."

Jack listened, making a mental note to check on the brother. He would have been investigated before Kit was given her security clearance and closing the loop on him would be straightforward. The ex-husbands could be involved.

"Beyond that, I don't know. I've had a few stalkers, people who send me creepy letters and make threats. Some who are borderline unnerving, like asking me to their prom or out on a date with some aggressive wording, but hard to consider that a real threat."

"I'll need to see those letters," Jack said. Leave no stone unturned.

Marissa sighed. "I'll ask my PR manager to send them to you. I don't read them. I quit that form of self-cruelty years ago."

"We'll figure it out," Jack said.

"I've never been more glad to be leaving the city," Marissa said.

Jack hadn't been given the details of this assignment yet and her travel schedule was news to him. "Where are you going?"

"I'm flying to Seabrook tomorrow morning for a jewelry shoot. Or rather, later this morning. It's a small coastal town in New Hampshire. I've been there before. It's a charming place," Marissa said.

"Who else knows your travel plans?" Jack asked. Worry pricked at him.

Two attacks had occurred in a short time frame. Jack knew too well how persistent and devious some people could be. More attacks could be coming.

"My agent. My bodyguards. The people who booked the gig. My stylist. My makeup artist. A few friends," Marissa said.

"Change the location and tell only the people who need to know," Jack said.

"Change the location? I can't do that. Seabrook is the hometown of the jeweler and the inspiration for his designs. A team is on location for the shoot already. A hundred-million dollars in jewelry is being delivered and guarded by a private security firm. The details have been in the works for months."

Marissa hadn't had time to fully process what had happened to her. An attempt on her life required extra precautions. "Call your agent. Have him or her get someone else to do the shoot," Jack said.

Marissa balled her fists and narrowed her eyes. "That's not possible. My professional reputation is at stake. If I don't show up to jobs, I won't be hired for future gigs. The modeling industry is small and everyone knows everyone. Rumors will spread. The designer who wants me to model his jewelry asked for me personally. I won't let him down."

"You're Marissa," Jack said.

Her hands moved to her hips. "What does that mean?"

Her fame, beauty and success came with benefits. "People will make exceptions for you."

"I work hard and honor my commitments. I've gotten where I am because I'm reliable and responsible." Hostility dripped from her voice.

He sensed pushing her more would send her over the edge. "I didn't mean to offend you. We'll change your flight and hotel. Maybe that will be enough to throw anyone following you off your trail," Jack said. Most of his previous clients were more calloused. His boss had mentioned that he could use some softening around the edges. This was his opportunity to show he could handle all types of clients.

"I'll agree to those changes," Marissa said. She sat again on the bed and looked at her alarm clock. "No point in going back to sleep now."

Being in her private space, he was aware of a boundary shifting. He shouldn't linger in her bedroom. It was making him think irrational thoughts, like of how it would feel to touch her or kiss her. "Rest while you can. I'll make the arrangements." He left her room, closing the door behind him before he did something he'd regret.

Marissa tilted her head back and turned it, arching her back. The sun's rays were beating down on her and the heavy sparkling diamond necklace she was wearing. Despite the brightness, in the crisp New Hampshire air, she was cold. A burnt orange bikini provided little protection from the wind. Outdoor heaters blew to keep goose bumps off her skin. The sounds of the waves rolling onto the beach were melodic and soothing. The beige of the sand swept into snow-dusted dunes and gray-and-tan marbled rocks.

The hardest task was keeping the sadness out of her eyes. Avery was dead and Marissa wouldn't have the opportunity to make amends with her. She'd heard people on the set whispering about the murder and her stomach twisted with grief. Clarice was working this event as well and she had much to say on the matter, eager to discuss it and vent some of her sadness. Rumors swirled despite not having any official information on the case.

Marissa's home intruder had admitted he was hired by someone he didn't know. He had been sent to kill her. Marissa tried not to let that sink too deeply in to her psyche. Except for the incident with Rob and Avery, Marissa didn't start trouble with friends or colleagues. Her divorces had been over long ago and any animosity had faded with time.

The wind blew across the water, sending a chill down her spine. Marissa thought of heated things. Soup. Hot chocolate. And Jack, who was standing about four yards away. He was wearing a dark coat that didn't hide his muscular shape. Strong shoulders and trim hips, his stride was powerful and every movement deliberate. Every few minutes, he changed his position, circling the area. She didn't believe that trouble had followed her. Jack believed it had. He had negotiated for the shoot to take place a quarter of a mile from the previously planned location. With the additional traffic the crew brought, it wouldn't be hard to find her.

Marissa felt safer with Jack. Serious, rarely smiling, he moved quickly and thought ahead. He didn't look at her much, but she found herself looking at him quite a bit. Marissa tried not to be arrogant about her appearance or assume that everyone found her attractive. Her job revolved around her looks and she had lucked out in that department. Most of the men on the set were staring at her. Jack was looking at everything else.

She had traveled from New York to New Hampshire with Jack and he had kept his questions and comments about her, Avery, the incident in her apartment and the changes to her travel plans.

She sensed she rubbed him the wrong way and wasn't his type. He would go for a rough-and-tumble woman, salt of the earth, low maintenance. Marissa was the definition of high maintenance. She liked sleep and her beauty products and her fitness regimen. When she was stressed, she liked time at a spa.

Jack wasn't paying attention to her and it bothered her. Not able to put her finger on why since he wasn't her type either. He hadn't shaved this morning, he didn't go out of his way to be charismatic or charming and he was not interested in her outside of their professional involvement. Dressed appropriately, his clothes lacked a fashion sense, but he wore them well. Dark gray pants and a black T-shirt; a black windbreaker that concealed his gun.

"Marissa, eyes," the photographer said.

Marissa had been squinting. Jack glanced in her direction. She refocused on showing the jewelry in the best light.

The photographer dropped his camera to his side and sighed. "This is boring. We need a different set. I want to do something daring. Not look like we're schlepping shopping-mall jewelry."

He snapped his fingers and pointed. Marissa stood. Three assistants started moving around the boxes and light reflectors.

Clarice jogged over with a plush robe. "Want this?"

Marissa shook her head. It was harder to get warm and then peel off the robe and be freezing again. Anyway, it would smudge her makeup and ruffle her hair. "Thanks, but I'm okay." The heaters were helping, but her toes were cold and she wiggled them.

"Probably only thirty more minutes with the sun's rays in the right position," Clarice said.

They had been on the set for hours. "I hope we have some good shots."

"Weird on the set today," Clarice said. "I can't stop thinking about Avery. She's on everyone's mind. It's hard to focus on other things. Business as usual feels strange."

"I know what you mean," Marissa said. It was simultaneously quieter, but with more behind-the-hand whispers.

"Have you heard anything else?" Clarice asked.

Marissa shook her head. "Avery's mother sent me a message about the memorial service." The woman didn't know she and Avery hadn't been speaking and she had asked Marissa to say a few words about Avery at the service.

"I've been asking around, but no one seems to know what happened." Clarice stared at her hard as if expecting her to reveal an important detail.

"The police will figure it out," Marissa said. She hoped they would soon. The man who had been inside her town house was denying any involvement in Avery's murder.

"What about the bodyguard?" Clarice asked.

"Jewelry guards, you mean?" Marissa said. The

jewelry had been escorted to the site by two burly looking, highly intimidating men.

"Not them. What about your new bodyguard? What's his story?" Clarice asked.

"His story?" Marissa asked. She didn't know much about Jack.

"Is he married or does he have a girlfriend? No wedding ring," Clarice said.

Marissa hadn't asked. "He was a referral." She was curious about him, too. Not her business, but he hadn't taken personal phone calls on the trip to Seabrook. A wife or girlfriend would call now and then.

"He doesn't talk to anyone. He looks around and watches," Clarice said.

"He's making sure everything and everyone is safe," Marissa said.

Clarice smiled. "After what happened to Avery, I'm glad for the extra eyes on us. But maybe when he's off the clock, he would be willing to talk more. When does his shift end?"

Possessiveness and a hint of jealousy nipped at her. Marissa tried to squash it. Clarice was being friendly. It was in her nature. "Not shift work. He's been hired to stay with me."

A puzzled expression crossed Clarice's face. "All right. I'll try to get his number and call him. I assume he'll have time off."

The photographer clapped his hands and Marissa hurried to the restaged set. Jack could be interested in Clarice. She was sweet and fun. Marissa looked at Jack again.

This time, he wasn't observing. He was running at her, screaming, "Get down, get down!"

Marissa heard sharp cracks exploding, like fireworks in the sky.

Jack caught her around the waist, throwing her to the ground and covering her with his body.

The cold sand pressed in to her back. Jack had his gun in his hand and was aiming it away from her and the water. Astride her while protecting her with his body, he reached to his other side and pulled out his phone, tapping the screen with his thumb.

"What is the meaning of this?" the photographer asked, marching forward. His hair was standing on end, as if he had run his hand through it too many times.

The squeal of tires from the parking lot.

Marissa struggled to sit. Jack hadn't moved. The heat of his body burned through her. She wiggled, trying to push him off her.

"He's gone," Jack said, rolling to his feet. He slid his phone away and slipped his gun into its holster. He reached for her hand to help her up.

"Who?" the photographer asked. "What is going on?"

The guards for the jewelry and her other two bodyguards had moved. They seemed unsure what to do, waiting for Jack to direct them. He had that type of presence. Confusion was clear on the faces around her. Jack had created a scene. Did he believe there had been a threat? Or had he overreacted to something?

Jack pointed to the crates draped in fabric behind him. Marissa followed his extended hand. Were those bullet holes in the pink-and-purple cloth? Three holes peppered the front.

"What happened?" Marissa asked.

"Two men approached from up the beach. Is anyone hurt?" Jack asked.

A murmur around them of "no" and "we're fine."

The photographer's mouth was hanging open. "Someone shot at me? Does this have to do with Avery?"

Jack cleared his throat. "Two men parked in the lot behind that sand dune. They were waved away by security to move farther down the beach. They circled back on foot. I'm sending a description of the attackers and their car to the police." He met Marissa's gaze. "We need to move to a safer location."

"We need to finish the photo shoot," the photographer said.

"You'll have to use one of the pictures you took. You have plenty," Jack said. He stared, waiting for the photographer to argue.

The photographer sighed. "A worse photographer would be dead in the water, but I'm sure I have something I can use."

Standing close to her, Jack escorted Marissa to the tent where the security guards for the jewelry helped her remove the million-dollar pieces and place them into protective containers. As they inventoried and inspected each item, Clarice brought her a pair of yoga pants and a zip-up hoodie.

Marissa put them on, along with her sunglasses. "Where to?" she asked Jack.

"I'll tell you in the car," Jack said.

He slung an arm over her shoulder and she winced.

"What's wrong?" he asked.

"I think I have sand burn on my shoulder from when you tackled me," Marissa said.

Jack faced her, and unzipped her hoodie. Though he had seen her wearing next to nothing a few minutes before, the action struck her as intimate. Her skin prickled and lust sent a warm shiver over her. Jack lifted the fabric off her shoulder and visually examined the scraped skin. "Hope this doesn't mean you'll have trouble at other jobs." He set his hand on her arm and the contact set off a shower of sparks.

The connection and the attraction were strong. His gaze lingered on her face and the heat in his eyes felt like a physical touch.

Marissa looked at her shoulder. The skin was red, but it would heal quickly with some ointment. "They can airbrush it out if it shows in pictures."

"You should call your sister in the car and let her know what happened," Jack said.

The idea of worrying Kit didn't thrill her. "Maybe we shouldn't bother her with this. She'll worry more."

"She'll read about it in my report," Jack said.

"You're sending my sister a report?"

"Daily reports under these circumstances are standard."

"Reports to whom?" Marissa asked. She was increasingly curious about Kit's work. Jack may give something away.

"Your sister is copied on the reports," Jack repeated.

"You work for the same company. What company is that?" Marissa asked.

"A car company," Jack said.

Marissa rolled her eyes. He was giving her the

party line, but she had time to work on him. "I'll call her. Is there someone you need to call?"

They had spent time together and she knew little about him. Usually, she built better rapport with the people in her life.

"No one," Jack said.

"Wife? Girlfriend?" Marissa asked, thinking of Clarice's questions.

"No one," Jack repeated. "I'll have someone pick up your belongings at the hotel."

Where would they spend the night? He was being evasive. "I need to be in New York tomorrow. It's Avery's memorial service." She couldn't miss it, although she was dreading it. She'd need to say goodbye and she wasn't ready to do that. Part of her was harboring denial.

"I'll get you there," Jack said.

Marissa bumped him with her hip. It was like moving against iron. "When you want to be amenable, you're a good guy."

Jack glanced at her, meeting her gaze. "You don't know anything about me."

His stare was intense and she felt it all the way through her. Her stomach tightened and warmth curled through her. "Are you saying you are not a good guy? 'Cause I'm pretty sure my sister wouldn't let a psychopath watch my back."

The jewelry guards were closing and locking the pieces of jewelry into containers, snap, click and lock. The waves beat against the sand and the hum of the heaters was low. Marissa was in her own space with Jack.

"I know how to do my job. That's all you need to be concerned about."

His tone was brusque. Marissa liked him, which fit a pattern with her. Her ex-husbands had been difficult people. The challenges of complex people intrigued her. Michael had been a musician and his volatile emotions brought intensity to their relationship. She had needed someone more calm and stable. Elliott had been sweet, but he had been possessive. Though his absolute attention and focus on her had made her feel cherished, he'd hated sharing her with the world and given her job, privacy had been in short supply. Marissa wished she could fall for a simple, even-tempered man.

Though Jack seemed in control of his emotions, she sensed a fire in him. Marissa went for broke. "Have I done something to offend you?" If they were going to be spending time together, better to clear the air.

"No."

It was hard to continue the discussion from a single word. "Then why are you being so abrupt?"

"I don't follow," Jack said. "You hired me to do a job. I've done that job. Twice."

He had performed well at his job. Most of the people she worked with, Marissa became close to over time. Jack wasn't having it. "Do I irritate you?" Marissa asked.

"You're a client," Jack said.

"That's not an answer," Marissa said.

"It is. I don't have feelings of any type for clients."

Marissa's heart fell and her emotional response told her she had developed a crush on him. Losing her head to someone she had known briefly under difficult circumstances was her specialty. Unlike her past relationships, Jack was bent on freezing her out.

Jack had protected dozens of people over the course of his career and Marissa was one of the most kind and considerate. She didn't keep distance between herself and who she worked with. She made millions of dollars having her picture taken. Under the traumatic circumstances, she had handled the shoot in New Hampshire well. No complaining about the weather or that she was wearing next to nothing or that she had almost been killed the night before.

That little bikini she'd worn would haunt him for the rest of his life. He hadn't seen a woman wear a few scraps of fabric so well. Jewelry held little interest for him, but the way she wore it made it entirely too appealing.

Marissa was nothing like Lacy. It had been seven years since Lacy had broken his heart and taken off for Los Angeles, hoping to score a job as an actress. The last he had heard, she was working as an assistant in a recording studio. Jack resented that she had thrown away their relationship for a chance to be an actress. She hadn't studied acting. Hadn't been in a play. Hadn't tried out for anything. Moving to Los Angeles and being the lead in a successful television series was the dream. Beautiful, and a head-turner in Springfield, couldn't compete with the thousands of beautiful, talented women already looking for those roles.

"You seem upset. Are you upset?" Marissa asked.

Jack kept boundaries with clients and she pressed them by asking too many questions.

"Someone attacked you. I'm concerned about who else might figure out where your next job is and try again," Jack said.

"Have you worked with other models?" Marissa asked.

She was digging around about his life and he wished she was more narcissistic. Droning on about herself would be easier. Didn't most people busy themselves playing games on their phones or texting friends or checking social media updates? Marissa rarely touched her phone. "You are the first model."

"How's that been so far?" Marissa asked.

"All that matters is that you're alive and unharmed," Jack said.

"Thank you, that is so nice," Marissa said with a genuine smile.

He wasn't aiming to be nice, only honest.

Marissa played with the hem of her shirt. "There will be a lot of people at Avery's service. What if one of them is her killer?"

"It's possible. But you'll be safe. You have me."

"Have you? I didn't realize you were mine." She winked at him and laughed.

Flirtation must come easily to her. Men probably fell at her feet. "I'm only yours until this is over."

Marissa frowned. "Won't be the first time a man walks away from me."

That gave him pause. "I would think you'd have no trouble finding relationships."

She smirked. "Finding them isn't the problem. Making them work is hard. I have terrible luck picking men."

He had read she'd been married before. It had gone

through his mind that she must be flighty. Unless her ex-husbands had something to do with Avery's murder, it wasn't his concern what had happened. "Your sister picked me to help you, so maybe this will work out okay."

Avery's memorial service loomed and weighed on Marissa. For now, sleeping soundly wasn't possible. Her agent had offered to contact her doctor for a prescription for sleeping pills. Not wanting for her thoughts to be cloudy, she'd declined. After showering, she dressed in a black high-neck sheath dress that fell below her knees.

She slicked her hair into a low bun, twisting her hair and pining it into place. Her makeup was simple and light. The musical jewelry box on her dresser pinged and Marissa's chest felt tight. Avery had given her the box for Christmas the year before. Marissa hadn't put jewelry in it and she had considered tossing it after Avery's betrayal. But it played one of Marissa's favorite songs and she had felt sentimental about the gift.

Marissa finished getting dressed, selected her handbag, shoes, a pashmina and a simple necklace. After checking her appearance, she decided she was ready.

She sucked in her breath at the sight of Jack waiting by the front door. He was wearing a black suit, white shirt and appropriately demure tie. He had shaved and his hair was combed and fell to the tops of his ears.

"The rest of your security team went ahead. The

funeral home has been swept and security is tight. We'll stay vigilant," Jack said.

He offered his arm and she took it, slipping her hand around his elbow and exiting the house with him. The warmth of holding on to him and the security of knowing he was protecting her were a comfort. He smelled of sandalwood, the light fragrance of his aftershave.

Leaning her head closer, she inhaled. "You smell good."

"Thank you. Same goes."

He opened her car door, helped her inside and circled to the driver's seat. It was a basic sedan with dark tinted windows and comfortable leather seats. She had purchased the car for transportation around the city when she wanted to go unnoticed and so there was nothing remarkable about the outside of the car and the inside was comfortable enough to sit for hours when she was stuck in traffic or when driving it to photo shoots closer than a plane ride away.

"Do you have any suspicions about who might have hurt Avery? I'm not looking for evidence and proof. I want to know who you think might have been involved. I can better protect you if I have an accurate picture of the situation," Jack said.

An accurate picture of her life included many volatile characters. Models, photographers, musicians and the occasional brush with professional athletes and actors. Some had built their reputation on being difficult and others liked to make headlines. "I don't know who will show up today. Less successful models were jealous of Avery. She was the face of famous brands and she worked the good gigs."

"Like you," Jack said.

"Like me, but also different. Avery dealt with problems more directly. When I'm working with someone who doesn't like me, I ignore it. Avery liked to engage and confront a problem. She would get into screaming matches and a few times, she refused to pose with certain models. Since Avery is more in demand than most others, she was responsible for lost jobs." Marissa didn't like to spread gossip, but Avery had worked with younger, less experienced models who had walked off the set in tears and had lost the booking and a six-figure payday.

"If you see anyone at the memorial who you know had a score to settle with Avery, give me a heads-up. Although it's unlikely an enemy will show up looking to offer their sincere condolences."

But on the off chance he or she did, Jack would be close by. Marissa was used to standing on her own. Even when she had been married, travel and work schedules meant she hadn't often been in the company of her now ex-husbands. That might have been part of their problem, no real intimacy or sustained closeness.

Marissa was determined to have loyalty, trust, intimacy and love in her next relationship. She'd move past lust and desire into real, amazing love. Her skin tingled at the thought of Jack as the object of her affection. To pursue Jack was a mistake. She had selected the wrong man time and again and when she next fell for someone, she would make sure it was real and lasting and not a fling.

Marissa hadn't known Avery to attend religious services of any type, but her memorial service was being held at Saint John's, a megachurch in downtown New York. The building was constructed of brown and beige bricks in a gothic style that was imposing and dark. Entering the church, Marissa felt she was transported to another place. As historic and unwelcoming as the exterior was, the inside was modern and fresh, the walls painted pale gray and covered in posters and prints about salvation and new life. Coffee and beverages were being served from carts. The memorial service was being held in the main auditorium, which seated three thousand. Chairs had been cleared from the center to allow mourners to mingle.

On the left stage, a band was setting up. On the center stage were life-size prints detailing the progression of Avery's career, from age fourteen to the present. Each photograph was angled under the best lighting, as if Avery herself was doing a photo shoot. It was unsettling how lifelike the photographs were.

The room was adorned in gold trim, the reflection from the metallic accents bouncing light around the room, the shine second only to the scent of flowers. Huge arrangements lined the stage, hung on easels, sat on posts and covered the floor space around the pictures.

Marissa cringed when she noticed the band's name. Her ex-husband Michael's band was performing. Avery's mother hadn't mentioned it. Though they had changed names and members over the last fifteen years, Michael was the lead singer and guitarist and proficient on the piano. He was iconic in the music industry. Though she and Michael had been married for about five minutes, it had been dramatic and heartbreaking. Their entire relationship had played out in the tabloids. Marissa had been young and naïve, and had given interviews about her relationship and said far too much. Two months into their relationship, she was claiming to love him and calling him her soul mate. Her words had come back to haunt her during their breakup and subsequent divorce.

The one detail that had never made it to the public eye was that after their quickie Vegas wedding, the following week, he had tattooed her name on his left posterior. Laser surgery would have removed it by now. Marissa and Michael hadn't spoken in years and that awkwardness arced between them.

Marissa bumped into Jack and straightened.

"Sorry," she said.

"What's wrong?" he asked.

"I see an old friend. Not an old friend. Ex-husband. The second one," Marissa said. She took a deep breath. Standing in a room with Michael shouldn't be hard. If he was sober, he would respect the space and remain reverent. If he was high, she expected rudeness, possibly some yelling.

"Could he have anything to do with this?" Jack asked.

Her exes didn't care enough to lash out at her. They gained nothing from killing Avery and then targeting her. Their divorces were final. Based on what she had seen, they had moved on with their lives.

"My ex-husband didn't kill Avery."

"Did he know Avery?" Jack asked.

She and Avery had been friends for decades. "Yes, but they got along with her."

"Tell me about your ex-husbands," he said.

She gestured around. "Here?" She didn't want to

talk about them. It made her feel silly at her age to be married and divorced—twice. The first time, she had been young, naïve and looking for something stable and real and Elliott had been grounded and calm. The second time, she had been caught up in a wild affair. Michael had swept her off her feet.

"Or elsewhere and later. Your call."

She wanted to put off the inevitable, indefinitely, but Kit may have already told him some of the more sordid details. For that matter, an internet search would fill in the blanks. "The first is a bar owner in Chicago. Elliott and I were married for three years. He hated my travel and after a while, it bothered him that I was too recognizable and that meant we rarely had privacy. The second is Michael, who is over there. He and I traveled too much to see each other enough to make it work. Opposite schedules." To list her marriages in those simplified terms, she felt like they were part of some past life. Each had affected her and every time, she had believed in love and forever.

A piano played a familiar tune and Marissa tried not to stare. Michael was seated at the piano bench, warming up for what Marissa expected would be a big performance. Michael didn't do small.

"We don't need to stress about this. Say goodbye to Avery now and give yourself this time to focus on her," Jack said. "Do you want me to keep him away from you?"

That wasn't necessary though having Jack at her side gave her a bump in feeling safe. "I can handle Michael." Marissa had enjoyed the distraction of the conversation. The situation was overwhelming. As she walked through the room, she sensed Jack at her back.

"Marissa!" Ambrose's voice. She spun on her heel and he wrapped her in a tight hug. Ambrose was slender and tall, with curly dark hair he kept cut short. It was graying around the temples. His eyes were blue and narrow and he rarely smiled.

"Ambrose, hi," Marissa said. "How are you doing with all this?"

Ambrose squeezed her hands in his. "Worried about you. It's a huge shock. I've been lying low and trying to process it. Do you know I've spoken with the police three times?"

"I've spoken to them, too," Marissa said.

"I see you've acquired a sexy new bodyguard. Tell me you're having an affair with him," Ambrose said, looking over Marissa's shoulder and lifting his eyebrows in interest.

Jack folded his arms across his chest. Though it was not likely his intention, his pumped biceps and forearms flexed beneath his suit jacket. The position was enticing and made her think irrational thoughts, like about running her hand along his arm.

"Of course I'm not," Marissa said.

"Disappointing," Ambrose said.

Conversation became impossible as Michael's band—the current formation calling themselves Silver Sundays—began a song. The lyrics, while not specifically using Avery's name, were about a beautiful woman whose life was cut short, but who lived forever in roses. They could have played a traditional song or a religious song. Marissa had a hard time keeping her composure through the poignant lyrics. She took a deep breath.

Jack took a step closer. Marissa didn't lean on him,

but they were standing close enough that the fabric of her dress brushed his pants leg. Reaching for his hand wouldn't be appropriate. Instead, she clasped her hands together in front of her.

When the song ended, Avery's mother joined Silver Sundays on the stage and spoke about her daughter. Her voice broke several times as she delivered a loving tribute. "And now, I have asked Avery's friend Father Franklin to pray with us."

Father Franklin, the rector at an Episcopalian church in midtown, walked onto the stage. It had been years since Marissa had spoken to him. He hadn't changed much, though he was carrying a few extra pounds around the middle and his hair was grayer than it had been. His skin was dark from the sun and his deep set eyes warm and welcoming. People felt at ease around Father Franklin, making his church one of the most popular in his neighborhood.

Marissa had introduced Avery and Father Franklin years before when Avery had needed someone to speak to whom she could trust. Marissa hadn't realized that Avery had kept the relationship going. Avery had been better at keeping people in her life, at least, everyone except Marissa. It was Marissa who had trouble holding on to relationships.

After his heartfelt prayers, Father Franklin stepped away and Avery's mother again addressed the crowd.

"Avery has a few friends who wanted to speak about her. Marissa? Are you here?"

Heads turned in her direction. She didn't know how many people knew about her falling out with Avery. It had run through the rumor mill. Marissa was angry with herself for not patching things up with Avery sooner.

Then she was standing on the stage. She hadn't been aware she had walked up the three steps, the maroon carpet soft under her shoes. A few hundred eyes on her, including Jack's. He was standing to her left off stage, glancing at her and looking around the room. If he wasn't there, she might have fallen apart.

Michael was behind her and he moved closer, standing to her right, his guitar slung around his shoulder and resting on his hip. He was watching and waiting. Though they had two feet of space between them, she felt his support. This was their first face-to-face meeting in years and she was surprised he was being friendly.

Putting aside thoughts of Michael and of Jack, she focused on the reason she was here, to honor her friend. Marissa spoke about Avery. She spoke of her love of fashion, her creativity and her contributions to the community. Avery had guest lectured at a few of Ambrose's college courses over the last two years, giving his fashion students her perspective on the topic. Marissa's throat was tight, but she finished her tribute.

She walked away from the microphone and a few others spoke about Avery. Then Avery's mother invited everyone to enjoy the celebration of Avery's life. With that, Silver Sundays began playing.

Marissa looked again at the photos of Avery. Jack was behind her, and she turned, took a couple of steps back and slid her arm around his. "I'm glad I'm not here alone." A shudder piped over her having him close.

She scanned the room for Father Franklin, eager to

introduce Jack to him. Father Franklin had filled a father figure role in her youth and having him meet Jack seemed important. In the crowd, she didn't see him and disappointment tumbled over her. This wasn't his church. He could have left already.

"I'm glad I could be here for you," Jack said.

She was especially glad a few minutes later when her most recent ex, Rob, approached. The man who might have been responsible for Avery's death and partially responsible for their fallout. His suit was impeccable and his brown hair slicked back. Dark circles rimmed his eyes. He was clean-shaven and had a strong jawline and aristocratic nose. In his younger years, he had modeled for clothing catalogs, but now he worked for his father's real estate company. Confident to the point of arrogant, Rob was sweet when he wanted to be and viperous when he didn't get his way.

"Can we talk?" he asked, hands shoved in the pockets of his pants. His stance was casual, but Marissa read the intensity in his eyes.

She had zero interest in talking to him. He had pointed the police in her direction, as if she could have killed Avery. Having a brawl now, in this space, was in poor taste. "This isn't a good time. I just want to say goodbye to my friend," Marissa said. Blowing him off was the high road. Tearing into him, the low one.

"Will there be another time?" Rob asked.

"I'm not sure what we have to say to each other. You told the police that I could be involved."

Rob appeared flummoxed. "I was out of my mind with grief. I said a lot of stuff I shouldn't have. I knew you were pissed at her and I was listing people who held a grudge against Avery. When my lawyer arrived, he shut me up."

Marissa considered walking away, but she was curious what Rob had to say.

Rob rocked back on his heels. "I've been thinking about what could have happened and who could have done this. Avery was secretive. She was hiding something."

Marissa hadn't known Avery to hold back. Bluntness and honesty were two of the traits she had liked most about her friend. It was why it had been so hard when Avery had lied to her about Rob and hidden their relationship. "What do you think she was hiding?"

"I don't know. Avery didn't answer her phone. She didn't return messages. When I asked what was bothering her, she was evasive."

Had Avery been dating someone else? "Which makes you believe what about Avery?" Marissa asked. If he had a suspicion, he needed to be direct. Avery was busy and in demand. None of his observations sounded strange.

"I don't know exactly. But it's a sense I had," Rob said.

"Did you mention this to the police?" Jack asked.

Rob shook his head. "I didn't have anything concrete to tell them. I didn't know what she could be hiding. But you knew her. Did you get the sense she was lying to you, at least, lying by omission?"

"You mean, when she was sleeping with you?" Why dance around the truth? Avery hadn't acted any differently around Rob or Marissa. The affair had been well hidden.

"That wasn't going on for that long. It was a slow build. When we started, it just happened. You were in Barcelona—"

Marissa held up her hand. "I don't need the details. Just think before you talk, Rob."

"I'm doing my best. I'm barely holding it together," Rob said.

If he wanted sympathy, he was barking up the wrong tree.

"I want to know what happened to Avery, too. She was my friend," Marissa said. A simplification, but she cared deeply. "This is not the time or place to discuss this."

Rob looked around her. "Another time, then." Without waiting for her answer, he walked away.

"You handled that well," Jack said. "And he backed down faster than I would have expected."

"Rob wouldn't hurt me," Marissa said.

"I wasn't concerned about Rob hurting you. I was worried about him. You don't carry much bulk, but you've got an iron core," Jack said. "I expected more drama. Screaming. A slap across the face at least."

"Not at Avery's memorial service," Marissa said. In the context of Avery's service, her anger at Rob was small and unimportant.

Marissa questioned her relationships in a larger sense. She'd let Rob go easily enough. Her marriages were part of the past. Losing touch with Father Franklin was another aspect of her life she regretted. She rarely spoke with her family and while traveling she missed birthdays and holidays. Those hadn't bothered her.

Until now. Now, she felt like she had given up too

many personal aspects of her life for success in her career. Starting with her retirement, she could make changes. "It's never too late to start over."

"Excuse me?" Jack said.

She hadn't realized she'd spoken aloud. "I was thinking about Avery. And wasting time. I want more in my life than work."

"I understand that sentiment."

Marissa heard something in his tone and for the first time since meeting him, she wondered if they were on the same path.

Chapter 3

Marissa turned on the television in her bedroom. The news was buzzing about Avery's death and reports about the memorial service. A crushing sense of loss poured over her. The autopsy had been released and the cause of death was a gunshot to the stomach. No one was coming forward stating that they had either heard or seen Avery being attacked or shot.

The media anchor stated the police had no comment on the matter. The report showed a clip of Marissa and Jack entering the memorial service. From the angle of the shot, they looked like a couple. The broadcast also featured Rob looking tired and devastated.

"Hey, Jack!" Marissa called to him. He was in the house, but she wasn't sure where.

Jack stood in the doorway, nearly filling it. "You okay?"

She was startled to realize he had been outside her room. "The news is talking about Avery." Having someone in her home staying so close was strange. "I can't believe she's gone. Avery and I were friends for so long. We met when we were sixteen. Or was I fifteen?" It had been long ago and the years blurred together. Jack didn't move from the doorway.

"That's a long time," he said.

Marissa patted the bed next to her. "Sit. I need to talk."

He didn't move from the doorway.

"Come on, I promise not to seduce you. I just need someone to talk to." She would control herself even if the idea lodged in her mind and got comfortable.

Jack took a few steps into the room and chose to sit on the chaise lounge next to her bed. It was better than standing six feet away. "Tell me about Avery," he said.

It was the invitation she needed to hear. Telling her and Avery's story to someone who didn't know Marissa, who didn't have preconceptions about her, was freeing. "We were competing for a modeling contract. We had been to the same four appointments that day. This was the fifth. We were tired and trying not to look it. The gig was for a college pamphlet." Marissa laughed at the memory. "After being passed over for every other one, this was it. If I didn't get the gig, I wouldn't have a paycheck. No paycheck meant struggling with the rent and bills for another month."

"You were living on your own at fifteen?"

Not exactly, although sometimes Marissa felt like she had been an adult her whole life. "I lived with my mom and sister and brother. My father walked out on us when my brother was four and I was seven. My mom had been working at an assisted living community in the dining facility. The upside was that she sometimes brought home leftovers." Leftovers that would have been tossed in the dump. "Even with that and Father Franklin at Saint Joseph's helping us out, it was still tough. My modeling gigs had bridged us a few times. I needed the job. Desperately."

Jack's brows furrowed in concern. "I didn't realize modeling was a must for you."

"Don't get me wrong. I loved it. I like the clothes and the fashion and the glamour. But at that point, it wasn't like it is now. I was new to the industry. I didn't know what I was doing. My mom tried to help me when she could, but she didn't know much, either. A couple times, I went to appointments that turned out to be for adult films. I knew to walk away from those. But anything else was fair game. If it paid and wasn't degrading, I did it.

"That day with Avery, she looked across the room at me and we knew we were competing for the ad. She had a much better chance than me, more experience, and while I had taken the bus and walked ten blocks, she had been driven there by her mother. I had a run-down look."

"She didn't have the same financial strains?" Jack asked.

"Avery was born with a silver spoon in her mouth. She loved modeling for what it was, not for the money. Her mother had been a model in the sixties."

"Who got the gig?" Jack asked.

"Avery did. But I got the next one. We had a similar look and so we often went for the same auditions. It wasn't until the eighth or ninth audition that I formally introduced myself and we had a brief conversation. Eventually, I broke out big when I secured a well-known makeup company sponsorship. I think I wanted it more. But Avery was the one person I could talk to about modeling. When I talked to other people about it, they just rolled their eyes, like I was a pampered princess complaining about having my picture taken. At the start of my career, it was hard. Never mind the number of photographers who wanted to swindle me. It was unreliable money for sometimes low pay, long hours and no guarantees of future work."

"I hadn't thought about it that way," Jack said.

"In any career, it takes time to build momentum," she said.

"I get it. New guy. Pay your dues," he said.

Since they were talking about jobs, Marissa wondered if he would give away anything more about his and Kit's. "How did you meet Kit?"

"Through Griffin," Jack said. His posture tensed. She was walking on shaky territory. He was holding back.

"How do you know Griffin?" Marissa asked.

Jack leaned forward, legs parted, elbows on his knees. "We met working overseas. He helped me out of a tight spot. I owe him."

"That's why you're here, helping me?" she asked.

"Not just that. I had an accident on my last job. My knee needs time to recover."

"What happened?" Marissa asked.

Jack touched his knee. "That's a story for another night."

Marissa sensed she had pushed him far enough.

She would ask more later. "Then you understand how people you meet on the job can come to be important to you."

"Yes."

Marissa waited to see if he would elaborate. When he didn't, she turned the conversation back to her and Avery. "Avery and I were lucky to be on some shoots together. We've done magazine spreads and high fashion and runway. We've traveled together, partied together and worked together. We were close. We shared clothes and shoes. That's why I can't understand who could have a grudge against her. Avery was chill and fun."

"You say this about the woman who cheated with your boyfriend."

That wasn't Avery's best quality. "It wasn't Avery's first affair." The words popped out of her mouth and Marissa felt disloyal for speaking them.

"She made a habit of dating unavailable men?"

"Sometimes," Marissa said. "She was attracted to men whom she couldn't have. They presented a challenge." Married men, other women's boyfriends and fiancés and once even a Catholic priest.

Jack leaned back and rubbed his hand over his jawline. "Since someone seems to have the same grudge for you, maybe it's related to a booking you've worked together. Have you and Avery done campaigns for big dollars that flopped?"

"Of course." Not every product they promoted did well. "We did a swimsuit ad last summer for a major clothing designer. It failed. Lots of accusations of unrealistic images by the public. Which they were. Totally edited."

"Does that bother you? When your photo is edited?" Jack asked.

"Sometimes. When I see my picture and it doesn't look like me. Or when I know some teenager is looking at it and wondering how she can get a seventeen inch waist and double-D breasts. But I also get why the ads are edited. The fantasy sells more product," Marissa said. "Avery told me that. She knew it was more important for us to appear a certain way, even if it wasn't who we were. When my personal life or my work became too crazy, she kept me in check. Stood by me through both my engagements and marriages and divorces. After all that, in the end, she died angry at me. We weren't speaking. I have to live with that." As a sob choked her, Jack stood from the chaise and set his hip on the mattress, wrapping his arms around her shoulders.

She grabbed on to his arms, wanting to draw strength from him.

"A relationship isn't defined by the last moment. It's the whole of what you did together. All the moments matter as much as the last," Jack said.

Marissa lifted her head to look at him, his sincere expression and handsome face. She pressed her lips to his. A kiss of gratitude, to express what words could not.

When their lips met, desire rose inside her, consuming her, dragging her under its spell. He did not deepen the kiss, but he did not pull away, either.

When she broke away, she stared into his beautiful gray eyes, seeing flecks of green.

Jack removed her hands from his arm. He stood. "I should check the house again."

Desire lingered and mixed with guilt. "Jack, I didn't mean to make you uncomfortable."

Jack inclined his head. "You're in a tough place. I know what it feels like to lose a friend. I've lost too many. I want to be respectful of your feelings."

Marissa didn't know how to respond. Perhaps kissing him hadn't been the best idea, but it had been a long time coming. He was handsome and sweet and kissing him had less to do with her emotions regarding Avery and more to do with how she felt for him.

The warehouse was plain and unremarkable from the outside, but the inside was set up for a photo shoot with hundreds of backdrops and props and lighting equipment. Camera stands and vanities filled with makeup were clustered in the middle of the open space. Jack had reviewed the schematics for the building and had spoken with the photographer's assistant. They had security covered and this job should go off without a hitch.

Jack preferred the logistics of this photo shoot to the outdoor one on the beach in New Hampshire. It was easier to control the variables. While one of Marissa's bodyguards watched the door and checked each person who entered, Jack searched the building. The doors and windows were locked. Unless someone blew a hole in the wall—a remote possibility—no one was getting close to Marissa who hadn't been screened.

Marissa had warned him that this shoot could take several hours. Jack needed something to think about or he would fixate on Marissa. She was classically beautiful, she dressed impeccably, her hair was long and shiny and she could strut in heels that were impossibly tall. Every man's fantasy and since she was the center of attention at the shoot, it was doubly hard to keep her out of his.

More than a job. Every tick of the clock made that obvious. He was into her *personally*. She was gorgeous and she moved like a dancer. Even when she was standing and waiting, she seemed to be posing. Being a model for so long, it must come naturally to her. Now that he had that kiss, that sweet, delicate kiss, playing on his lips, it was that much harder to see her as just a client.

Few of his clients were ever just a client. He put his life on the line for them. Devoted his every waking hour. But this was the first time he had kissed a client. She had gotten to him, gotten under his skin. Her beauty was impossible to ignore, but he could have resisted that. It was her warmth and her charm that had lured him into kissing her. He wouldn't let it escalate. It had been a mistake that he wouldn't repeat. Compartmentalize the issue and stay focused on his work. He was good at that.

This photo shoot involved several other models. They were gathered on the set, posing with their hands on their hips while the lighting was checked by the photographer's assistant.

A male model stepped onto the set. He was wearing a black pair of boxer briefs and nothing more. Marissa appeared and took her place close to the nearly naked man. Jealousy struck Jack unexpectedly. This was her work and he was not her boyfriend. No place for feeling possessive.

The photographer was barking instructions and

the models positioned themselves, following his commands.

Marissa and the male model were staring at each other. They moved as if in slow motion, reaching without touching, gazing at each other with longing. The intensity of their expressions made Jack feel like he was watching a private moment playing out in a bedroom. Marissa had sex appeal and her white dress and glittery makeup made her appear ethereal. The male model set his hand on her hip and she stepped closer until they were nose to nose, their mouths inches apart.

The possessiveness that ripped through Jack was only because she was a client. Anyone close to her was a potential threat. Not that the male model could be hiding a weapon; his attire concealed next to nothing. Jack forced himself to look away. He walked around the area trying to burn off the unwanted emotion and looking for anyone new or anything out of place.

When Jack looked at Marissa again, she was standing with the other female models and the male model was being photographed alone. Marissa had added a pale yellow scarf to the white dress. The other women were wearing similar outfits in light colors, only theirs were more conservative.

"It's pretty boring, right?" Clarice stood next to him holding a clipboard. She had been on the set in Seabrook and had struck up a conversation. Her name had been mentioned in connection with the incident at Ambrose's fashion show.

Jack didn't know what to make of her. In control on the set, her clipboard her constant companion, she should know if something had been wrong at Ambrose's show. Jack had read the statement Clarice had made and she had indicated that she'd noticed something wrong when Avery wasn't waiting to walk the runway.

"They take hundreds of pictures of the same thing," Jack said.

"Each picture is different. Facial expressions and the lighting," Clarice said.

"What are they selling?" he asked.

"The shoes," Clarice said.

Jack looked at the shoes the models were wearing. He hadn't noticed them before. Tall, strappy and each appeared wildly uncomfortable. Jack couldn't picture anyone buying those impractical shoes. "I wouldn't have guessed."

Clarice laughed. "San Terese shoes. Very hot right now."

"Not my style. I'm a sneakers or boots kind of guy," Jack said.

"I can see that," Clarice said. "Marissa said you work around the clock. Guess that means you need more practical shoes."

Saying he worked around the clock was technically true. He could call in backup from the West Company if he needed a break. Based on his instructions from Griffin and Kit, he was only to rely on Marissa's bodyguards for appearances. They were not trained in the same manner he and his colleagues were. "For now."

"Why?" Clarice asked.

Jack didn't like giving away details about his job. "She hired me as part of her team."

"None of the other guys work around the clock," Clarice said.

None of her other bodyguards worked for the West Company. Connor West, owner of the West Company, held his employees to a high standard. They were experts in their field and had a higher than average success rate at accomplishing the jobs they'd been hired to do. With his injury keeping him from overseas work, Jack wouldn't make a mistake that would throw doubt on his abilities. "We're being extra careful."

Clarice looked away and Jack caught something in her eyes. Did she know more about Avery than she had told the authorities? "Something on your mind?" he asked.

Clarice fiddled with the clipboard. "I was there."

"At Ambrose's fashion show?" Jack asked. He had known that. If he gave her enough space, she may provide important information.

"I was working. It's my job to know what the models are doing and if they're ready or not. I should have been keeping better track of Avery. If I had..." Her voice grew tight and she brought her hand to her throat.

Jack couldn't discern if the guilt laced in that statement was because she'd had a hand in the incident or she incorrectly believed she could have prevented it. "You couldn't have known what would happen. You can't blame yourself." Unless she had something to do with Avery's death.

"I keep rethinking the day and trying to figure out if I missed something. Someone had to have noticed something." Clarice touched her earpiece and sighed.

"Excuse me. Wardrobe issue." She hurried off. Jack turned his attention back to the set and to Marissa.

The photographer was again taking pictures of Marissa. She was standing in front of a black backdrop contrasting her white outfit. A fan was blowing her hair and she was looking at the camera, her expression serious and her eyes piercing.

"Could we try a different angle?" the photographer asked. "Let's try bedroom eyes. Sultry expression."

Like flipping a switch, Marissa lowered her head and pouted her lips. Jack would call that hot. Definitely sexy.

"Isn't duck-face out?" one of the other models said to another. The three giggled.

Jack moved closer. He wasn't here to defend Marissa from jealousy, but he didn't like the cattiness. Before meeting Marissa, he would have assumed it was par for the course and every model was vicious and undercutting to others. But Marissa didn't have a bad thing to say about anyone.

"My agent told me they want to replace her on this campaign," a red-haired model said.

"Her thighs are huge. Talk about needing editing," another said.

"I think her hair is going gray," said another.

The vitriol in their comments rolled off him. He guessed they spoke this way about anyone more successful than they were. From what he had seen, they were the accessories. It was Marissa and the mostly naked guy's show.

Jack cleared his throat and the three models glanced at him. They straightened and turned, adding him to their circle.

"Hey there," one said.

"Haven't seen you around before," another said. She winked at him.

Jack had wanted them to stop talking crap about Marissa. He had no plans to exchange pleasantries. "I'm new to the modeling business. Learning what I can."

"Are you a model?" one asked.

"Nope. I'm working security for Marissa," he said.

"What is she like to work for?" one asked.

"She's great. Not demanding. Professional. She's had a tough time, but she rises above the petty."

Suddenly, they wouldn't make eye contact and were busy patting their hair and inspecting their nails. After a few awkward moments, they walked away. Jack didn't pursue the conversation. If they wanted to pout about his unwillingness to spread vicious gossip about Marissa, he was fine with that.

The photographer snapped his fingers. "We need a break. I need my other camera. Other camera! And change this set. Next one." He strode in the direction of his assistant.

A flurry of activity moving the set and the lighting while Marissa walked toward him.

"Everything okay?" she asked.

"I see nothing to worry about," he said. The set was secure.

"What do you think of the shoot?" she asked.

She was wearing more makeup than he was used to, especially around her eyes. Her outfit was flowing, almost like a Roman toga. "It's different than anything else I've seen."

Marissa took his elbow and led him a few steps away. "I heard some of the other models talking about me. Was it about Avery and me and our falling out?" Worry creased the corners of her eyes.

"No."

Her shoulders slumped. "I'm trying to focus on the shoot and not let Avery's death bother me. I'm trying to forget that someone wants me dead." She blew out her breath. Grief leaked from every pore. "But I'm tired. I'm tired of this. I'm tired of all of it."

"Do you want to leave?" he asked. He could whisk her off the set, claiming a security breach. Since the attack in her home, Marissa hadn't slowed down to process it.

Marissa swallowed hard. "I can't. Let's get through this and then we'll go."

At the rate she worked and with her limited free time, she was heading for a breakdown. He was worried about her. "You've been through a lot and I've seen this play out with other clients. The stress will get to you. You need to take a break."

She crossed her arms. "I can't. I have to honor my obligations."

"I admire that commitment. But I've seen your schedule. We'll slow down some. Work in some breaks," Jack said.

"Tell you what. After this, we'll run away for a few hours just you and me."

She was called back to the set. She winked at him and Jack was left thinking about time alone with Marissa. Lust hit him low and hard. He'd keep it in check. He couldn't give in to temptation.

Reporters were standing outside the photo shoot with cameras and lights. For days, Marissa had been waiting for the hammer to drop and for them to pursue the story of Avery's death more aggressively with her. They shouted questions at her, asking about Rob, Avery and for her to speculate about the affair and Avery's death, as if the two were linked.

Jack's arm slid around her shoulders and she held her sunglasses over her eyes. They hurried to Marissa's car, Jack slipping in behind the wheel. When she was inside and he pulled away from the warehouse, she relaxed.

She hadn't sorted her feelings about Rob and Avery's affair. She felt bad about it. Bad that they had started it, bad they had continued it and bad about how it had affected her friendship with Avery. She and Rob had only dated for six months, but they'd had fun. It had been serious enough for Marissa to factor him into her short-term plans, but not serious enough for her contemplate a distant future.

"You okay?" Jack asked from the driver's seat.

"I expected it. I need them to lose interest. Usually, it takes another Hollywood scandal and I'm forgotten about," Marissa said.

Jack's phone beeped through in the car communication system and the number appeared on the dashboard. Pressing a button on the steering wheel, he answered the call.

"Bad time?" the voice asked.

"I'm in the car with Marissa," Jack said.

"Hi, Marissa. I'm Abby. I work with Jack and Kit. I'm following up on an item about your case. Your business agent forwarded us threatening mail addressed to you. We haven't confirmed the sender."

"What kind of threats?" Marissa asked. She'd received threatening mail before. On the heels of the break-in to her house, those letters took on a different meaning.

"The threats have to do with you being responsible for and paying for hurting Avery. One of the threats mentions your jealousy over Avery and Rob's relationship and making you pay for seeking revenge. I want you to understand the seriousness, but also know that Jack won't let anything happen to you."

A chill went down her spine. She and Avery had been friends who'd had a falling out. Who would be obsessing about Avery, especially now that she was gone? "Was there anything else?" She felt sick to her stomach, but she needed to know.

"The letter most concerning to us says that Avery got what she deserved and you're next."

Dizziness made her head spin.

"Abby, let's talk about this in more detail later," Jack said.

Marissa's mouth went dry. She reached into the pocket in the back of the seat for a bottle of water. She twisted off the top and took a long swallow. "I was planning to retire at the end of the year. Maybe I should retire now. Move out of the public eye. Hide somewhere no one can find me."

Jack appeared surprised. "Staying out of the limelight until this is resolved is a good idea, but you can't let some nutjob force you into permanent retirement early. What happened to Avery was terrible, but I'm here to keep you safe."

The warmth in his voice touched her and her nerves calmed down a notch. "This business is brutal," Marissa said. She had worked hard for years and wanted time for leisure travel and painting and relaxing. Explore the world at her own pace, keep no schedule and follow where her interests led.

"You've climbed your way to the top of it. Remember how strong that makes you."

Marissa wasn't sure what to say to that. During her career, she'd had some great experiences. Working with creative designers like Ambrose, inspired photographers and talented models. She'd traveled the world and had attended movie premiers and celebrity weddings. Five years ago, she had taken a painting class in Paris and had fallen in love with the medium. From that point forward, painting had been in her plans. "I could publish my memoirs. A behind the scenes look at the modeling industry," Marissa said.

"You want to add bestseller to your résumé?" he asked.

She was too self-conscious about her painting to mention it to Jack. Which may have been silly, but so often she was dismissed as just a pretty face. "It has a certain appeal. Although if I write with too much honesty, I'll be blacklisted and destroy friendships. I'll have to move to a small town and hide out. Now that I'm saying it, it doesn't sound that bad."

"We'll call that plan B. Plan A is to find Avery's killer and stop him before he can strike again."

Chapter 4

After a hard workout in her home gym and a massaging and hot shower, Marissa went to bed. She kept her phone on her night table. When it buzzed against the wood, she considered ignoring it. Few people had her private cell number and most didn't call her after nine in the evening.

She reached for the phone and looked at the message. It was from Rob.

You awake? Call me when you get this.

Marissa wasn't in the mood to talk to him. She ignored the message and deleted it.

She was tossing and turning forty minutes later when she heard a tap on her door. Rest was elusive as she tried to sort her thoughts.

"Marissa?" Jack's voice. "Your mother is here. She needs to speak with you."

Her mother elbowed Jack to the side and came barreling into the room. Lenore was wearing a wrap around print shirt and a pair of navy trousers. Faux fur lined boots were pulled up to her calves. Her hair was cut short and dyed a deep auburn color. "What is going on with you? You haven't been answering my emails."

Marissa shoved a hand through her hair. She'd been busy and sorting emails often fell to her assistant to take care of. "Thanks, Jack." Letting him know he didn't need to listen to this conversation.

"She said it was an emergency," he said, appearing apologetic.

Marissa didn't blame Jack. Her mother had a key to her house and Jack wasn't her screening service. Everything with her mother was an emergency. "I haven't had time to reply to emails."

Lenore huffed. "You didn't have time to call me about what happened with Avery? I was in Paris and I had to read about it in the newspaper."

"I knew you were traveling and I didn't want to interrupt your trip."

"When someone is killed, you interrupt me no matter what."

"I'm sorry. It's been tough on me," Marissa said.

Her mother sat on the bed and put her arm around her shoulders. "I was worried. The news is saying the killer is targeting models. That's why I had to see you."

"I know, Mom. But I'm okay. Kit and Griffin referred Jack to me and he's doing a good job."

Her mother sighed and leaned against the headboard. "Your brother is in trouble."

"What has Luke done now?" Marissa asked. Her brother had been a financier for a large investment firm. Marissa was sketchy on the details, but Luke had lost his job when the company he'd worked for had downsized. Unable to find work, he had moved in with a friend, was sleeping on the friend's couch and he was floundering professionally.

"His girlfriend is pregnant," Lenore said.

Marissa hadn't been aware her brother had a girlfriend. Luke had been dating since he was fourteen, a never-ending line of women, all vaguely similar. "I don't think I should get involved." She had given her brother ten thousand dollars the year before. He hadn't paid her back and as far as she could see, he hadn't been prudent with the money.

"We have to get involved. This will be a huge scandal," her mother said.

Marissa disagreed. Maybe thirty years ago people cared about the length of a relationship and marriage before having a baby. She was a shining example of how marriage vows now were meaningless to the public. "No one will care. They'll wish him and his girlfriend well. Is she someone we know?"

"I met her. Once," her mother said. "She's loud. And brash. She hugged me. Her name is ridiculous. Zoe Ann. Two words."

Marissa liked the name. "I hate to be rude, but how do Luke and Zoe Ann's issues pertain to me?"

Her mother straightened. "I thought you would want to know. I'm upset about this, Marissa. I don't have anyone else to talk to about it. I can imagine what your sister will say. She'll think it's nice."

"It will be nice. A baby in the family."

"If we're allowed to see the baby. You know how your brother is. He'll do something stupid, torpedo the relationship, and I'll lose my only grandbaby."

"We need to get to know Zoe Ann. Be her friend. Don't insult her. Then if Luke does something stupid, we'll be in her and the baby's lives," Marissa said. It had worked that way with several of her former sisters-in-law and mothers-in-law. She'd had better relationships with them than her ex-husbands.

"I want them to stay with you," her mother said.

Marissa cringed at the idea. "Excuse me?"

"Luke is still sleeping wherever he can find a spot. And his girlfriend is on the outs with her parents over this. Luke asked to stay with me, but I have a two-bedroom condo and I need the extra bedroom for my office."

"Mom, this isn't a good time. With what happened to Avery, it's not safe here."

"You have five bodyguards," her mother said.

Her mother was exaggerating. At any time, she had one or two around at most. "There's a reason for having security," Marissa said.

"You're being unreasonable and selfish," Lenore said.

That was Lenore's response whenever Marissa didn't capitulate. "Let me think about it." It would be easier in the short term to rent Luke and Zoe Ann a place to live.

"My place is too small for all three of them. A baby needs room," Lenore said.

"Babies are also loud," Marissa said.

Lenore seemed to contemplate the thought, but not how it would affect Marissa. "I'll talk to Luke."

After catching up with her mom on a few more family topics, her mother stood. "I needed to know you were okay."

"I know," Marissa said. She appreciated that her mother cared so much.

"I'll see you soon. I won't travel for a while. You may need me."

"I'll be okay," Marissa said.

"Still. I'll be around."

After her mother left, Jack appeared in the doorway. "Should I have kept her from coming upstairs?"

Marissa shook her head. "That probably wasn't possible. She's my mother. She's a force all her own. What do you think I should do?"

"I only heard parts of the conversation. What do you want to do?"

Living with her brother would be a challenge. They hadn't lived together since they were teenagers. Add to it a total stranger, a pregnant stranger, and Marissa worried she would feel crowded. "Is it safe for anyone to live with me?"

"As safe as I can make it," Jack said.

"Luke has been unemployed for over a year," Marissa said. "And every time I've seen him, he looks worse. He's drinking too much. Sleeping all day. He's depressed. I could rent him an apartment, but he should work this out without me interfering." Marissa hated when her mother tossed a problem at her feet and left it there.

"I don't know the details of your relationship with

Luke. Maybe instead of leaving your mom in the middle, you should talk with him directly."

Marissa would try that. Maybe Luke and Zoe Ann had thought of other arrangements. "Do you have siblings?"

"I have three, two sisters and a brother," Jack said.

"You'd let them live with you?" Marissa asked.

"If they needed to," Jack said.

Marissa hadn't been great at cohabitating. Her ex-husbands could attest to that. "I'll call my brother and speak to him. He may have other options."

Jack moved toward the door. "That sounds like a good plan."

Marissa didn't want him to leave. As she was thinking of a reason to make him stay and talk, she heard a thump from somewhere in the house. "What was that?"

"Not sure. I'll check it out." Jack left the room. When he returned, his expression was serious. "A lamp was on the floor in the living room. I checked with the other bodyguard. No one in or out except your mother and she didn't knock over a lamp."

Marissa wouldn't overreact. "Could someone be in the house?"

"I will look around again and check the house. Wait here."

Jack disappeared.

Marissa sat on the bed, taking deep breaths and trying not to let her imagination run away with her.

Jack reappeared in the doorway. His strong body was a source of comfort. With him close, she felt safe. "All clear."

Relief tumbled over her. "Could you stay with me

until I fall asleep?" She was cold and wished he would remain in her room all night. Desire and fear mixed in a potent cocktail and she wanted him to stay with her.

"I could do that." His voice was tender.

He managed to be both strong and gentle with her, a combination she needed. "You're not a sentry. Why don't you come closer?" Marissa asked.

Jack glanced over his shoulder. "Giving you privacy."

"I appreciate that. But could you relax a bit?" The kiss they had shared replayed in her thoughts. He could be nervous about that happening again or he could feel like she did and be looking forward to it. With their connection and chemistry, it was inevitable.

Jack took a few steps toward the bed.

Marissa's heart fluttered in anticipation and warmth curled in her stomach. Marissa patted the mattress. "Lie here with me until I fall asleep."

He folded his arms and the bulges of his muscles drew her attention. "You wouldn't prefer space?"

Marissa didn't. She slept alone most nights, rarely having boyfriends spend the night. It had been a challenging day. She needed Jack tonight.

He settled onto the bed next to her, keeping a foot and a half of mattress space between them. Marissa shifted closer, drawn to him. She was under the covers; he was over them. She could smell him, the scent of sandalwood and she closed her eyes and let sleep claim her.

Jack wasn't on the schedule as the main bodyguard and Marissa wasn't scheduled to be out this morning. But he couldn't stay in bed late. His training prevented it. He had things to do and he wanted to spend time on the exercises he'd been given to strengthen his knee.

Marissa had a home gym and she'd given him permission to use it.

When he entered, Marissa was inside. The flat-screen television was on in the corner of the room playing an exercise video. The walls of the room were painted a bright yellow. She had five weight machines and two cardio machines, plus free weights on a ten-by-ten open area and a sound system. One of the walls was lined with mirrors and a waist-level, silver bar ran along it.

Marissa was on a turquoise foam mat, following the video. Jack had expected her to have a personal trainer. She wore a skintight outfit in black, purple and white with matching sneakers. Her hair was in a ponytail and pieces had escaped and framed her face.

The elliptical was his first choice. Though he preferred running—or better, running outside—he couldn't keep a hard pace for a long period of time on the sidewalk these days. His knee would occasionally still give out. To get back in the field, he needed to build the muscle around his knee.

Marissa turned to face him. "Good morning."

"Am I disturbing you? I can come back later," Jack said.

Marissa walked to the elliptical, tucking stray hair behind her ears. "Not bothering me. I was disappointed you left last night."

She was direct. He liked that. "I waited until you were asleep." Which had been her instructions.

"You should have stayed. I didn't sleep well."

His body heated and lust enveloped him at the idea of sleeping beside her. "You were safe."

"I know I was." Marissa smiled at him and he felt like a hero.

"Want to do some yoga with me once you're finished warming up?" she asked.

"Never tried it."

"My trainer swears by it. This is his video. He'll be by later today for a live session. You can participate if you want. He has great energy. Helps get me motivated."

"Sounds promising. I'll see how the day goes."

Marissa returned to her mat. She followed the trainer on the screen, stretching up. Jack's machine beeped. He had come to a complete standstill. He started moving again, trying not to fixate on the gorgeous supermodel leaning and reaching her lithe body into difficult positions. To fix his knee and get back in the field, he needed to do this. Requalifying to be an operative for the West Company required a level of physical fitness and conditioning he didn't have now. He wanted to get it back.

He started his machine again, this time, careful to keep his eyes on the miles and off Marissa.

A guard stood on Marissa's kitchen balcony, another at her front door and Jack was in her office. Paperwork was piled on her desk and her file cabinets were begging to be cleaned out. It wouldn't happen today.

"Do you have time for a meeting with your agent to discuss the mail?" Jack asked.

Marissa shook her head. "Not today." For a number of reasons, but first among them, she didn't want to talk about hate mail.

"Your schedule is empty today," Jack said.

Marissa set her handbag on top of her desk. The handbag was a gift from a friend and it was one of her favorites. Bright yellow and large enough to carry more than the essentials. "Once a month, I clear an afternoon for me. It's nonnegotiable."

"What does that entail?" Jack asked.

"Anything I want. I go see a movie. Shop for friends' birthdays. Lots of options," she said.

"And today's pick?"

"There's an open-air flea market about thirty minutes from here. I've seen signs, but I've never been. I'd like to go."

"That sounds like an uncontrollable situation," Jack said.

"No one knows I'll be there. I haven't told anyone. I only decided what I wanted to do this morning while you were pretending not to watch me doing yoga," Marissa said.

His cheeks darkened. "I wasn't watching you."

"Sure you were. I'm used to being watched. I know what it feels like," Marissa said.

Jack seemed flabbergasted.

Marissa patted his cheek. "It's okay. I'm giving you a hard time because you're so cute when you're flustered. What do you say? We try out the flea market?"

"If that's what you want," Jack said.

"By ourselves? Usually, I go without my security. I wear a hat and glasses and I'm largely ignored. With what's happened, I'm okay with you coming with me, but as a friend."

Jack whipped out his phone and started tapping on the screen. "I need to let the security team know where we'll be. I want them standing by as backup."

She didn't need backup, but she didn't argue. It was a small victory. Her monthly outings were the one time she could disappear in a crowd and spend time with her thoughts. Though her personal assistant handled most of her shopping, she liked to buy certain things herself.

"I'll drive," she said.

She took the keys to her sedan from the peg board on the wall. The keychain gave her pause. It had been a gift from Avery. The small bejeweled half heart had Marissa's initials on it. Avery had the other half of the heart. Avery had given it to her when she'd bought the sedan. Avery may have still had the other half and the idea sent a wave of grief crashing over her.

Marissa sat in her office chair.

"What's wrong?" Jack asked.

Marissa held up the keychain, letting it dangle from her finger. "This was a gift from Avery."

"The car?"

"The keychain," Marissa said. "She was always buying stuff like this. Loved personalized trinkets."

"I'm sorry. I know you miss her."

She did. She truly did. Marissa gathered herself. Spending the day wallowing wouldn't help. Going outside, walking in the fresh air, would give her a new perspective. "I do. It was stupid to let the problem fester between us. But let's go. I need to be back by six to meet my trainer." She stood and after Jack exited the room, she closed the door behind him. Obsessing over what had happened with Avery would take her to a dark place. Coping with what she had done and how their relationship had ended would haunt Marissa for the rest of her life.

She opened the garage bay door. "We'll take the sedan. The trunk is bigger than the sports car's, so if I score anything awesome, I can fold the backseats down and haul it home." Retail therapy and getting her mind off the terrible events of late was her primary goal.

"I didn't picture you as a flea market type," Jack said. "Everything in your home seems polished."

"When I was younger, Kit and I used to pull junk from the dumpster. We had some good finds. We'd bring it home, clean it, fix it and either use it or sell it. It became a hobby. My place was decorated by an interior designer, but I've added pieces myself." In some cases, her guests didn't know the difference.

Thirty minutes later and having enjoyed the easy conversation with Jack, Marissa parked on a grass field, the lot marked with orange tape. She was next to a sky blue minivan with rust around the door edges and she tried to remember that detail. Checking her sunglasses and hat in her reflection in the window, she felt sure she wouldn't be recognized. She adjusted her wool scarf over her mouth. Her coat covered her outfit and her boots were pulled to her knees.

Ahead of her were rows of tents providing shelter from the wind for the vendors. She pulled the small, rolling collapsible trolley from her trunk.

Jack laughed. "You come prepared."

"I sure do. Can't waste time walking back and

forth to the car. We could miss something good." Jack took hold of the trolley's handle and Marissa let him.

The aisles of the flea market were crowded with shoppers with canvas totes, wagons and carts similar to hers. She stopped at a table selling records. "Oh, look at this! Old records." The vendor had various genres.

Jack moved closer and slipped his arm around her shoulder. His touch burned through her. She leaned into him, curious about the intimacy.

"There's a group of women pointing at you. Make your purchase and then we need to move. They may have recognized you."

Marissa was dressed like everyone else, her hair in a wool hat, and sunglasses covering her face. In case Jack was right and she had been recognized, she bought several albums and they hurried down the line of tables, making quick decisions about her purchases. It annoyed her to feel rushed. The purpose of the day was to get away from the frantic pace and take a stroll.

After filling her trolley, Marissa and Jack walked to the car. The group of women Jack had spotted hadn't said anything to her.

As they walked back to the flea market, two teenaged girls ran to Marissa, their phones in hand. "Are you Marissa?" they asked in stereo.

Marissa obliged most fans. They were the reason she was successful. But not on her one free afternoon a month. Today, she wasn't a model.

Jack's arm went around her waist. "You're mistaken. Happens. Come on, honey, the kids are waiting at home." She and Jack hurried away from the girls. "We should consider that a warning."

"You handled it. We'll be fine," Marissa said. "Nice line about the kids." She didn't want to give up so soon and return home. Visiting this flea market had been on her wish list for months.

"I thought it sounded domestic," Jack said. He was wearing a jacket, scarf and gloves. The gloves were tight and she wondered if could handle a gun with them.

His hand on her waist felt natural and Marissa pressed against him. Even with their coats between them, she felt the heat radiating from his body.

Tents were set up to form uneven paths and all manner of items were for sale. Marissa and Jack strolled through, looking at various treasures. Pots, chairs, frames, lamps, antique electronics that may not work, and children's toys were laid out for shoppers to peruse. Hard to decide what else she wanted. Some of her visions didn't work how she pictured them and she ended up selling the project or giving it away.

About a third of the way down the line of vendors, she spotted a hidden treasure swinging from the back of the open canvas tent. A crystal chandelier with colored gems strung together with silver metal. "How much?" she asked.

"Two seventy-five," the bored-looking man said. He stroked his chin, appraising her, maybe trying to figure out from her clothing if she had money.

"That's too high," Marissa said. She didn't know much about the item, but she could negotiate. It was one of her favorite parts. "Two twenty-five."

The man studied the chandelier. "Two fifty. Final offer."

Marissa took off her sunglasses to look closer at the chandelier. She didn't have a place in mind for it. It was an unusual piece. The man's jaw slackened and she heard whispers behind her and turned.

Removing her sunglasses had been a mistake. The teenaged girls who had approached her earlier had their phones out and snapped a picture.

Marissa slid her sunglasses back on. It was too late. Others had recognized her and were taking pictures.

"Two fifty? You want it?" the man asked.

People were closing in around her, putting their cameras in her face and asking if she wanted to take a selfie with them for their social media sites. Her stomach knotted and her blood pressure soared. Marissa backed away, only to bump into others. Their voices were getting louder and more insistent. Her toes curled and panic clawed at her. "Jack?" The question escaped her lips, shaking and small.

Jack's hands slipped around her waist in a touch that was protective and strong. She leaned into him and he moved her through the crowd, elbowing people out of the way as they walked.

"No pictures please," Jack said.

Marissa's thoughts jumped around her brain. What if the person who had killed Avery was in the crowd? Her vision blurred and her heart was racing. Something felt off about this, like a dark presence was circling and bad things were about to happen.

"Jack?"

He hadn't left her side. Marissa kept her head down and put her arms around Jack's waist. When they were through the crowd and to the car, Jack helped her into the passenger seat.

No one had followed them this far. She released a weighty breath.

He knelt next to her on the grass. "Are you okay? You look pale."

Marissa's hands were shaking. "I think Avery's killer was there."

Alarm registered on Jack's face. "How do you know? Did you see someone?"

"This might sound silly." She felt ridiculous saying it. "But I felt something bad was about to happen."

Jack stood and looked around. "We're out of here."

"Maybe I should go back and see if I recognize anyone," Marissa said.

"First priority is your safety."

She groaned. "My chandelier."

"There will be others."

She laid her head against the back of the seat. "Not like that one. It was unique with the colored gems."

Jack circled the car and climbed in the driver's side. Thirty seconds later, they were pulling onto the main road. "I'm sorry about the chandelier."

"I shouldn't have taken off my sunglasses. I wanted to see if the chandelier was in good condition. It was dirty and needed a good polish, but it would be great." Marissa reached across to Jack and set her hand over his.

He turned his hand over and squeezed hers.

"Your hands are strong," she said. "When you're close to me, I feel safe."

"I'm glad you feel that way. You're still trembling."

Her imagination might be overactive, but feeling

someone lurking near her was unsettling. "I know it seems irrational, but I felt something dark."

"Can you focus on that feeling? Was it more than a feeling? Maybe you caught a glimpse of someone and it triggered that worry. Someone who was there the day Avery was killed."

His confidence in her was a shot of adrenaline she needed. Marissa closed her eyes and thought about the flea market. The feeling of worry had wafted around her. She could have seen someone in her peripheral vision who had unsettled her or she could have caught a glimpse of someone familiar. Hard as she was trying, she couldn't recall what had set off the feeling of unease.

She looked at Jack and another emotion rolled through her: desire. The warmth she felt for him, the closeness and the connection they were forming wrapped around her, binding her to him. They were a team in this.

"I'm sorry. I can't think of anything specific I saw," Marissa said.

Jack drummed the car's steering wheel with his finger. "I want to run something by you. Kit suggested it and I've been holding off on asking." He took a labored breath. "Would you be open to going to Avery's apartment and taking a look around? The police have searched her things looking for a connection to something or someone who led to her death. Her financials look clean, although she had almost weekly transactions in the ten-thousand range both expenses and payments. Nothing on her home computer or phone to indicate trouble."

“What were the police looking for exactly?” Marissa asked.

“Prescription pills, drugs, gambling debts, excessive alcohol present, or any type of blackmail.”

Marissa pictured Avery’s apartment. She had an entire room that had been remodeled into a closet with racks and drawers and shelves. She and Avery used to walk through and look at pieces Avery had saved from the eighties and nineties, relics from another era. Many were gifts from designers, couture pieces worth thousands. “I could do that. But I don’t see how I would find something if the police didn’t.”

“You were her friend. You might notice something new or missing and make a connection,” Jack said.

Marissa was willing to try. If they didn’t get to the bottom of who killed Avery, Marissa wouldn’t have peace.

A police officer met them at Avery’s apartment, located in a trendy neighborhood and occupying the eleventh floor of a renovated, brick-sided canning factory. Avery had lived in the space for the last eleven years and she had made it her own.

The apartment was modern and spacious, the kitchen open to the rest of the living space, with the exception of her bedroom, which was closed off by a glossy, reflective sliding white door. The walls were white and the kitchen cabinets and countertops were white. The couch, marble floor tiles and curtains were white. The only splash of color was the teal couch in the middle of the room, Avery’s statement piece. The throw pillows on the couch had Avery’s initial’s embroidered on them in silver, the glass vase on the counter had Avery's name etched into it and the prints on the wall were black-and-white canvases of photos of Avery, her career highlights.

This place was hers. The sadness that descended on Marissa brought tears to her eyes.

"Does everything look the same?" Jack asked.

With the exception of the stale scent in the air, it was as she remembered it. "It has been a few months since I've been here, but it looks the same. Can I check the bedroom?"

Jack nodded.

Marissa pulled open the barn-style white door and was struck by the brightness of Avery's private sanctuary. Whereas the main room was stark and white, this space hummed with color. The throw rugs over the marble tile were bright pink. Her bed was covered with an orange-and-yellow comforter. The walls were painted light green and the adjoining room that served as her closet was as vibrant.

Grief tightened Marissa's throat. She had borrowed clothes from this closet. Traded accessories. Made last-minute switches for different clutches and scarves. Regret followed close on the heels of grief and sadness.

Jack's hands touched her shoulders. She closed her eyes and wiped away the tear that had formed. She sagged into him, grateful he was with her.

"If it's too much, we can come back another day," Jack said.

Marissa mustered the strength to push away her sadness and do this for Avery. "I couldn't say if anything is missing. But I doubt Avery was having money problems. She has several pieces in this room she could have sold for thousands if she'd needed money."

"Jewelry?" Jack asked.

Marissa shook her head. "Some of the garments are original designs from major fashion houses."

"That's pretty wild," Jack said.

In the center of the closet on top of a set of drawers, Avery had stacks of fashion magazines and sketch pads with her original designs and ideas in them.

Marissa walked through the closet, looking at the dresses and costume jewelry. "I don't see anything out of place, but I didn't memorize the contents of her closet or her house. All I can tell you is that she told me she had never once used her kitchen. Her caterer did a few times, but Avery didn't like to cook." She whirled to face Jack. "I'm sorry. I wish I could give you more. I wish I had the answers you're looking for."

Compassion touched the corners of Jack's eyes. "We'll figure this out. I promise you. And I'll be here with you until we do."

Chapter 5

Marissa held up a brown basket and a roll of shiny blue ribbon. "Help me?"

"What are you working on?" Jack asked. If she was doing arts and crafts, that wasn't his jam.

Marissa had spread out various items on her kitchen table. Ribbon, scissors, tape and glue along with envelopes and wrapped gifts.

"I need to assemble this for a charity event tonight," Marissa said.

"You're selling a basket?" He had seen the event on the schedule, but it hadn't listed details about what Marissa was doing at the event.

"I am selling *me* with the basket."

That got his attention.

"I decorate this and fill it with prizes and goodies and then people bid on it. Proceeds go to charity and whoever bids highest gets the basket and an evening with me."

Jack didn't like the idea. Not because he was attracted to Marissa. His concerns were security related. "You're planning to run off with a stranger?"

"Not run off. Just have dinner in the private dining room of the hotel where the auction is being held. I need to participate. I'm the chairperson of the event," Marissa said. She was threading the ribbon through the weave on the basket.

"You waited until now to make this?"

Marissa pulled the ribbon through. "I bought the basket and the decorations and the items to fill it. I just need to organize it."

Jack settled at the table and glanced into the bags. "All this stuff has to go in?"

Marissa opened the flip-top lid of the basket. "I may have overbought. This is the biggest one I could find. I want to set a good example. The better the auction item, the more money we raise."

"What are you raising money for?" he asked.

"A children's research hospital," Marissa said.

He was surprised that she had time to chair an event and that she was taking a personal role in it. "What are you putting in the basket?"

Her smile was bright and excited. "It's an entertainment gift assortment. I have movie tickets, concert tickets, baseball tickets, football tickets and gift cards for a few restaurants. Plus, bottles of wine and chocolates. To personalize it, I put tickets to the swimsuit show this spring. I've decided against being in the show, but I'm giving up my second ticket. Whoever bids the most gets a front row seat next to me."

"I have security concerns." Multiple concerns ranging from crowd control to monitoring whoever bid highest. And he was in tune enough with his emotions to recognize jealousy. Whoever won her basket won time with her. Though he had that in spades, their time wasn't as he would have spent it were they in other roles.

Marissa smoothed the ribbon. "What security concerns? Everyone coming to the event tonight was vetted by the fund-raising committee."

She was in a better mood than he had seen for the last several days. He didn't want to dump on it. "You knew most of the people backstage at the fashion show, too."

She winced. He didn't mean to put too fine a point on it.

"You'll be with me and if I feel the slightest bit uncomfortable, I'll signal you."

She began filling the basket. He handed her some of the larger items and she carefully arranged them. When she was finished, she sprinkled sparkling curls of ribbon around the items. The she closed the lid. "What do you think?"

"Whoever wins that basket is one lucky man and I'm thinking you're going to start a bidding war."

Marissa grinned. "That's the idea."

Tonight's charity event was the shot in the arm of morale Marissa needed. She had pulled strings to host the event at the best hotel in the city even if Thursday was an odd day of the week. The men and women who had agreed to offer themselves as dates for the evening had come through. The baskets were beautiful and elegant and stuffed with unique items.

For the purposes of this event, the dining room had been decorated in whites and blues. She hadn't wanted it to look like a wedding. The blue tones were soothing and blended with the natural decor of the room. The room to the right would serve as the location for the auction and the cocktail hour. It was also decorated in blues, although she had intentionally kept the flowers and decorations in the cocktail area understated, so her guests were blown away by the ballroom.

Marissa had also scored a major coup by convincing five billionaires to attend. Two were married and at the event with their spouses, but she hoped they would bid big on a basket in any case. It was for a great cause and 100 percent of the money raised went to the research hospital. Plus, the men and women she had asked to donate their time and a basket were great conversationalists. While the event had an element of romance, every match-up didn't need to be more than a great night with a fun person.

As Marissa mingled, thanking attendees for coming, she watched Jack out of the corner of her eye. He was staying to the side of the room, but moving with her, keeping her in his line of vision.

When he looked at her, she felt tingles over her body. She was wearing an Ambrose design, one that hadn't been in his spring collection. He had kept it for her, insisting it was perfect for her, made for her. She'd saved it for a special occasion. Tonight's black-tie affair was that occasion. The emerald green dress fit her snugly—a one strap design, clinging to her thighs and then opening in a series of cascading ruffles that moved when she walked. She had her hair clipped to the side and twisted up, old-world romance. Everything about this night had to be perfect because much was riding on it.

Marissa glanced at Jack. In his tuxedo, he blended well. Did he have experience with this type of event? The extent of what she knew of his background was that he had three siblings and worked with Kit and Griffin at a car company.

She strolled to him. In this room of actors and actresses, reporters and media moguls, models and photographers, she wanted to be with Jack. He seemed always at the ready and he was darkly good-looking with midnight eyes and a commandingly powerful build. “You are welcome to socialize tonight.”

Though he called no attention to himself by being loud or boisterous, she couldn’t stop looking at him. “I’m working. I’m good here.”

Marissa admired his work ethic, but security was tight. Everyone in attendance was on her list. They were friends and colleagues and special guests. She wouldn’t start living her life being suspicious of every person in the room.

On a more selfish level, if he relaxed, she could enjoy time with him. Of all the people in the room, he interested her most.

Marissa had bought tickets for her mother and a date and her brother and his date, who Marissa assumed would be Zoe Ann. Marissa hadn’t made up her mind about allowing her brother and his pregnant girlfriend to live with her, but speaking with Zoe Ann would help Marissa to understand if they needed help, or if her mother saw trouble where it didn't exist.

"I wasn't suggesting you disappear at the bar, but you look stoic. Maybe smile and blend," Marissa said. He could drop the tense readiness for a few hours, couldn't he? She wondered what he would be like on a date. Tense, ready and careful or could he let down his guard enough to let her in?

The corners of his mouth lifted slightly. "How is this?"

Marissa laughed at the forced expression. She touched his arm and felt heat lightning moving through her at the connection. "Okay, you tried. I want everyone to feel relaxed and in a generous mood. The hospital needs funding. They lost a big donor last year and haven't made up for it."

Jack was looking at her but watching around them, as well. "This has personal meaning to you?"

She was invested more than she could express. It felt important for him to recognize that she was more than her beauty. Though she was accustomed to being underestimated, she cared about people, most especially those charities she had committed to helping. "Of course. I've been planning this evening for nine months. I've called in every favor with every celebrity and pseudo-celebrity I know. I even called an old boyfriend from college who works at one of those big financial firms to get him to give me the personal contact information for big name clients."

"That's generous of you." His eyes seemed to convey appreciation of what she was doing.

Attaching her name to the cause was only to bring

interest. "If I don't do something like this every year, I get helplessly caught up in my own stuff."

"Meaning?"

How could she explain it without sounding narcissistic? She was self-involved to a large degree and people around her promoted that. Unmarried and without children or pets, she had only herself to consider. "My manager, my agent, my mom and most of the people around me are all about me. On a photo shoot, everyone is looking at me. After a while, I get wrapped up in my problems. My contracts, my cash flow, if I miss a workout and eat a piece of cake. Which is a miserable place to be. I do these events to get outside myself. If a magazine cover I was on gets terrible reviews or people send me hate mail about looking too thin or too fat, it goes to my head. But this event keeps me grounded. Makes me remember that a troll calling me ugly online is unimportant."

The more he got to know her, the more he liked her. "The event looks lovely. You should be proud."

She was. She had secured amazing guests for the night. The lights dimmed once. Marissa's heart hammered. What happened in this room in the next two hours would be critical to the hospital. The waiters and waitresses would be serving appetizers and drinks to stave off hunger and irritability. Once the baskets were paired, those who were matched up would move to the formal dining room in which small tables were assembled to provide for private conversation.

As the first basket was set in the front of the room on a white linen–covered table, excitement ping-ponged inside her. Her good pal, a news anchor for a top television broadcast, was first. The news anchor was intelligent and beautiful and a wonderful speaker. Marissa wanted to start the bidding high by having a great first candidate and set the tone of bidding high for the rest of the night.

"First basket was created by Abigail Stevens."

A whoop of approval from a table of suit-wearing men.

The contents of the baskets were a mystery, but dinner with Abigail this evening was worth at least several thousand dollars.

The bidding began at one thousand dollars. The table of men seemed to be in competition with each other, driving the price high. Within minutes, a portly gentleman with gray hair had forked over eight thousand, five hundred dollars for the basket and dinner with Abigail. Abigail hugged the man and by the genuine warmth and easiness between them, Marissa guessed they were friends or at least friendly.

The next basket was set out for bidding to begin. Then another. Each basket netted more money than the last.

Marissa's anxiety touched down as she tracked the donations. Her goal was a quarter of a million dollars and she had the right people in the room to do it. She would match the donations, a fact she hadn't disclosed to the hospital and would do anonymously.

Her palms started to sweat when her basket was placed on the table. She smiled as the auctioneer spoke her name. Several heads turned in her direction. Relaxing her shoulders and keeping her expression calm, she gave a demure wave. Posing for pictures was easy, but she felt on display and the importance of the night was not lost on her.

The bidding started at one thousand dollars. At the four-thousand-dollar mark, Rob stood, raising his paddle and offering twenty thousand dollars.

Marissa's heart almost stopped. She hadn't known Rob would be attending the event. He hadn't been on her guest list, although he could have gotten a ticket from someone. Rob didn't have twenty thousand dollars. This wasn't a game. The hospital needed the money. Irritation and indignation struck her.

The idea of sitting across the table from Rob made her physically ill. She couldn't deny him or make a scene; this was her event. She would have to be a good sport.

She felt Jack behind her and glanced at him. Rob and another man, Thomas Thurlow, were bidding, raising the bids by a few hundred dollars each round.

"How do you know Thurlow?" Jack asked.

Their relationship was casual. "He's an executive at a fashion magazine I've modeled for. Nice guy, easy to work with. Probably figures I don't want to spend the evening with an ex."

Marissa didn't want a confrontation with Rob or to be forced into a conversation with him. People were watching her and she kept her face neutral. With Avery's death making headlines, Rob's presence was a fresh reminder of what had happened between Rob and Marissa. "I don't think I can talk to him for more than a couple minutes, but I don't know what choice I'll have."

When Rob bid thirty thousand, Thomas sent Marissa an apologetic looked and sat in his chair. Panic flared. Could she bid on her own basket? She would rather sit alone than be with Rob. Plus, he might not have the money. He was terrible with finances. He made money, squandered it and invested poorly and recklessly. Grief and frustration surged through her and she worked to hide it from her expression.

Jack stepped forward to stand slightly in front of her. "Fifty thousand."

Marissa gasped. Fifty thousand dollars? From a car dealer or bodyguard or whatever he was? For dinner with her, which he could have for free most nights? She was simultaneously shocked and grateful.

The amount was so high it also brought the total raised above the quarter of a million dollar mark. Many emotions careened through her. Happy to have met a goal she hadn't believed possible, gratitude for the generous people in this room for opening their hearts and wallets, relief at being rescued from Rob, worry about Jack spending so much money, and lust and desire at the anticipation of being alone with Jack.

Rob was staring at her, openmouthed. Marissa shook off her emotions and smiled.

The auctioneer declared Jack the winner of her basket. Jack circled the room, accepted the basket and brought it to where he had been standing.

The entire room was staring and whispering, but the only thought in her mind now was that Jack had saved her again.

"Jack, please, let me reimburse you the fifty thousand," Marissa said.

Jack tried not to be insulted. He understood how a charity auction worked. This was his first event of the kind and he was happy to make a donation. The children's hospital did great work and he wanted to support Marissa. The bonus was putting her in a position to avoid Rob.

Rob had cheated on her. Jack wasn't convinced that Rob was innocent in regards to what had happened to Avery and what he knew about it. He had to know what his girlfriend had been involved with or at least have a suspicion. The West Company was staying looped into the police investigation and Rob had not given anything away yet.

Marissa might be worried Jack couldn't swing it. Working fifteen years in special operations, without a permanent home or many possessions, Jack had accumulated a large sum of hazard pay, salary and bonuses. Fifty thousand wasn't a big deal. He wasn't sure what he would do with his money anyway. It might as well go to helping a children's hospital.

"I'm happy to support the cause," Jack said.

Marissa blinked at him. "I'm sorry if I'm being rude or if I seem ungrateful, but I feel like you were forced into bidding."

The idea incensed him. "No one forces me to do anything."

"It's so much money," Marissa said. "Were you planning to bid?"

"No," Jack said. He made quick decisions and lived with them. "I'm pleased to make the donation although I feel like I cheated."

"Cheated?"

"I had a sneak peek of what was in your basket," Jack said. "I knew I was getting my money's worth."

Marissa laughed, the sound like the soft ringing of hand bells. “I can reimburse you.”

He held up his hand. “Really, it’s fine.”

Marissa slipped her arm through his. “Tell me what it is my sister and you do that makes fifty thousand dollars a reasonable amount to donate.”

“I don’t do the same work Kit does. We have different jobs. I’m a bodyguard.” He couldn’t give her more than that. If Kit wanted to divulge to her sister what she did and who she worked for, that was her decision. At the West Company, silence was the default answer.

Marissa rested her head on his shoulder. “You are more than a bodyguard to me. You’ve become a friend.”

A friend. He pondered that word. He hadn’t before thought of a client as a friend, but everything about this assignment was new. He had assumed this assignment would be easy. Compared to an environment with exploding bombs, sharpshooters, traitorous partners and general chaos, it was simpler. It presented other challenges, like keeping Marissa close while keeping her at a distance. “How do you know I didn’t bid on the basket so I could keep you close? For professional reasons?”

Marissa appeared surprised. “Was that the reason? Just your job?”

He shook his head. “I would have hovered near you regardless. This just makes it easier. Plus, I won’t have to listen to Rob jawing off about his issues.”

Speaking of Rob, he approached, walking fast, hands knotted at his sides, his cheeks red with anger.

Jack stepped between them, intercepting Rob. "Cool off."

Rob pushed at him. Jack didn't budge.

"This doesn't concern you. I need to talk with Marissa," Rob said.

"She's my date for the night. Those were the rules," Jack said. He took some delight in antagonizing the other man.

Marissa moved around him. "Rob, calm down. Why don't you go outside and get some fresh air?"

"I bid on your basket because I need to talk to you."

"We have nothing to say to each other," Marissa said. Her eyes were flat and her tone frosty. She had indifference nailed.

Rob leaned close. "It's about Avery."

Jack's interest was piqued, but he wasn't certain Rob was telling the truth. Discussing Avery could mean anything.

Marissa's shoulders tensed. "If you have some information pertaining to the case, you should contact the police."

Rob ran his fingers through his hair, leaving his hair poking in various angles.

People were staring. Tossing Rob out was tempting, but creating a scene would embarrass Marissa.

Marissa tapped her heel. "It's almost time for dinner to be served," Marissa said. "I need to handle my duties."

"Your duties? Is that your way of saying you want to sneak off with your bodyguard?" Rob asked and his fists balled at his sides.

Marissa inhaled sharply. Jack's temper flared, but

he kept his voice low. "Enough. This is a nice event for a great cause and you're creating a problem. I'll give you the opportunity to walk out on your own accord. If you don't move in the direction of the exit immediately, I will haul you out. That will make a nice picture for the gossip columns."

Marissa folded her arms and looked at Rob expectantly. "Leave. Go now."

Rob's eyes flared with anger. He turned on his heel and fled the ballroom. The door banged against the wall as he exited. The door closed slowly.

Marissa took a deep breath and let it out slowly. "Let me announce the start of dinner and check that the waitstaff understands their cues."

The faster she could move this situation along and distract everyone, the better. The best part of the night was the dinner, a chance for all the bidders to enjoy a meal with great conversation.

Marissa hurried away and Jack followed at a distance, keeping her in his line of vision. She was shaken by the encounter with Rob. Jack should have punched the guy. He could tell the night was important to Marissa in the way she was fussing over the details.

Marissa's mother approached, wineglass in hand. "What did Rob want?" Lenore asked.

"To talk to Marissa," Jack said.

"About what?"

Jack was in the middle of the situation and would rather not be. He had his hands full with protecting Marissa. "You should talk to Marissa about that." Before her mother could chase her down, Jack touched

Lenore's arm. "Except not here. She worked hard for tonight and she should focus on being hostess."

Her mother gave him a long look. "You're protective of Marissa."

"Protecting her is what I was hired to do."

Lenore stared hard. "To protect her physically. But you care about her. On a personal level."

"She is a good, hardworking woman," Jack said. That was as far as he could let anyone know he had developed feelings for his client. Personal feelings of any type were distracting and inappropriate. His closeness to his last partner had almost gotten him killed. He had trusted Bianca too completely.

"Marissa is a good person. Not everyone sees it. They see her beauty. That's impossible to miss. But few see her for who she is. Do you?" Lenore asked. She leaned forward as if the answer was written on his face.

"I barely know her," Jack said.

"Yet you threw a small fortune after her to keep her away from Rob," Lenore said.

"That wasn't the only reason. I am duty bound to protect her." This conversation was making him uncomfortable. It was circling around a developing emotion he didn't want to discuss.

"Tell me how a bodyguard has that much money. Did Marissa give you the money? Did she put you up to bidding?"

Marissa and her mother were worried about the money. Why? As long as he could write a check to the charity, it wasn't a big deal. "It was not Marissa's money." He would leave it at that.

"I see. Then you are not who you seem."

"I am exactly who I seem. I have not misrepresented myself," Jack said.

"You're friends with Kit and her fiancé, Griffin, right?"

Jack nodded.

"Kit seems to think I live under a rock. Like I'd believe she works for a car company. Please. There was an incident last year at Marissa's birthday party. It made it pretty clear that Kit was more than a florist. She gave me some line about going to work for a car company. She won't say which one. I've put the pieces together. Kit is smart. If she says you're right for this job, then I won't question her judgment. But I know you are not a bodyguard. You're more than that, and I mean that about your job and about how Marissa cares for you."

Before Jack could respond, the music stopped and he turned. Marissa stood at the microphone at the front of the room. She was blindingly beautiful.

"Excuse me. If I could have your attention. I hope you've had a few minutes to introduce yourself to your companions for the evening. If you would please take your seats in the next room, dinner will be served."

Four sets of trellis-scrolled doors opened and guests moved into the adjacent room.

Marissa joined him and her mother. "Oh, no. What did she say to you?" Marissa gave her mother a wry look.

"Marissa, don't be dramatic. We were exchanging pleasantries. Speaking of pleasantries, I see your brother and Zoe Ann. Please make yourself available to speak with them about that matter I brought to your attention."

Marissa's shoulders tensed. "After this event, I will speak with Luke."

Her mother walked away leaving them alone. Jack extended his arm to Marissa and they followed the other guests into the dining area.

Dozens of small sweetheart tables seating two to four people were set around the room, the linen-topped tables different colors with flower arrangements set in the middle. A string quartet played softly and waiters in white gloves circulated to the tables, taking orders and delivering drinks.

He and Marissa found an open table. Jack held out her chair and Marissa beamed at him. "Thank you."

She took her seat. "The hospital will be thrilled about this. They need money for new machines and want to renovate the inpatient suites. Thank you again. I don't know what I would—"

The sound of the fire alarm cut the air. Marissa flinched.

Jack stood, taking Marissa's arm and scanning for the nearest exit and the source of the fire. He didn't smell smoke and he considered that emptying the hotel was a way of exposing dozens of high-profile, wealthy individuals to whatever may await them outside. The alarm could also be a false alarm, too much steam in the kitchen or steam from a shower. The hotel was old and perhaps their systems weren't up to date.

Guests could use the emergency exit from the ballroom or exit through the adjoining room and into the main lobby. The emergency exit was closest, leading onto a blue, green and white pavers patio. It was five steps from the patio to the street.

Other guests in attendance had security as well and would make their decisions. It was Jack's priority to keep Marissa safe. Jack guessed many would be hustled to their cars.

Jack tucked her close and they hurried toward the exit.

Marissa pulled away. "I need to make sure that everyone gets out."

He didn't want to wait too long. "When a fire alarm goes off, everyone knows what to do."

A flash of indecision and then Marissa followed him outside.

A light drizzle of snow sprinkled down on them. The air was crisp and cold. Jack needed to get Marissa somewhere covered.

A man's scream interrupted Jack's train of thought.

"Marissa! Marissa!" Rob was standing in front of the hotel's main door, bellowing. Passersby moved around him, ignoring him. The lights from the hotel lobby and the street lights illuminated the sidewalk. Rob's jacket looked rumpled, his tie loose around his neck. His pants had lost their crispness.

Rob was involved with the fire alarm. Whether he had set it off by pulling it or starting a fire was anyone's guess.

"He's drunk. Don't talk to him. Get in the car," Jack said. Being out in the open left them at greater risk for an attack.

"He's making a spectacle." Marissa looked around. The guests from the charity event were glancing at her and whispering amongst themselves.

"Let him make a spectacle." They needed to go.

The sound of sirens approaching filled the air.

"Please check that my mom, brother, Zoe Ann and our guests made it out okay. I need to find out what happened." She started in Rob's direction, walking quickly, purpose snapping in every step. Jack stayed close to her. The night had taken a bad turn.

When Rob caught sight of Marissa, he rushed to her. He was babbling, making apologies. He knelt on the ground in front of her. Jack wanted to tell him to stop making a fool of himself. Marissa had told him to go home, not to stay around the hotel to start drama.

People on the sidewalks were pointing at the hotel. The sound of the fire alarms could be heard on the street and the swell of guests vacating the hotel was filling the sidewalk.

"Get up, Rob," Marissa said quietly but firmly.

Jack grabbed Rob by the lapels. "Did you pull the fire alarm?"

"It was the only way to get to her," Rob said.

"You idiot! Someone could be hurt. There could be a stampede," Jack said.

"I did it for her. She wouldn't talk to me. She shut me out." His blathering continued and Jack released him and turned away. When the police arrived, Rob would be arrested.

"This is not the time or place to have this conversation," Marissa said.

The fire truck pulled to the front curb. An employee of the hotel rushed forward and Jack jogged over to explain what happened. Marissa appeared distressed. Her guests had left and her fund-raiser was in shambles.

Marissa was tapping on her phone with shaking hands. "I need to call everyone. They could come back. I can beg them not to withdraw their donations. Maybe I can offer something else or reschedule the dates."

Jack draped his suit jacket over her shoulders, but the shaking was likely her nerves. Jack set his hand lightly on her wrist, if nothing else, to get her attention. "It's okay. Relax. We'll figure it out. We'll get the guest list and your mom, your brother, Zoe Ann and I will make the calls. Only a jerk would ask for a donation refunded. The dinner was a fun incentive."

Rob was now in handcuffs in the back of a police cruiser.

Zoe Ann, Luke and Lenore met them at the car. Zoe Ann was wearing a black wool wraparound cape and knee-high black boots with a silver buckle accent. Her hair was straight and long down her back. Luke wore a three-piece black suit and a purple tie tucked in his vest. His black shiny shoes and scarf were flecked with water droplets.

Lenore's hair had been styled into large curls, but the snow was weighing it down, making it uneven and flat.

"I told you Rob was trouble," Lenore said. She fluffed her hair, which did not make it look better.

Jack wasn't stepping into this conversation. It was far too close to told-you-so.

"You say every man I date is trouble," Marissa said, sounding irritable.

"That's because every man you've dated has turned out to be a loser," Lenore said.

"Not true. I've dated some nice guys," Marissa said.

"Going on one date that your manager arranges for promotional reasons is smart for your career. I don't count it as dating," Lenore said.

"Let it go, Mom. We have a lot going on now," Marissa said.

Zoe Ann reached for Marissa's hands. "Marissa, I'm so sorry about this. How can I help?"

Gratitude flooded Marissa's face. She held up her phone. "Can I message you some numbers? I want to let our guests know what happened."

Luke sighed. Zoe Ann punched his shoulder lightly. "We're happy to help," she said.

Luke glanced at Zoe Ann. "I can make calls."

Lenore lifted her chin. "Send me some numbers."

By the time the firemen were comfortable allowing guests to return to the hotel, over an hour had passed. In that time, they had huddled in the car, sending messages to everyone they could. Only about half of the guests had returned. Zoe Ann and Luke had gone back inside and Lenore was searching for a bathroom to reapply her makeup.

Marissa appeared exhausted, her dress was rumpled and her expression pained. "I texted my contact at the hospital that we raised a ton of money. Now, I'll have to tell him it wasn't nearly the amount I'd promised."

Jack slid his arm over Marissa's shoulders. "Your worry might be unnecessary. No one wants their money back. Maybe the guests we couldn't reach decided to relocate with their dates to a restaurant."

Marissa smoothed her hair behind her ears, pushing the snow-dampened strands away from her face. He hadn't seen her disheveled. It wasn't just the weather, her eyes were sad and wide and her mouth drawn into a frown. Despite that, she pulled off the look and managed to be insanely hot and tempting. "You think? I hope so. Otherwise, they'll refuse to help in the future."

Her voice broke and she closed the distance between them, laying her head on Jack's chest.

"The circumstances tonight were not your fault. You couldn't have known Rob would act this way." He wrapped his arms around her.

"I don't know what's going on with him," Marissa said.

"Is he addicted to drugs? The police may test him. He's acting unhinged."

Marissa rubbed her arms. "I don't think so. He was an occasional user when I was dating him. He was in control of it."

"Could he have gotten Avery into drugs? I know you said she avoided them, but could that have changed? Even recreationally?" Jack asked.

"Definitely not. She wasn't even much of a drinker. She worried what it would do to her weight and her face," Marissa said.

Jack filed the information away for later and made a mental note to follow up on Rob's erratic behavior. "Let's get back inside and finish the evening the best we can."

Marissa remained close to him, her hand around his waist under his suit coat. "I'll say something to make this right. I can turn this night around." She kissed his cheek and then climbed out of the car. Marissa hurried into the dining room and Jack followed, her kiss scorching desire through him.

Marissa stood behind the microphone. "That was unexpected excitement tonight. We'll have fresh drinks and dinner out soon. Thank you for your patience. The children at the hospital will be helped by your generous donations."

Another ten minutes and cocktails were rolling out of the kitchen. Marissa has stopped in the bathroom and had done something with her hair, returning to looking beautiful and put together. She was circulating through the room, stopping to talk at tables, smiling and laughing as if she had nothing weighing on her. Jack gave her points for commitment. She wanted this to work and her drive and determination would see it through.

Two hours later, Marissa strode to their table. She set her hands on his shoulders and lowered her mouth to his ear. "You look hot right now."

The bluntness caught him off guard.

"Could you get the car? I want to go home. With you."

Chapter 6

Anticipation crackled around him. Marissa had told him she wanted him. It seemed impossible. As he held open the door to the car, Jack struggled with his desire for Marissa. Telling her no, when all he wanted was to tell her yes, required strength he didn't know if he had.

Jack closed her door and circled the car. After climbing inside and starting the engine, Jack fastened his seatbelt. As they pulled away from the hotel, Marissa adjusted her seatbelt and slid closer.

"We could go to a hotel if you'd prefer," she whispered.

"We're leaving a hotel," he said.

"A different hotel where we're unknown and the chances of someone setting off a fire alarm in an attempt to speak to me is nil," she said.

Jack used every ounce of focus to keep the car on

the road. Her breath tickled his neck and the nearness of her hand to his thigh drove lust straight through him. He pressed the gas pedal harder, accelerating. "Not a hotel. The rest of the security team is expecting you. If we change the plans, we'd have to explain." He wasn't telling her flat out no, and that worried him.

He had the short drive to her town house to make a decision that could have a huge impact on his career and his life. If he denied Marissa, if he summoned the strength to turn her away, he would regret it. If he did what every fiber of his being wanted, he'd need to resign his position. While the second option wasn't sounding that bad, he didn't trust anyone else to keep her safe how he would.

"You seem tense. You have no reason to be tense," Marissa said. "Let go. Let this happen. Stop fighting it."

Jack turned into Marissa's neighborhood. Her hands moved over his chest, her fingernails grazing across his shirt.

He pulled around the back of the row of town houses and pressed the button to open the garage door. After turning into the garage, he shut off the car and closed the door behind him. It closed with a thunk.

Marissa unfastened her seat belt. "This is much easier."

She moved on top of him and he caught her in his lap. This was making it harder to think. Her body was a wicked combination of lean and muscled and soft and feminine. The dam of restraint collapsed.

She smelled of fresh air and rain and a light floral scent wafted from her.

Their lips met in a thoroughly arousing kiss. He was instantly lost. She was everything he wanted in a woman and she was here, with him.

She tugged at the tie around his neck, loosening it and then pulling it over his head. She tossed it into the backseat of the car.

Her adept fingers unbuttoned his shirt and her hands slid inside. Her skin connected with his. The heat of her body was a brand, searing him.

Long kisses and slow kisses, steam forming on the windows of the car.

Jack reached into her hair and removed the pins holding it back.

She watched him, reaching to finish the job. Her hair was a mix of curls and long strands falling down her body as it came free. She shook her head, letting her waves tent around them.

"You are so beautiful," he said.

"I've been told," she said.

"I imagine you have. But I've been thinking your beauty is a reflection of who you are. What you did tonight was amazing. No one else could have pulled it off with as much success. Grace under pressure," Jack said.

"Thank you. That means a lot to me," she said. She slid back to her seat and set her hand on the car door handle. "Come inside."

Jack followed her into the house, disabling the alarm, shutting the door and enabling it. He checked in with the West Company and her security. Marissa had disappeared into her bedroom.

Did she want him to follow her? He heard the shower and decided not. Had halting what they were doing in the car caused her to think twice? Being away from her had not lessened his need for her. He could picture her smile, hear her laugh and imagine the light, clean scent of her skin.

Even in another room, she lingered around him, tempting him. He sat on the couch and began typing his notes about the evening. Putting himself fully into his work, he found Marissa entering his thoughts. Finding the words to describe the evening without fixating on her was hard.

Then she exited her bedroom wearing almost nothing. His heart stilled and then broke into a sprint. Her pajamas, if he could classify them as sleepwear, consisted of enough scraps of white fabric to cover her, but baring her flat, toned stomach and long, lean legs.

"Is this outfit enough to hold your attention?" she asked.

"You've had my attention since we met." Truer words had never left his mouth.

She set her hand on her hip. "You think about your job more than you should."

"You are my job," he said.

Marissa walked toward him. He closed the computer and set it on the coffee table.

"Working again?" she asked.

He nodded. "Case notes. Reports."

"See? More work. It's break time." She laid her finger over his mouth. "And before you tell me that you don't get breaks, I declare that preposterous. The Department of Labor would agree. So classify tonight as off the clock. If you want me to message your boss and tell him or her, then fine. But no talking about work. Try not to think about work. Tonight, I'm a woman who has a crush on you and wants to see how that goes."

At the present, she was his entire line of thought. That outfit, her body…wow. His yearning for her elevated to unmanageable proportions.

She extended her hand to him. "Let me show you a few things."

Marissa was being forward with Jack. She was used to going after what she wanted. She had dated losers and she didn't have a good explanation for it. Too often, she ignored her instincts about men. She'd known Michael was too into drinking. She'd known Rob liked that she was a model, maybe more than he'd liked her. Half of her relationship centered on the upside in the media and not any deep, genuine feelings. But she was finished with using her personal life to forward her professional agenda. That hadn't gotten her satisfaction. The media wanted to see famous faces fall in love and get married, but Marissa wanted the real thing. She wanted honesty and a connection with someone.

That someone could be Jack. Jack was a good man. No drugs or excessive drinking, no embarrassing her or causing a scene, no demanding she make appearances or be photographed with him. He had seemed put off by her career when they'd met. Winning him over meant he saw more to her than a model. Her connection to him was genuine and strong.

If she didn't press the relationship with Jack, he would hold on to his professional boundaries. She wanted him and for once, she was going after the man she wanted for that reason alone. He made her feel precious and smart and respected.

Jack couldn't help her career. He wasn't famous. And after tonight's display, she didn't believe he had interest in her money. It was a connection different than every other one she had experienced.

His hand was strong and firm in hers. She was leading him to her bedroom, leaving him no doubts what she had in mind.

She wanted to seduce him and she wanted him to enjoy it. She had confidence in the bedroom. It stemmed from being told she was beautiful and that men seemed to want to do the work in bed. A few years ago, she'd taken control and realized how to get what she wanted.

It was a rush of power, finding her rhythm and not just following someone else's.

She'd lit candles and the air was filled with the light scent of jasmine. Jack was still wearing his dress shirt and pants. Marissa unbuttoned his shirt and pulled it from his pants. Jack watched her with interest. He did nothing to hasten her actions.

She liked that he wasn't grabbing at her in desperation or complimenting how she looked. While a well-timed compliment was nice, a pet peeve was men repeating their comments about her body in a pseudo-worshipful manner.

She peeled Jack's shirt over his broad shoulders and down his sinewy arms. She draped the shirt over the footboard of her bed. Running her hands over his chest, she could feel the roped muscles of his strong body. His abdomen was flat and chiseled.

Marissa brushed her hands over the waistband of his pants. After removing his belt, she set it over his shirt.

"Why me? Why tonight?" he asked.

How to answer his question. The connection between them was immediate and intense. He was a stranger to her in a many aspects, but she trusted him. "You're you. That's enough of a reason. And tonight, because I've wanted this to happen. The longer I've waited, the more sure I am. I can't wait anymore."

He swept her into his arms and kissed her. He was holding her against his lean length, her breasts crushed to his bare chest.

He carried her toward the bed and laid her down. Her lingerie bunched around her hips. They stayed together, kissing, touching. His hand moved from her hip, down her thigh to her knee. Back again to her hip.

She craved more. She reached to his pants, unbuttoning and unzipping them. Working them down his hips with her feet, she shuddered when his hips came to rest between hers.

"Arc you surc about this?" he asked.

She could stop this with a word, but the only word on her mind was *more*.

"I'm sure," she said.

He removed his boxers and then unlaced the front of her lingerie, letting the sheer fabric part. With a shrug, she let it fall from her shoulders. In her bedside table, she found a foil packet for protection. Carefully, she opened it.

She scooted up the bed and Jack followed. His eyes flickered with fiery provocation.

When he was covered, he again kissed her, using his hands to work her up.

"Please, hurry," she said. She lifted her hips, encouraging him. The slowness was driving her mad. Perhaps that was the point.

His hand went to her hip. She went still. Their eyes met and Jack pushed inside her. Erotic pleasure overtook her. And then he began to move.

For the first time, she knew consuming and absolute pleasure. She held on to him, wrapping her feet around his legs. His thrusts became more insistent, and then she was free-falling into ecstasy with him right after her.

Marissa awoke alone in her bed. Disappointment speared her. Where was Jack?

After the night they had spent together, she had expected him to be beside her in the morning. Breakfast together, even going for a run would have been welcome.

She slipped on her robe and a pair of fleece pants and went in search of him.

He was sitting in the downstairs living room, his computer open in front of him.

"What are you doing?" she asked. He could have woken her before he'd left if he'd had work.

"I needed to catch up on a few things," Jack said. "Your appearance in Las Vegas has brought to light some security concerns."

Her visit to Las Vegas had been on her calendar for months. Jack was changing the subject on purpose. "I promised Barry I would do the opening. He's an old friend. I won't back out."

"I wasn't expecting you to. But I need to prepare."

Marissa didn't want to talk about Las Vegas. She wanted him to mention the night prior. "What time did you get up?"

"Five," Jack said.

She had slept soundly and hadn't heard him leave. "It was a late night. Are you tired?"

"No. Do you want coffee?" he asked.

She could make coffee. He could have brought her some. Or done anything to show a scrap of affection. Irritation nipped at her. "Have you had breakfast?"

"Yes."

Boldness last night had worked to a point. She went for it again. "Are we going to talk about last night?"

He looked at her. "What is it that you would like to discuss?"

"I don't need to discuss anything. You're acting weird."

He lifted a brow, like he had no idea what she was talking about. "I'm working."

"You left without saying goodbye."

"I didn't leave the house," Jack said.

"You left my bedroom," Marissa said.

"I didn't realize there was a protocol," Jack said.

"It's not a protocol, it's common decency. You sleep with a woman, you're nice to her the next day. You do not sneak off like a bandit, as if you've done something wrong," Marissa said.

His cheeks colored.

"Is that it? Do you feel like you've done something wrong?"

Jack stabbed his fingers through his hair. "It's my

job to protect you. I take that job seriously. Obviously, I'm attracted to you. You're smart and sincere and beautiful and my God, you're good in bed. But I'm trying to mesh that with what I'm supposed to be doing here. I've been in a situation before where a personal relationship weakened my instincts on a job and it cost me."

Her anger touched down a notch and she wondered what had happened. "What job?"

"I am not at liberty to discuss that," he said.

Her curiosity piqued, but she sensed not to press him about it now. "I told you that you were off the clock last night."

"Am I ever off the clock? Until we figure out who killed Avery and who is after you and stop him, I'll be worried. I'll want to protect you."

"That's sweet, Jack, but I have a team of security personnel. I made last night happen." Now she wanted him to show her a modicum of warmth. It wasn't expecting too much.

"What do you want from me? If there's something I can do or say to make this right, please tell me what that is," Jack said.

"Stop acting cold and distant," she said. Simple and to the point.

Two of her other bodyguards appeared in the living room. They exchanged glances.

"Sometimes I hate that I'm not ever alone. I don't have privacy. There's always someone around." She was being rude and emotional, but she hadn't had enough sleep or any coffee and she was too tired to deal with this problem.

If Jack wanted to pretend like the night before

hadn't happened, then she would indulge him. A part of her heart broke, but that's what happened when she got involved with a man. Thinking Jack was different might have been a hopeful delusion.

The bright lights of the Las Vegas Strip were blinding. The crowds, the screaming raucous laughter and heavy traffic were more intense than his urban security training had prepared him for. Jack hovered close to Marissa. He couldn't see in every direction around them and a threat could be lurking close by. On the plus side, the disorienting lights would make it hard for an assassin to pick Marissa out of a crowd.

Jack had been beating himself up since they'd left the house that afternoon. Sleeping with Marissa was the stupidest move Jack could have made.

She was everything he wanted in a woman. Being with her was a fantasy and he could envision spending time with her. But he worked for her and that made his feelings for her inappropriate. A personal relationship with her would cause him to lose objectivity.

They were no closer to finding the person who killed Avery and while the threats against Marissa had waned, she wasn't safe until Avery's killer was caught.

Thousands of strangers milled on the streets making it impossible to verify that none of them had it out for Marissa. The casino where they were staying, the Lucky Strike, was equipped with high-tech cameras and surveillance. The Lucky Strike had provided security to some big name celebrities without incident.

Marissa was in town to promote the newly renovated casino. New slot machines and luxury accommodations, a five-star restaurant and an exclusive, high-end spa. They had added a VIP area with high dollar tables and top-shelf drinks. Marissa had been hired to show up, promote the games and accommodations at scheduled events and spend time in the casino.

Jack and Marissa entered the Lucky Strike through a side entrance under a green-and-gold awning. They were escorted by a bellhop in a green uniform to a private elevator with gold doors. Inside the elevator, the concierge inserted their keycard into a slot. The elevator opened into their suite. A sunken living room, two large televisions, a patterned forest green rug that contrasted the geometric prints on the wall felt sumptuous.

"Your attire has been placed in the closets in your rooms. Is there anything else I can get for you?" the bellhop asked.

Marissa looked around the room. "This looks great. Thank you."

Jack tipped him and the bellhop left. The elevator doors closed and Jack and Marissa were alone. On the far end of the room, three sets of sliding glass doors presented an amazing view of the Las Vegas Strip.

"I guess you're used to places like this," Jack said.

Marissa shrugged. "I still get a kick out of cool hotel rooms. Some of them blend together, but this one claims to have a hot tub with a view overlooking the mountains and twin soaking tubs with massaging jets and surround sound. Barry hooked us up with one of the best suites in the place. Give me a minute to change," Marissa said.

"I'll do the same."

Marissa went into the main bedroom. Jack found a tuxedo waiting in the second bedroom's closet. He changed into it, impressed how well it fit. This was their place for the night and he wondered if he'd have the discipline to sleep in the second bedroom when Marissa was asleep in the main one. She had been chillier toward him since they'd slept together and he'd left without saying anything to her. He had disappointed her and he hated that.

When she exited the bedroom, Jack couldn't take his eyes off her.

She was the epitome of glamour. Her dress was green with a high slit and straps at the top that twisted together. Marissa spun and Jack had to compose himself. The back of the dress was almost nonexistent, dipping to her lower back and accenting the womanly curve of her rear.

"Do I look too much like a leprechaun? I took a peek at the outfits the casino arranged for me. Every single one is green. Like head to toe green." She smiled.

"You look amazing," he said.

Marissa tipped her head and smiled. "I was starting to think you'd lost interest. That maybe one night slaked your curiosity and you'd moved on."

He hadn't lost interest. He was upset at himself for not keeping professional boundaries. When he was close to her, he wanted to bend and break the rules, touch her, lean in close and kiss the soft skin at the base of her neck, wrap his arms around her slender waist and hold her against him. "I didn't add to my report what went on between us."

"Why would you? You weren't working. It doesn't concern anyone else. Just you and me," Marissa said.

It wasn't as black-and-white as she painted it.

He inhaled deeply and calmed himself, pushing his libido aside and focusing on his job. One of the most beautiful women in the world was a red-hot temptation and he had to keep his hands off her. "I heard from the head of security at the Lucky Strike. They've added security at the entrances to where you'll be making your appearances. They will be sticking close to the list of invited guests. No time to vet every person who walks through the doors, but we'll do our best."

Marissa strode to him and set her hand on her hip. She swiveled her body close. "If you want to stay close, you should pose as my boyfriend."

"That will invite questions," Jack said.

"I can handle it," Marissa said.

Her boyfriend. That idea was wildly appealing. "No doubt. But it's better I don't."

Hurt flickered in her eyes. "Why are you pushing me away?"

He owed her an explanation. "Because if I don't keep you at a distance, I will do something to make a spectacle of you. I'll kiss you or look at you with obvious lust and the whole world will know about us."

"Is that bad?" she asked.

Never mind the professional problems stemming from it, they would have to deal with pressures from being in the public eye. "We're trying to keep a low profile." He was on the job and would not split his focus.

"I'm doing nothing of the sort. The reason for

me being here is being in the public eye. The casino wants me to draw attention to this place."

Jack removed her hand from him. "I think it's best to keep it cool."

Her eyes narrowed. "In public or in private?"

She wasn't afraid to ask the hard questions. He liked that about her. "Public."

A smile turned up the corners of her mouth. "When we're alone, does that mean we can do what we want to do?"

They were consenting adults. His inability to say no to her was his problem. "Yes," he said.

"Kiss me."

Could he stop at just a kiss? "We know it will be more." Heat traveled over him.

"Then let it be more."

The seduction in her voice flowed through him. "You're due in the casino in ten minutes. That isn't enough time to let this go further."

"They expect me to be late. We can say we were late to throw off anyone plotting against me," she said.

Tension knotted his shoulders. "Don't joke about that," Jack said.

"I'm not joking, but I am asking you to kiss me."

She wouldn't let it go until she got what she wanted. He wanted the same thing. Why fight it? Jack set one hand on the back of her neck and the other on her hip. Bringing their bodies thigh to thigh, hip to hip, he kissed her the way a woman should be kissed. He traced an outline of her lip with his tongue.

Her mouth opened beneath his and he deepened the kiss. His entire body heated. Her hair brushed his hands, silky strands that tickled his skin. The generous curves of her body seemed to fit against him and with the right movement, he could take them to paradise.

Desire charged in his veins and possessiveness and lust nearly destroyed him. The fabric of her dress was silky and tight around her body. He imagined too easily sliding it off her and letting that rich-looking fabric pool on the carpet. Grappling for his control, he slowed his escalating thoughts. This wouldn't end with her back on the mattress and his body over hers. She would let it happen; he could read it in her reaction and in her eyes. He would be the one to stop it.

People were waiting for her. He shouldn't be doing this.

When he broke the kiss, she had a slightly dazed expression.

"You'll be late." His voice was gruffer than he'd intended. Everything south of his belt wanted to stay in this room with her.

"Will you stay close to me tonight?" she asked.

"Yes. Nothing will happen to you. Not on my watch."

"Then we should go downstairs."

"In that dress, it will be hard to keep people away from you."

Marissa turned, showing him the back. She looked at him from over her shoulder. "I think that's the point."

Marissa erased her feelings for Jack off her face. She had to look like she was having the best time. Casually flirt with the men and be delighted with every press of the slot machine buttons. This wasn't her first time making a paid appearance. She knew the ropes, though she almost had declined the job. Her old friend Barry was the casino's general manager. A slick-looking guy in his forties, he had salt-and-pepper hair and his clothing was impeccable and expensive. His shoes were shiny black and he moved with confidence in his swagger. Marissa and Barry had met back when she was modeling for a clothing designer who was selling her fashions in a boutique store in Las Vegas. Barry had been a security guard at the Lucky Strike and had been working the photo shoot as a side gig.

"Welcome back to the Lucky Strike. We're glad to have you here," Barry said, kissing her cheeks.

"It's great to be back. It's been too long. I'm thrilled to be part of this," she said. People were taking her and Barry's picture and listening to every word.

"You look beautiful," Barry said.

"This place is beautiful," she said.

Barry's eyes glittered, appreciative of her comments. "We have a surprise for you. We invited a dear friend to dine with you tonight."

Marissa's chest grew tight. A friend could mean a number of people she would rather not see. "Oh? Who?" She tried to keep her voice light and failed.

"Declan Ambrose," Barry said.

Genuine delight swept over her, followed by relief. "That's great. I haven't seen him in a while." She almost said, "Since Avery's memorial service," but her words were supposed to be happy and uplifting.

Barry took her on a tour of the renovated wing of the casino. She was given a VIP card attached to a gold bracelet to use in the machines. She carried her green clutch and hoped the cameras were snapping shots of both the bracelet and the clutch. Waitresses in tiny white-and-green outfits delivered drinks and Marissa took a sip of one. She wasn't a beverage connoisseur, but she wanted to look enthusiastic about the service.

Jack had the ability to fade into the background, but Marissa sensed him close to her, watching. She felt secure knowing he was with her.

"Tell me about the handsome man following you. He does not take his eyes off you," Barry said.

Marissa didn't have a problem with anyone knowing of her personal relationship with Jack, but she'd respect his wishes to keep it quiet. "Since what happened with Avery, we've taken additional security precautions. He's a bodyguard."

Barry lifted a brow. "I'm never wrong about these things. I see a spark. I see something in his eyes. Not just an employee."

Barry was perceptive. "He's become a friend."

"I see," Barry said.

Marissa swatted lightly at his shoulder. "Don't go spreading rumors about me. There's nothing in my life right now except work."

They paused to have their picture taken by a four-sided hand-carved wood beverage bar positioned in the middle of the floor. The lights around the top of bar shimmered and bartenders in tuxedos with glittering green vests and ties moved swiftly, pouring drinks and not spilling a drop.

Barry straightened his black suit jacket. "I won't say anything to the media about your personal life.

Thank you again for doing this. My boss is thrilled with me. Having you at the Lucky Strike might earn me a promotion. I've got my eye on an executive position at one of our sister properties."

Marissa slipped her arm through Barry's. "I hope you get it. Anything I can do, you know I will."

"How about a sex scandal in our hotel? Something that will bring big press."

Marissa laughed. "Almost anything. Not that."

"I'll think on it. But I owe you. This means a lot to me."

She had known her appearance at the Lucky Strike would pay below her usual fee. Her friendship with Barry was more important than that. "I'm holding you to that. I'm planning another fund-raiser next year and I'll need a premier place to hold it." Many of her guests who had attended the last basket auction wouldn't blink at flying to Las Vegas. The wheels in her head started turning as she considered the possibility and how much money she could bring in for the children's hospital.

Barry nodded appreciatively. "A star-studded event is right up our alley."

They finished another round of promo photos and Barry escorted Marissa to the new restaurant. The floor was polished black-and-white marble. The tables were covered in green linens and the C-shaped booths created private places to dine. The lighting was good, illuminating the table without being glaring and casting darkness around each table to make each feel like its own part of the restaurant.

Ambrose was waiting for her at the bar and happiness rushed through her. He stood resting one hip on a bar stool and held his drink glass with a relaxed wrist. His suit was incredible, the gray the right hue and his tie and white dress shirt polished. Marissa strode directly to him and hugged him. His suit fabric was crisp and he smelled of pine.

His arms went around her. "I've been worried about you, old friend."

Marissa held on to him, feeling grief rolling off him and the words. He was continuing on with life, like she was, but Avery's death had affected them deeply. She searched for words that would help ease his mind and came up short. Finding something to heal her own grief was hard.

"How have you been? Really, tell me," Marissa said.

He set his glass down and rubbed his forehead. "Avery's death meant a ton of free publicity for my show. I can't get my clothes out fast enough. I have waiting lists seven months long. My new designs are in demand and I haven't even created them yet. That success feels good, but I can't stop thinking that it wouldn't have happened if Avery hadn't died. And then I feel guilty, like I'm benefitting from her death."

Marissa took Ambrose's hands in hers. Losing Avery was as unexpected as it was hard. "You cannot think that way. You've worked harder than anyone I know. You deserve this success. It would have happened no matter what."

Ambrose looked over her shoulder. "Still traveling with the bodyguard?"

Jack was more than a bodyguard, but those thoughts stayed private. "No choice."

"Someone still coming for you?" Ambrose asked.

No recent threats, but Marissa wasn't convinced she was in the clear. "Not sure. We're playing it safe."

"Why would Avery's killer want you dead? It's not like you know anything," Ambrose said. "Or is that the part I'm missing? Did you see something? Did Avery tell you something was going on in her life?"

Marissa shook her head. Like the investigators seemed to be, she was in the dark. "I wish I knew something. I have nothing to help the police. I even went by Avery's place and I was useless. I don't know why this happened."

Ambrose patted her shoulder. "We're all doing the best we can to make sense of a senseless tragedy." He stood and shook himself off, as if trying to forget the hurt. "Ready to eat? I've eaten nothing all day in anticipation of stuffing myself with five-star food. I skipped the meal on the plane and they were serving shrimp."

Jack appeared next to her. Ambrose glanced at him. "Will you be joining us?"

Jack shook his head. "No."

Ambrose sighed and set his hand on his hip. "You plan to stand over us and watch us eat? That's intolerable. Tell him, Marissa."

"Pretend I'm a waiter," Jack said.

"I can't pretend that. I know who you are," Ambrose said and took a swig of his drink, emptying the glass.

"Jack, sit with us," Marissa said. "I'm safe in this restaurant and you've had a long day."

She was curious to see how Jack would get along with her dear friend. She and Jack were different people from opposite worlds. Did any part of those worlds collide? Sharing her bed with him wasn't the same as sharing her life, but Marissa was looking for something meaningful, even if abbreviated.

They took their seats, positioned in plain view of anyone walking by. Bad for security, good for promotional purposes. They were three of the first patrons to eat in the restaurant. The grand opening was the following day.

Barry stood next to their table. "Please, order anything and I want an honest critique. If something isn't to your liking, tell me."

"Barry, everything has been exquisite. Will you join us? I'd love to catch up," Marissa said, gesturing to the empty section of their booth.

Barry looked at his watch. "Unfortunately, I have an appointment. But if you need anything, I'm at your beck and call. You have my cell number."

They said their goodbyes and focused on the menu.

As the courses were served and they ate, Jack seemed to relax. He followed the conversation and appeared interested in the topic even when she and Ambrose had been speaking about fabric for ten minutes.

"Tell me, Jack, do you have an interest in fashion?" Ambrose asked.

"Only as it relates to Marissa and this job," Jack said.

He meant nothing by it, but Marissa felt a tingle. What was his interest in her? Long ago, she had understood that sleeping with a man didn't translate into genuine emotions. With Jack, sleeping with him had been an expression of her feelings. Desire and lust for him were her constant companions.

"I am working on some new designs and I have an

outfit that would look great on you," Ambrose said to Jack. He delved into details about the outfit and Jack listened, nodding along.

Marissa watched Jack, taking in his strong jawline and perfect cheekbones. His hair, though not styled with precision, was tousled in a just-got-out-of-bed manner that was sexy and masculine. His tuxedo wasn't designer label, but fit him well.

Her skin heated thinking of the night they had spent together and imagining peeling his jacket off his body and examining his tattoos. Jack had been caring and attentive in bed and out. He had looked at her in a way that had made her feel like he could see who she was beneath the makeup and the clothes and the hairstyles. The woman she was behind the pictures, a side of herself few people knew well.

Jack then abruptly turned, stood on the bench seat and launched himself behind her.

Marissa whirled. Jack was on the ground grappling with another man. In the man's hand was a knife.

Jack slammed the man's hand against the ground and the knife popped free. The man flipped Jack onto his back as the two struggled. Two of Marissa's bodyguards and men from the casino security swarmed close to help. Within seconds, Jack had subdued the man. Marissa's bodyguards pulled the man to his feet.

The knife-wielding stranger glared at Marissa.

"Who are you?" Jack asked. He took a step back. His shirt was torn, but he seemed otherwise unscathed.

The man answered in a language Marissa didn't recognize.

"Who hired you?" Jack asked.

The man answered again, shaking his head with his statement. Jack was staring at the man as if trying to understand.

Casino security boxed out passersby and photographers, but they were snapping pictures, lifting their cameras over their heads aiming them at her. This would be in the paper. Those photographs would be worth a ton and would reignite interest in Avery's murder. Marissa's heart clenched. She had wondered if she could put the murder behind her for a few hours. It was still haunting her and without Jack at her side, it would kill her.

Chapter 7

The man who had tried to attack Marissa in the Lucky Strike's VIP restaurant had been questioned for five hours by the local police. He had spoken to Jack in German, but Jack only knew a few words in the language and hadn't understood him. A German translator had been brought in, and suddenly, the assailant didn't speak German. He was utterly silent. He wasn't giving his name or any information about who had hired him or why he was after Marissa. A specialist from the West Company who lived locally had been brought in to observe the questioning and he was frustrated with the assailant's silence, as well. Video and audio recordings from hotel security were being reviewed. The assailant's photo and fingerprints were being run through criminal databases looking for a match.

Marissa was in her hotel room with her other bodyguards. Jack hated leaving her alone for even a few minutes, worried there would be another attack. But he needed to meet with his contact at the West Company and brief them on the situation. Two assailants and neither was admitting to killing Avery, so they may be looking for a third. The two in custody were silent on the matter. They were loyal to someone. Unbroken silence meant they were afraid to talk or knew they'd be taken care of in the legal system if they stayed quiet.

Jack returned to Marissa's hotel, churning over various theories of the case. Two of her bodyguards were waiting at the elevator.

"Is she okay?" he asked.

The guards nodded and one pointed to the master bedroom. Jack was eager to see Marissa, anxious to see for himself that she was safe. Hired assassins didn't give up and pursued until the target was dead. The meeting with the West Company had made it abundantly clear Jack should anticipate more problems.

Jack knocked once on the door and entered.

Marissa was lying on a massage table, her lower body draped in white sheets, receiving a massage from a pretty brunette. The room smelled of spices and flowers. Soft music was playing.

A second table was next to hers. Another woman dressed in white gestured to the identical, empty table. "Marissa has requested a couple's massage."

Jack looked from the woman to the table. "For me?" He hadn't before had a massage.

"Relax. We're alone," Marissa said from the table, her voice sounding muffled.

Jack's knee twanged where he had been shot as if in reminder. A stranger's hand all over him didn't appeal. "No, thank you, though."

"Jack." Marissa's voice was filled with a protest. "I want you to relax. You saved my life today. Again. Get a massage. For me."

"I don't see how getting a massage helps you," Jack said. He had theories running through his head and wanted to write everything down and draw connections. This had gone on long enough. Professional assassins were harder to find and stop than run-of-the-mill thugs, but the West Company had provided more intel he could use.

"Your being tense makes me tense," Marissa said.

"I don't have time for a massage," Jack said.

"Sure you do. You work for me. This is next on your task list," Marissa said.

Jack sighed. "You won't let this go, will you?"

"Not a chance."

Jack was too tired to fight her. A quiet massage would give him time to organize his thoughts. "How do I do this?"

"I will turn around. You may remove your clothing and lie down. I will drape this sheet over you," the masseuse said, holding up a sheet.

No chance of that. Being naked in the same room with Marissa, even if they weren't touching was a position he wouldn't put himself in again. "The clothes stay on."

The masseuse frowned. "Will you remove your suit jacket? And take off your shoes."

That was as far as it went. This was odd to him. People couldn't find being naked and rubbed by strangers relaxing. "Okay." So much reluctance, it was hard to force out the agreement.

He did as she asked and lay on the table. He felt ridiculous. Then the masseuse went to work and Jack felt like he was melting into the table.

"Do you like it?" Marissa asked.

He wouldn't lie. "It's good." As the masseuse moved down his body, he tensed when she came close to his knee. "Skip the knees." He didn't want her pressing on his injury.

The masseuse did as he asked without comment. It was nice to have someone listen to him without question. He let his mind wander.

The West Company was looking into connections between the assassin and motives for the attacks. Striking out at two of the most well-known models in the world threw suspicion to other models, businesses they'd had relationships with and men they had dated. Rob was high on Jack's list, although Rob struck him as impulsive and out of control of his emotions. Hiring two assassins, although not two good ones, took time and effort. It wasn't like Rob could open a web browser and search for them by trade. He'd need connections and money and patience. Jack wasn't convinced Rob had any of that.

When the massage was over, Jack rolled off the table. His back felt loose and limber.

Marissa was sipping a glass of water with lemons and limes floating in it, reclining on a settee under the large window. She wore a white robe.

"How do you feel? Like you wasted an hour?" she asked.

"That was an hour?" he asked. It hadn't seemed that long.

"Goes by fast."

The masseuses were packing their tables. Jack tipped them both as they left the room.

"You look less tense," Marissa said.

"I feel less tense," Jack said.

"Was that your first massage?" Marissa asked.

"Was I that obvious?" he asked.

"Painfully so. What's wrong with your knee? Did you hurt it today?"

"Not today. Old injury that bothers me sometimes," Jack said. He did not want to discuss this. Bianca's betrayal was a topic he hated revisiting.

"Sometimes?" Marissa asked.

"Yes, but I'm okay," Jack said. He enjoyed her curiosity except for now when he wanted her to let this go.

"Want to tell me about it?" Marissa asked.

Jack shook his head. "I can't."

"The top secret work at the car dealership."

He let the comment pass. "I want to talk to you about this evening and what happened in the restaurant. That was pretty scary." He wanted the observation to draw her out, for her to confide in him how she felt. They had grown closer since they'd met the day of Avery's death. He could help her with this, help her put her head around it. She could have a detail locked away that she either didn't know was important or she was subconsciously afraid to confront.

"It was intense. I thought hotel security had everything locked down," Marissa said.

"They're reviewing their security procedures and trying to figure out how he came into the VIP area because only approved names were to be permitted in the area."

Marissa stood and crossed the room to a silver tea cart. She poured more water into her glass. "Modeling is competitive. I've been stabbed in the back. Betrayed. Nothing compared to this."

"It's unsettling," Jack said.

"If Kit hadn't called you, I don't know what I'd do."

Jack considered telling Marissa some of the truth about what he did for a living. Letting her into his confidence might encourage her to do the same. He sensed she was deeply upset about recent events yet she hadn't opened up to him.

"You know I don't work for a car company. I work for a firm that specializes in providing help to those who need it. The help is often special skills. Odd skills."

"And what odd skills do you have aside from being an army ranger?" Marissa asked.

She had remembered that detail from their first meeting. "The skills I learned in the service come in handy in difficult situations. I carry the promise of working hard, tirelessly and energetically into my current role."

Marissa poured him a glass of water. He took a sip.

"Does that mean you'll stay with me? You won't give up?" Marissa asked.

He sensed she was asking about their future, not just about this case. The minute he had touched her, kissed her and held her, he had opened the door to it. How could he make her understand that his life was ever changing? Leaving the country on an hour's notice, working in hostile territories, going long weeks where he was out of communication. That wasn't a life many women would accept in their partner. "I will find the person who wants to hurt you and I will shut him down."

She stared at him, her gaze unwavering. "And then what about us?"

"Tell me how you see the future." He didn't want to hurt her by telling her the best he could offer was a weekend now and then, and that he would miss more time than he would be with her. The truth might be better. But he was afraid the truth would break them apart.

"I want to retire from this life. Not because of what happened to Avery. Not because of what's happening to me now. Because I've been thinking for the last year that I'm tired. I've been on a diet since I was twelve. I work out every day. My personal life is on display. I've traveled the world and missed holidays with my family. Now that my brother will have a child, I want to be an aunt. Not just an aunt in name. I want to be there. I want to be an artist, take some classes and explore that part of my talents."

Not what he was expecting from her. He was impressed. "Art school?"

"I want to study various media. I've played around with paints, but I'm interested in more than painting."

"You should follow those dreams. You've proven you know how to chase them down. Do it again."

Marissa smiled at him, her eyes wide. "You're the first person who has ever said that to me. Everyone else thinks I should be happy to have money and I should spend the day sunning myself poolside." Marissa set her water on the windowsill. She pushed on his shoulders and he sat on the settee. She knelt over him and brought her mouth to his.

Their mouths met in an explosion of passion. He'd had the internal dialogue. He should slow this down. He should stop.

But she was in his head, silencing his protests and when her hands slipped beneath his shirt, he was lost to her.

Marissa's phone rang. Her manager Tobin's name splashed on the screen. Marissa wanted to crawl beneath the soft pale blue bedding and ignore the world. Just a day away, where no one spoke to her, called her or demanded her attention. A day with Jack. She answered, hoping for a quick call and knowing she couldn't avoid her life.

"Are you with Jack?" Tobin asked.

Marissa glanced at Jack. He had been sleeping, but now his eyes were open. "Yes. Why?"

Tobin sighed. "I received another letter. It was forwarded by our PR department. Usually, we toss a signed picture into an envelope or throw out jealous messages, but this is more disturbing than the other ones. I needed to call and warn you and Jack."

Tobin wasn't dramatic. For the purposes of his job, he was calm and cool under pressure.

"In what way was it disturbing?" Marissa asked, a chill going down her spine.

"Maybe I should talk to Jack about this. I wasn't sure..."

Jack's gray eyes watched her. He could likely hear

what Tobin was saying. "You can talk to me about it. Just tell me," Marissa said.

"It was a picture of you from the photo shoot you did for San Terese shoes."

The photos from that shoot were scheduled to run in a campaign starting in a few months. "From the photo shoot?" she asked, needing to confirm. Marissa's mind flipped into overdrive as she thought about who had been on the set. Someone could have hacked the photographer's computer or snapped a picture themselves.

"There are several. Each has a warning written on the back. It's upsetting."

"I'm not upset about it," Marissa said. "I've received hate mail before. People send me all types of letters. They think I'm a sellout, that I promote body issues and eating disorders for young girls. I've heard and read it all."

"This isn't like those. It's certainly filled with vitriol and I'm sure the person is unbalanced. But this is over-the-top," Tobin said.

Marissa wasn't sure she wanted to know the specifics. While she had been through years of negativity and her skin was thick, it bothered her. If it was that disturbing that Tobin had to call her at seven in the morning, it would weigh on her and she would have nightmares about it. "I can mention it to Jack."

Jack's hand went to her lower back in a supportive gesture.

"Tobin, let me talk to Jack and call you back. I'm sure he'll have questions." She disconnected and faced Jack. "I received more hate mail. My manager seems to believe it is more disturbing because the messages are scrawled on the back of photos from the San Terese footwear shoot I did recently."

A muscle in Jack's jaw jumped. "That might narrow down who is sending the threats. We have the list of people on the set. We can look into them."

"The person responsible wasn't necessarily on the set. Someone from the photographer's office could be responsible. A hacker. Someone from the designer who ordered the shoot. Graphic designer in the ad department. At this point, hundreds of people could have had access to the photographs."

"I'll call Tobin and talk to him." Jack opened his arms and she moved into his embrace. She wanted the warm comfort of him. She closed her eyes, shutting out the world.

Jack's nose traced along the back of her neck. "I know you have a booked calendar over the next few months, but maybe you should consider dropping out of sight for a few weeks. Lie low. Let us look into this matter further. You could rent a villa far away from this and relax. I'll arrange for a masseuse to come a few times a week to help keep your tension low."

Marissa heard the wisdom in his words and she appreciated he was trying to help her, but she couldn't stop living her life. "It might start that way. A couple of weeks. And then what? What if this person still isn't caught? If I go off the reservation, he won't be able to find me and your leads might dry up. As long as I stay in the public eye, he'll keep reaching out to contact me, and every time he does, he risks revealing something about himself."

Jack's armed tensed around her. "I don't like this. He's getting closer."

She hated it, too. But the person threatening her would make a mistake. Kit and Jack were involved. The police were investigating the matter. Casino security had resources on it. Someone would uncover a mistake and out this person. "My idea is the opposite. I am supposed to go to the Daytime Show Awards tomorrow in New York. Anyone who wanted to would know that I am scheduled to attend. Why don't you come with me? Something might happen. If he comes at me, you'll be there, like you've been every time."

Jack shifted behind her. "You want to be bait."

She craned her neck to see his face. "Yes."

His frown and narrowed eyes said it all. "I don't like it. It's risky."

"Until he is caught, I have to keep looking over my shoulder. I can't do that for the rest of my life. Please, do this for me." She was asking more than for him to accompany her to the awards show. She was asking him to trust her judgment. Asking him to help bring this to a close so she could move on with her life.

Jack inhaled deeply. "I'll do this for you. But if I catch a whiff of something we can't handle, we're out of there."

The Daytime Show Awards were being held at a theatre built in 1905 and renovated to include big screens, ideal acoustics and modern HVAC and wiring, while maintaining an early twentieth-century feel.

The red carpet extended from a drop-off location where cars and limos pulled to a curb and then into the front doors of the theatre. A blue awning covered the last four yards of the walk. The fifty feet between the drop-off and the awning worried Jack the most.

Security was tight, but for television broadcast reasons, the arrivals of the guests were timed and scheduled. A schedule that was available to dozens of people. Jack had suggested that Marissa skip the walk down the red carpet and enter the theatre from another door. She had rejected the idea.

She had wanted him to walk beside her as her date. Though his vantage point would be poor, he could use his body to protect her if needed. Excited fans were crowded in wood boxes, like corrals. Security for the event had ensured the people waiting around the red carpet weren't armed.

"Do you want to stand on my left or right?" Marissa asked.

"Either." He wasn't her boyfriend and his appearance at her side would drum up gossip. Marissa had attended dozens of events like this one in the past without security glued to her side.

Their driver pulled to the red carpet and stopped. Jack reached for the door handle. The noise from the crowd was deafening.

Marissa stopped him. "Are you here as my date or my security detail?"

Jack hated the worry in her eyes. "I'm here as your security."

Her eyes went wider. "Why do you think Ambrose sent you the suit?"

Jack looked down at the crisp black suit. "I thought he wanted me to blend. To go unnoticed."

"He wanted you be photographed next to me, wearing one of his designs."

The crowd was cheering. They should get moving. Marissa was picking a strange time to discuss this. "I will stay with you tonight," he said.

"But you can't stand like you're my bodyguard, hulking over me. Don't try to blend into the background. I want you to hold my hand and smile at the cameras and maybe look at me adoringly."

"I need to be looking around for a shooter," Jack said.

Marissa picked up her clutch from seat. "Do what you need to do."

Jack climbed out of the car and circled around to open Marissa's door. He took her hand and helped her step onto the red carpet–covered sidewalk. She was wearing tall slim heels and seemed poised on her feet. Her pink dress fluttered around her legs as she stood.

He offered his elbow and she slid her hand through the crook of his arm.

"I'll be okay," Marissa said. She smiled and waved, speaking to him from under her breath.

"Because I'm here."

"I feel safe with you."

"It's when I'm not with you that I'm worried about," Jack said.

Cameras flashed and reporters came close to her, shoving their microphones in her face. Marissa answered questions about which designers she was wearing and her jewelry and shoes. The reporters glanced at Jack several times, but didn't speak to him. They would have a hard time confirming his identity. His work for the West Company meant he didn't post information about himself online. An internet search of his picture wouldn't reveal much.

Marissa answered a few more questions and then Jack led her toward the front doors.

"Do you want to talk to more reporters?" he asked quietly.

She shook her head. "I'll stare at you and pretend I'm too enamored to notice anything or anyone else." Marissa blinked up at him and he had to smile. He enjoyed her playfulness.

Once they were inside, the atmosphere changed. It was darker inside, fewer people, many Jack recognized from television shows and movies. Floor-to-ceiling red curtains hung between the windows and the blue-and-red carpet was set in a puzzle pattern. The lobby was smaller than he had imagined it, but four bars were open and serving drinks.

"Thank you for walking in with me," Marissa said.

"I want you to be safe." He also wanted to be near her in the case another attacker chose this event to strike.

Marissa was the most beautiful woman in the room. Other men looked in her direction, letting their gazes linger. Their reaction to her made Jack unreasonably territorial.

He shouldn't be. He had told her he was here as her bodyguard. No personal implication.

Marissa was wearing a pink strapless gown and her hair was long and loose around her shoulders. She wandered to the bar and requested a glass of wine.

Jack asked for a soda water. "Have I told you that you look beautiful tonight? Everyone in this room has looked at you at least once." The drinks were poured quickly.

Marissa took a sip of her white wine. "Everyone is eyeing everyone else."

"I feel better having you inside." He stopped speaking when his gaze landed on Rob. It was beyond his comprehension how Rob slithered into A-list events. After the incident at the children's hospital charity dinner in New York, Jack hoped Rob would have learned his lesson to keep his distance or he would have been blackballed from these events. He may have weaseled his way out of criminal charges for pulling a fire alarm in a hotel, but Jack wouldn't forget Rob's recklessness.

Rob approached and Jack felt his irritation rise. Rob wouldn't do anything to hurt Marissa, but he might make a scene.

"Marissa, I can't believe you're here with him. The guy who bid on your basket at the auction?" Rob sounded like he had been drinking, his words slurred.

Marissa narrowed her gaze on her ex. "You're bold to bring up the auction after your behavior."

Rob sniffed. "That was a misunderstanding."

"Let's not do this here," Marissa said.

Rob held out his hands. "Relax. I wanted to apologize. I was out of line."

Jack didn't comment. It wasn't his place. But which incident was Rob thinking of? His behavior over the last several months was out of line.

"I've moved on. I'm here with someone," Rob said.

Marissa set her hand on her hip. "Moved on? Avery died less than a month ago."

"Things weren't going well between us. I was mostly over her anyway." Rob shifted.

Marissa's hands fisted at her sides. "You know,

what, Rob? I would tell you to have respect for her memory, but you have no idea what that is or what's entailed with giving a woman respect."

A blonde in a red gown approached. She kissed Rob on the cheek and slipped her arm through his. "Hey, babe."

The intimacy between them was startling. Marissa had made a good point. Rob had moved past his grief fast to be in a new relationship.

Stuttering over his thoughts on Rob, it took Jack a moment to place the woman. She was one of the models from the footwear photo shoot who had been bad-mouthing Marissa. Jack moved closer to Marissa, sensing venom from the other woman and wanting to pull Marissa away before the night was ruined.

Rob introduced them to his new girlfriend, Bella.

The woman lifted her chin and zeroed in on Marissa. "We've met. Marissa and I have done a few photo shoots together." Her tone was cool.

Marissa extended her hand. "Right. The San Terese footwear shoot was the most recent. Good to see you again."

Bella appeared surprised. Maybe she had expected Marissa to behave like a prima donna or not recall they had worked together.

"Are you presenting tonight?" Bella asked.

Marissa shook her head. "Not this year."

"I've heard you had some trouble."

"Trouble?" Marissa asked.

"Getting campaigns. I've heard fresh faces are more in demand." The venom seeped from her words.

Marissa inclined her head. "Are you implying I'm too old?" It was her turn to add a chill to her tone.

That was putting Bella's insinuation bluntly and Jack applauded her. He loved that Marissa spoke her mind.

Bella straightened and took a sip of her drink. "You've been around a long time. Advertisers want to appeal to a younger audience. They want to see something they haven't before."

"Excuse me, I see someone I need to speak with," Marissa said. She strode away. The snap in her walk gave away her aggravation.

Jack caught up to her. "Don't let them get to you."

Marissa turned to face him. She appeared calm and he guessed it was an act she had perfected after hundreds of hours in front of a camera.

"They are outrageous for different reasons and the two of them together offend me. Rob, dating? Didn't he care about Avery? And Bella with her criticism of my career? They are here together when Rob should be grieving for Avery."

"Everyone grieves in their own way," Jack said.

"Don't defend him," Marissa said.

"I'm not defending him. He's a total loser. They deserve each other."

Marissa took another swallow of her wine. "Bella is right, though. There are some designers, ones new to the industry, who don't want me to model for them. I've lost big campaigns to younger women."

"No one can be the face of every new designer. You're still getting plenty of bookings. I've seen your schedule. I'm the one who has to plan security around it. Declan Ambrose picked you to work with him."

Marissa rolled her shoulders back. "I'm not upset about my work. Rob pissed me off and then Bella hit a nerve. I'm not over what happened to Avery. I miss her. I wish I could have talked to her about things before she died."

"I know that's been hard," Jack said.

The lights in the lobby dimmed briefly.

"That's our cue to find our seats," Marissa said.

"You sure you don't want a few more minutes to vent?" Jack asked. When they were in the crowded theatre, conversations could be overheard. They wouldn't be able to speak privately inside.

Marissa shook her head. "I'll be fine."

Jack followed her into the hall. Marissa had a great seat close to the stage. On either side of her were two big-name actors with their dates.

As they settled in their seats, Marissa smoothed her dress. "I'm glad I wasn't asked to present this year. Public speaking isn't my thing."

"Yet your face is everywhere," Jack said.

"My face. Not my voice."

"I like your voice," Jack said.

Marissa squeezed his hand, warmth written on her face. After several minutes, the host for the show walked onto the stage wearing a white tuxedo and black bow tie with shiny black shoes.

This was Jack's first awards show. He didn't watch them on television and he wasn't sure what to expect. The host chatted with the audience, told some jokes, and then the first presenters walked onto the stage.

Ten minutes into the show, the actor seated to Marissa's left won a big award and collected his prize onstage. He thanked his family and his fellow actors. Clapping and hoots of approval thundered from the crowd. He started toward the steps to return to his seat.

The lights went out.

"Is this normal?" Jack asked, alarm sharpening his senses.

"Can't say I've experienced this before," Marissa said.

The audience was silent. As the seconds ticked by, whispers grew louder. Jack sent a message to the security team. They had no knowledge of a planned power outage. As the seconds ticked by, Jack's nerves tightened. He took Marissa's hand. Taking her somewhere safe took the highest precedence.

Then flames shot up from the stage. Jack's adrenaline fired. How could he protect Marissa?

Marissa squeezed Jack's hand.

The lights snapped on and a giant spotlight was pointed at the center of the stage. A five-man band kicked off a high energy song about heartbreak.

Jack relaxed next to her.

"It's okay. We're okay," she said.

"They should have given us warning," Jack said.

"Negates the shock effect," Marissa said.

As the band performed their song, Marissa had trouble focusing. At any point, the camera could pan around the room and her face would be on the large screen to the left of the stage. Her expression should be interested and amused.

All she could think about was Jack's hand holding hers. He might not be aware he was still grasping it. If the camera took a picture of her now, she guessed her expression would be akin to shocked and confused.

It felt great to have Jack close, his shoulder rubbing hers and her hand clasped in his. She set her free hand over theirs and he looked at their joined hands. Calling his attention to it was a mistake.

She read a dozen fleeting emotions in his eyes, among them worry and uncertainty. He pulled his hands away and set them in his lap. She left her hand on his forearm, needing the contact.

Marissa leaned closer, letting her body press against him. He didn't move away and she was grateful for that. She craved his touch and wanted to feel his hands on her. They had spent another night together and then he had backed away—thrown up his walls again. She hated it. She wanted an explanation and an opportunity to talk him out of whatever reason he had given himself for not pursuing their relationship.

The longer she thought about it, the more urgently she wanted to know why he had shut her down. The heat and connection was still between them, in the air around them, sparking and heating. He was choosing to actively ignore it.

He unwrapped her fingers from his arm. She hadn't realized she had been tightening her grip on him. He shot her a questioning look.

"Later," she mouthed.

When the show was over, they were having a frank and honest conversation. They couldn't keep circling each other. She had a pull on him and he had captured her interest. The complication of their professional relationship wasn't enough to smother her feelings for him. She wasn't sure anything was.

* * *

Marissa posed for publicity pictures after the awards show. Jack watched her, waiting patiently. She had been invited to a number of parties and was hesitant to mention them to Jack. He wouldn't want to attend and he wouldn't want her to attend without a thorough security screening.

No time for a security screening. She had promised Ambrose she would attend his party, being held at the Burgundy Hotel, a five-minute drive from the theatre.

"We have a hotel room at the Burgundy," Marissa said.

Jack lifted his brow. "That wasn't on the schedule. We've made overnight arrangements for you at a hotel outside the city."

Marissa smiled, not because she was happy, but because people were taking her picture. Images of her scowling at Jack would be gossip section fodder. "I'm not used to telling anyone else where I'm going and what I'm doing. Before you, my security followed me and handled whatever came my way."

"Death threats have been made. This situation is escalating," Jack said.

"It's Ambrose's party. I promised him I would be there," Marissa said. He had assured her the party was invitation only, guests were being screened at the door and lots of extra security personnel would be on hand.

"You're the boss," he said.

"That was almost too easy. You took some of the joy from me."

"If you had an argument prepared, go ahead," Jack said.

She kissed his cheek instead. "No, thanks. I know

this might seem crazy, but I need a night to dance and blow off some stress."

"A loud party with hundreds of people is relaxing?"

To her, the crowd meant anonymity. "Yes."

He shrugged. "Lead the way."

Twenty minutes later, Marissa was in the master bedroom of the grand suite at the Burgundy that Ambrose had reserved for her. Like its name, the hotel's decor centered on shades of red from the throw pillows, to the furniture, the wallpaper and the throw rugs. A bottle of Burgundy was on the coffee table, along with two glasses with rose gold trim.

Ambrose had hung three dresses in the closet for her to choose from. She couldn't wear the same clothes she'd worn to the awards show—fashion mistake. She slipped into a short red dress. The neckline scooped low and the hemline was high. She changed her shoes, too, and after putting on her jewelry, she met Jack in the living room of the suite.

"Ready to go?" she asked. He had seemed anxious about this addition to their plans. She didn't want him to be upset.

He looked her up and down. "You changed your clothes."

"Yes." She pivoted and looked at him over her shoulder. "Like it?"

"It's really something else," Jack said.

"Something good?" Marissa asked. She was fishing for a compliment, but also wanted to be sure Jack wasn't upset with her about the changes to their plans.

"You look amazing," he said.

Satisfied with his answer, she strutted toward him. "Can I help you to be more comfortable?" She loosened his tie and removed it. Then she took off his jacket. She unfastened the top two buttons of his shirt, opened the collar and rolled the cuffs of his sleeves. "It will be hot. You'll feel better like this."

"Thank you," he said. He studied her, and she read questions in his eyes.

"Can we talk about what's going on between us?" They were alone. They weren't in a rush. This was the time to discuss.

Jack shifted and his shoulders tensed. She wasn't letting him out of the conversation that easily. "What do you want to discuss?" he asked.

"You've been distant since we spent the night together," Marissa said. It hurt to speak the words, but she wanted to know where they stood.

"I crossed a line. I'm aware of it. I've considered admitting to Kit what happened between us and then asking her to find someone to replace me," Jack said.

Mild alarm skittered through her. "Why haven't you said anything to my sister?"

"She and Griffin asked me to do this because I'm the right choice. It was a onetime thing between us. It won't happen again and I can stay focused on your protection."

Marissa didn't think of it as a single, isolated event. She wanted their relationship to be more and deeper. Spending time with him, she had seen strength and tenderness, focus on keeping her safe and intensity when he looked at her, and he made her feel fascinating and special.

The seriousness in his eyes made her yearn. She wanted him. As excited as she had been about attending Ambrose's party, now she was thinking about blowing it off and staying with Jack in this amazing suite. "Jack, I appreciate everything you've done. How much of your life you've put on hold to help me. I'm worried about the person who is after me, but also I'm certain you and I can have a relationship and have it not impact my safety."

"You're my client. I can't get distracted. It blurs the line of my responsibilities." He knew the consequences of losing absolute focus on the job. His friendship with Bianca had blinded him to her treachery.

"I want the other night to happen again. I don't think we should let something that great end." She traced her finger down his cheek.

He closed his eyes. "It was."

Marissa slipped her arms around his neck. "Don't you want it to happen again?"

"I've thought about it. A lot," Jack said.

Marissa brought her lips close to his. "Stop fighting me so hard. Go with it."

Chapter 8

Jack didn't reach for her, but he didn't pull away.

Marissa brushed her lips against his and then kissed him hard. It took several seconds of her lips coaxing his before he responded. And then a firestorm lit between them. Jack's hands went to the small of her back and he pressed her against him, walking her backward toward the couch.

She fell onto it and kicked off her shoes. They hit the floor with a thud. Jack covered her body with his, unbuttoning his shirt.

"Careful, that shirt is worth a few thousand dollars," she said.

"For a shirt? I will never understand fashion." He resumed kissing her, his lips moving seductively over hers.

Marissa helped him remove his shirt, admiring the

fabric briefly, Jack's body thoroughly. She ran her hands over his chest and stomach, enjoying the roped muscles of his chest and the flatness of his abdominals. His skin was hot and taut. Her fingers brushed the top of his belt. Desire swirled through her.

She slid the end of the belt out of the loop and moved the prong out of the hole.

He finished the job and finally, his pants were off. They fell to the floor and he stepped out of them, losing his shoes and socks. An amazing specimen of a man, he was something to look at.

She tugged up the skirt of her dress around her waist, hot and eager for him. Wanting him had been a slow simmer in her soul and now that she could have him again, she was ready. Slipping her thumbs into the sides of her thong, she slid it down her legs and tossed it on top of his pile of clothes.

"I am so turned on by you," Jack said. "Everything about you. Your voice, your body, the way you care about the people around you."

She hadn't often heard those words about her. Men obsessed about her legs, her breasts, her body. Jack saw more to her and that was special and meaningful.

He moved to her, running his hand down her bare thighs. He stroked the backs of her calves and his fingers grazed the apex of her legs. Her body tensed in anticipation.

"Please hurry. You've made me wait long enough," she said.

Jack covered himself with protection and turned her on the cushions. She knelt on the couch, grasping the back of it. He pushed on her shoulder blades and she arched. The last time they'd had sex, it had been hot and simple. This was spicy and raw emotion. Her heart was racing and her body felt primed.

He gripped her hips and came into her in one smooth glide. She shuddered as sensations overwhelmed her.

"I love how I feel when I'm with you," he said.

He grasped her hips and moved, keeping a perfect rhythm. The friction, the pressure, the speed were exactly what she needed.

"You look so sexy like this," he said.

She looked at him and their eyes connected. The emotions and words of affection swelled inside her. He was what she needed and wanted in her life. It had been tragedy that had brought him to her and her feelings for him that kept him close. Jack meant more to her than she could have anticipated.

Her emotions poured through her and she came apart in his arms. Pulses of pleasure consumed her and he followed her into completion.

"Wow." A simple statement that summarized how she was feeling, too.

His arms went around her and he held her against him. The couch itched her bare skin and she shifted. "Want to move to the bedroom?"

"Yeah, I do," he said. In one rolling motion, he came to his feet. She wished she could have snapped a picture of him, raw masculine energy, pumped muscles, delicious man.

Her phone buzzed and she reached for it on the coffee table. It was Ambrose. Guilt plucked at her. He could be worried about her. She answered, trying to sound nonchalant. "Hey, Ambrose."

"Where are you and that fabulous bodyguard?"

It was difficult to hear him over the music. "We're on our way. I'm getting changed." She wiggled, trying to pull her dress down and hoping the wrinkles didn't give her away.

"Getting changed together? Did that cause a delay?" Ambrose sounded amused.

She laughed, pretending his question was ludicrous. "I wanted to make sure everything was good. The dresses you left for me are beautiful. Hard to decide which one to wear. But we're on our way." She shot Jack an apologetic look. Tumbling into bed held a great appeal, but she couldn't let Ambrose down after he had gone through all this trouble to ensure she'd attend the party.

"Good. I need you here!" Ambrose said.

"See you soon." She disconnected. Marissa's legs felt weak, as if she had run ten miles. "Ready to party?"

Jack stood. "Is that an invitation to the bedroom or are we heading out again?"

His preference was retreating to the bedroom and catching some rest. "Ambrose arranged this for me. We need to go to his party."

Jack was dressing. His shirt was wrinkled. He still made it work.

Marissa checked her hair and makeup in the bathroom mirror and made the necessary adjustments.

When she was ready, Jack was waiting by the door. "Are you sure you want to go?" he asked.

The seriousness in his voice gave her pause. Jack was with her and this was Ambrose's party, but something could still go wrong. "I want to go. If anything feels off, we'll leave." Being alone with him held a different excitement and promise, but loyalty to her friend was important.

She slipped on her shoes and took Jack's hand.

Marissa entered the party and excitement bubbled over her. There were enough famous faces that hers was nothing special. This was a place she could relax and dance and not worry about being photographed. The party area was two stories, with a second story that wrapped around the perimeter of the room and the dance floor in the center opening to a cathedral ceiling. A well-known DJ was spinning records, and waiters wearing leather pants and waitresses wearing black bikinis circulated with drinks, their wrists covered in light-up bracelets, making them easy to find in the darkened room.

Marissa took Jack's hand. "Dance with me."

He shook his head. "I don't dance."

He had moves. She knew it. No man who made love the way he did could claim to be missing rhythm. "Come on. We're here to have fun."

Jack drew her close and whispered in her ear. "If I dance with you, I'll forget that I need to be watching the people around you to keep you safe. I'll just watch you."

Her cheeks heated. "I'm safe here."

"I want to keep you that way," Jack said.

A friend called to Marissa from the dance floor. She looked at Jack and he nodded at her to go. "I'll keep an eye out."

Marissa wanted to stay with Jack. She wanted him to integrate into her world, but he seemed bent on staying at the fringes. He'd argue it was his job, but he was holding back.

"Who's the hottie?" Kristen asked. Kristen was a television actor between shows, but the last three series she had been on had been huge successes. She was looking over Marissa's shoulder at Jack.

A rush of possessiveness struck her. "He's a bodyguard."

Kristen lifted her brows. "Oh really? Just a bodyguard?"

Marissa wasn't comfortable answering the questions. Jack had come to mean more to her and she didn't want Kristin going after him. Admitting they were sleeping together would be great gossip and Kristen wasn't known for keeping her mouth shut. "He's off-limits," Marissa said.

Kristen laughed. "Then something is going on with him."

"Nothing serious, but I would like it to be." Until she said the words, she hadn't known they were true. She wanted something with Jack. More than their professional relationship and trysts in between events.

"Wait, stop the presses. Are you telling me you want a man and he doesn't want you in return?" Kristen asked.

Kristen had dated at least a dozen actors. Men flocked to her. "You're one to talk. You break up with someone and ten men call your agent to ask for an introduction. And I didn't say he didn't want me. I said I would like for our relationship to progress. Right now, it's in employer and employee mode."

"Nothing sexy about that," Kristen said.

Everything about Jack was sexy. "Have you ever dated someone you worked with?"

Kristen held out her hand. "Guy who does my lighting. Guy who delivers my scripts. Guy who works in my press manager's office. And actors. Can't seem to stay away from actors." She ticked off the list on her fingers.

"Doesn't that get complicated?" Marissa asked.

Kristen shrugged. "For me, not really. By the time I ended it, they were ready to move on, so no hard feelings. Or the relationship fizzled because there wasn't enough to keep it going and neither of us cared it was over after the sex got boring."

Marissa wasn't sure how to keep a relationship going. To date, she hadn't had any long-term relationships lasting longer than three years and her marriages were not something she was proud of. "How do you keep it going?"

Kristen held up her bare left hand. "If I knew that, I wouldn't be at this party alone. But I don't want to talk about my incessant singledom. I wanted to tell you that I heard that Rob is in deep, deep crap with a couple bookies."

Talking about Rob put her in a bad mood. At the same time, Marissa was intrigued by Kristen's information and wanted to know more. "Rob doesn't gamble."

"Sure he does. Big time. He and Avery did. I'm not speaking ill of the dead. It's just a fact."

Avery had expensive tastes, but she had the career and the salary to back it up. She loved being the center of attention; it gave her a thrill.

Marissa could imagine Rob gambling. His finances were tighter and the idea of a big payday could be motivating. "What did they gamble on?"

Marissa wasn't sure if she believed this rumor. She would tell Jack about it and see if he could sniff out more.

"I heard they were gambling on sports," Kristen said.

Kristen had to be mistaken. Avery hadn't watched a day of sports in her adult life. "That doesn't seem like Avery. Rob, maybe."

Kristen waved to someone over Marissa's shoulder. "Oh, I see Clarice. I need to talk shop with her for a few minutes. Be right back." She kissed Marissa on the cheek and dashed off.

Marissa kept dancing, thinking about what Kristen had said. Had Avery been gambling and gotten in over her head? Rob used to go to the bar with his buddies and watch games from time to time. He hadn't been a big fan of any team that she knew about.

This rumor didn't fit with the events. If Avery had gambling debts, she could have paid them back easily. Killing her was a sure way for a creditor to not get his money. Marissa didn't know much about gambling or how loans were repaid if delinquent.

As Marissa moved through the room, saying hello to old friends and making idle chitchat, she scanned for Jack. She wanted to tell him what she had heard about Avery and Rob. Not seeing him, she sent him a phone message, asking him to meet her at the bar. He said he would stay close. The room was crowded. Marissa regretted separating from him. He wouldn't leave, but he had the option of calling one of her other guards to stay with her.

Out of character for him to do so without telling

her. To this point, he had been there every time she had needed him.

Jack appeared at her side. "Are you all right?"

Relief and happiness engulfed her at the sight of him and the sound of his voice. Marissa led him to a less crowded part of the room where they wouldn't be overheard. She related what Kristen had told her about Rob and Avery gambling.

"If she's right, their financials should show it," Jack said.

"Can you find out?" Marissa asked.

Jack nodded once. He tapped some buttons on his phone, typing on his on-screen keyboard. "Good news and bad news."

Marissa waited.

"Avery's financials are being investigated. She frequently moved huge sums of money into and out of her accounts. Tracking every transaction is taking time. But that movement of money was being investigated as a possible lead."

Not a new lead they could prove, but Kristen's words rang true for Marissa. "What about Rob?"

"His lawyer has blocked any investigation into Rob's financials."

That surprised her. "How?"

"The investigators have nothing to link Rob to the murder and no judge will sign off on a warrant allowing the police to go on an exploratory mission."

"Rob did not kill Avery. He wouldn't do something like that. But he and Avery could have been involved with someone who did. That's the connection. If I speak to Rob, maybe he'll understand why we want to look at his financials."

Jack shot her a look. "Rob will not be that reasonable. You are not calling him and opening yourself up to that."

Marissa opened her mouth to answer and was interrupted.

"That red dress works!"

Marissa turned at the sound of Ambrose's voice. He was wearing faux-alligator printed pants and a black T-shirt. In his right hand, a cane with a silver alligator head mounted to the top. His shoes were also alligator print with silver toes.

Ambrose wrapped her in a hug. "What do you think of this party?" He released her and gestured around him, pride obvious on his face.

Marissa had a hard time disconnecting her thought process from Avery and Rob. She mustered some enthusiasm. "Fantastic. You did a great job."

Ambrose clasped his hands together on top of his alligator cane. "Everyone who is anyone is either here or planning to be."

Being accepted in this world was another marketing tool for Ambrose's designs. The right people being photographed wearing his clothes and his collections would ensure continued sales. "You've done it, Ambrose. Congratulations."

He grinned. "Who'd have thought that an immigrant working in a fabric manufacturing plant would be able to live this life?"

Marissa put her arms around his shoulder. "You've arrived. I'm so happy for you."

Ambrose kissed her cheek. "I need to mingle. I'll catch up with you later." He walked away, practically skipping on air.

* * *

It was after three in the morning when Ambrose's party ended. Jack was grateful they had a hotel room waiting for them upstairs at the Burgundy. He wasn't sure he could drive Marissa home. The noise, the crowd and the watching for threats for hours was exhausting.

"You didn't dance with me," Marissa said.

She was standing at the double glass door leading to the balcony of their hotel room, frowning at him.

He wished he had a camera. Snapping a picture of her right now, the emotion on her face, would create a work of art.

"I was working tonight," Jack said. That was his counter. That was the one fact he could hold up as proof he was doing what was right and needed. Being close to her and not touching her wasn't easy for him.

"You're not working now. I'm in no danger."

She had a hopeful look in her eyes and he hated being the man to disappoint her. Caught between his duty and his feelings, Jack strode to the room's stereo system. He cranked it on, flipping the tuner to a station he knew played soft, sweet songs. He offered his hand. "Dance with me? It's not the same as dancing in a crowd of hundreds of your friends, but it's something."

Their view of the city was picturesque. The skyline was lit by the skyscrapers of the city and by the moon.

The sadness disappeared from her eyes. They brightened and her mouth curved into a smile. "Yes, gladly." She stepped into the circle of his arms and rested her head on his shoulder. "Sometimes, I get the feeling that you're intentionally keeping distance between us. Like you don't want to be part of my world."

He wasn't part of her world. Marissa fascinated him, but the rest befuddled him. A picture couldn't capture who Marissa was and therein lay her true beauty.

After his knee was healed, Jack would return to working for the West Company in an international special operations capacity. He would be sent on a mission for weeks or months. He would work completely in secret and try not to be seen or noticed by anyone. He didn't belong in a world of champagne and thousand-dollar ties and constant pictures. "I feel out of place," he said.

"You do? Now?" Marissa said.

"Not when we're alone. When I'm at a photo shoot or a party like tonight, I don't fit in."

Marissa's arms tightened around him. "That's what you tell yourself. But you do fit."

"I'm wearing a borrowed suit I wouldn't pick on my own. I had never heard of three quarters of the actors and actresses who won awards tonight and I didn't know any of the songs that were performed," Jack said.

"What about what happened between us?" Marissa asked.

Their relationship worked for him on many levels. "That was pretty special."

Pointing out they were different seemed like stating the obvious. Yet he was here, in her hotel room, one of the most unlikely men to be dancing with a supermodel.

Marissa liked Jack sleeping in her bed.

His big body was warm, heating the sheets. She

liked leaning into him as she slept. But tonight, even with him close, her thoughts were restless and she had a hard time calming herself down. After getting a glass of water, she watched the rise and fall of Jack's chest. He was a restless sleeper, too, tossing and turning, sometimes groaning. What was he dreaming about?

He had mentioned his injury. Marissa hadn't had the opportunity to inspect it closer. She longed to know the story. He had been shot and he was secretive about the circumstances.

Marissa considered waking him, but decided against it. She searched for the words that would convince him to confide in her. The idea of calling Avery for advice shot through her mind and on its heels, the quick stab of grief. She couldn't talk to Avery. She was gone.

Marissa settled back into the pillows and closed her eyes. She extended her leg over to Jack's, sliding her calf over his. Spending the night with him was comfortable and easy. With him, she was safe. Nothing bad would happen.

The sound of her mother's voice hit her.

Marissa sat up, her heart racing and the jolt to her nerves making her hands shake. A glance at the clock told her she had drifted off to sleep. It was nine in the morning. Jack was on his feet in seconds.

"It's my mother," she said. What was her mother doing here? How had she gotten inside her hotel room?

Marissa grabbed a hotel robe and slippers from the closet and exited the bedroom. She hadn't slept enough and she needed water and coffee. "Mom? What are you doing here?"

"Didn't you see the news? Were you there when it happened?" her mother asked.

A heavy sense of dread fell onto her shoulders. "What happened?"

Lenore straightened. "Are you alone?"

That didn't matter. The threat of bad news hung over her. "I'm never alone lately." Marissa's stomach clenched. The interruption and the five hours of sleep she had gotten made her nervous and edgy. "Tell me quickly. Please."

"Clarice was killed last night."

Marissa felt like the air had been sucked from her lungs. Setting her hand over her rib cage, she inhaled a shaky breath. "How?" Clarice had been at Ambrose's party last night. Kristen had mentioned needing to talk to her, but Marissa hadn't spoken to her. Assembling the facts into a reasonable explanation was impossible.

"I don't know the details. I heard it on the news," Lenore said.

Jack stepped out of the bedroom, phone to his ear.

Her mother frowned in Jack's direction. "I see your bodyguard is taking his job seriously."

Marissa wasn't in the mood for a lecture. Discussing her and Jack's relationship wasn't high on her priority list. "Don't start, Mom." She had other concerns. Like Clarice's family and how they were feeling and what they were going through.

Jack slid his phone into his pocket. "I spoke to my employer. The authorities believe Clarice was killed after she left Ambrose's party at this hotel. Security footage shows her leaving alone. She got into a cab. The police have spoken to the cabdriver, but he claims he dropped her at her apartment. Her phone wasn't found on her. The police are looking for it."

It didn't make sense. Who would want to hurt Clarice? She was hardworking, helpful, in-demand and kind. "How was she found?" Marissa asked. As many times as Marissa had worked with Clarice, she was embarrassed to admit she hadn't known her well. She could have a family and children or a live-in boyfriend.

"She had planned to meet a friend for breakfast before a shoot this morning. When she didn't show for either, her friend got worried and went to her apartment, found her and called the police," Jack said.

Marissa sat on the couch, her legs not feeling strong enough to support her. "I can't believe this. I need to call her parents. Maybe I can do something to help. Did she have a boyfriend or children?"

"She lived alone," Jack said. "I don't have other details." Jack crossed the room to her and sat beside her.

It was what she needed. Just someone who she knew was on her side to give her a minute.

"Jack, will you excuse us? I need to speak with Marissa alone."

Emotions swirled inside Marissa, grief, sadness and fear. The robe felt like it was suffocating her. The room was too hot.

Clarice had been on the set the day the Avery had been killed. The connection wasn't clear, though Marissa kept trying to piece it together.

"I'll make coffee," Jack said.

Caffeine would help, but the day would be rough.

"Mom, we can talk on the balcony." She and her mother walked onto the balcony and Lenore closed the door behind them.

The cold air was a relief. Marissa inhaled, enjoying the crispness of the air. They looked out over the city. Usually, a sense of awe and excitement struck her. Today, she felt dirty and sad.

"Marissa, what are you doing with your bodyguard? Before you lie to me, let me remind you that I have eyes. I can see something is going on between you two," Lenore said.

Marissa didn't roll her eyes, but she wanted to. "Jack and I have become close." And her relationship with him didn't involve her mother.

"He's a bodyguard."

"I am aware of his job."

"Why are you involved with him? Does this have to do with Rob? Because I can speak to your manager and we can brainstorm men you could date. Appropriate men you could date."

Marissa had explained to her mother before that she didn't want to be set up on a date. Matching someone on paper didn't translate to chemistry. The last man her manager had set her up with had been gay. They'd had a good laugh about the ridiculousness of the situation, two adults with successful careers agreeing to a date for the purpose of headlines. "I don't need to be set up on a date."

"If you want to stay relevant, you need to keep the public interested in you." Her mother continued talking about modeling and how more than being pretty, she had to be interesting.

It was a lecture her mother had given her many times before.

"Are you listening? Jack isn't famous. Does he have any film credits? Has he ever been part of a fashion campaign? Does he know anyone important? Have any important connections?" her mother asked.

That didn't matter now. Avery was dead. Clarice was dead. Her mother was fixating on the wrong problem. "He knows Kit," Marissa said.

Lenore sighed. "Don't be difficult. Kit has followed her path in life. She's not someone I understand. She's in her own world and she rarely confides in me. But you are different. You're a star."

Kit had the right idea, keeping her life private. "A friend, someone I respected, died last night. My primary concern isn't Jack or my relationship status or how many times my name appears in the news." Marissa felt grief and anger welling inside her. She should excuse herself and get some sleep. She should eat and focus on helping Clarice's family. Yet, she couldn't silence herself. "I think it's terrible that you barged in here, gave me heartbreaking news and judge how I live my life."

"I am not judging. I am trying to prevent you from making a mistake."

If her mother was a great judge of character, she was not perfect in that regard. She had been blinded by the man she had married. Despite Marissa's success in her field and her contributions to their family, Marissa carried the guilt that she owed her mother. Her mother had started her on this path into modeling to help the family and Marissa took those responsibilities to heart. "What makes you think I am so terrible at making decisions?"

"You are better suited for someone else. Come on, Marissa. Look at him. He's friends with Kit and you know they are probably more alike than not. That's about as different from you as possible. Before I met him, I hadn't heard his name."

Her mother had touched a nerve. "I am jealous of people who have anonymity. Whose names aren't printed in daily gossip sections."

"You want to be a nobody?" Lenore asked.

Like her face could either be everywhere or she didn't exist. She wanted something in between. "I don't see it that way. I've spent the last twenty years on my career. I want a break."

"You don't mean that. You're saying that because of what happened to Avery and Clarice," Lenore said.

It could be part of it. She couldn't pretend those friends hadn't died. "Even before Avery died, I was thinking about leaving the business. I don't want to be in the spotlight anymore. I did this for our family, but I want to do something else now."

Lenore set her hands on her hips. "You love modeling and you sound like a spoiled child."

Marissa didn't hate what she did. But she had often dreamed of pursuing her artwork, becoming an artist. Going to art shows and hanging out with local artists. "I am glad I took this path, but it came with a price. At times, it was stressful and hard. I never got to be a regular teenager. I missed school to go to interviews. I would workout and eat right even when I'd rather flop on the couch with a tub of butter popcorn."

"Are you blaming me for your unhappiness?" Lenore asked.

She was so defensive, she wasn't listening. "I am not blaming anyone for anything. I'm not unhappy. But I'm ready to take the next step and that means putting my career on the back burner."

"You'll quit? Walk away and turn your back on your friends?" Lenore asked.

Her mother was ever dramatic. "I am hardly turning my back on my friends. I might work in the industry in a more behind-the-scenes capacity. I helped Ambrose with his last collection and I enjoyed every minute of it."

"I can't believe this! There are so many opportunities around the corner. Walk away now and they'll give those campaigns to another model. Someone younger and who is willing to work more for less."

Marissa had considered that. "What if they do?"

Her mother recoiled as if Marissa had physically struck her. "You should be grateful."

"I am."

"You don't sound it," Lenore said.

Marissa wasn't making any headway with her mother. "My thoughts are a mess. Could we talk about this more later?"

Her mother seemed appalled. "I wouldn't start the rumors that you're quitting. Watch the bookings dry up. You'll lose your sponsorships. Think this through, Marissa. Don't be impulsive and reckless." Lenore fled the balcony and left the hotel room without saying anything to Jack. Marissa hated that she couldn't help her mother to understand her. She had tried in the past, but her mother was incapable of listening and seeing that modeling wasn't the entirety of who she was.

Marissa looked at Jack through the glass doors. He was working on his computer with a steaming cup of coffee next to him.

Entering the hotel room, she sat beside him and he pointed to the mug. "For you. The way you like it."

After the conversation with her mother, she needed coffee or something stronger. "Thanks." She took a sip and felt a little better. "I'm sorry if my mother was rude to you."

"She's protective of you. It's a notion I understand."

Marissa's thoughts cleared and emotion bounced around her head. "I'm heartbroken for Clarice's family."

"I know you are," Jack said. "I'll do everything in my power to find who did this. And I will stay with you until I do. I give you my word."

Chapter 9

After Clarice's funeral, Marissa could only think about getting away. Somewhere out of the city, away from her work and her family and her friends. She couldn't run away for good, but a few days in another place would help. Give her a fresh perspective. Take her away from the hurt and grief. Except she didn't want to run from Jack. Him she wanted at her side.

As Jack drove toward her house, the car was quiet and only the sounds of car horns and the hum of activity in the city were audible.

She'd pitch the idea. She had nothing to lose. "Let's go away somewhere."

"Where?" Jack asked, concern creasing the corners of his eyes.

"An island. A beach. Somewhere no one will recognize me," Marissa said.

"Your problems will follow you," Jack said.

"I can hide from them for a few days," she said.

"You're scheduled to be in Boston tomorrow," he said.

She could count on one hand the number of times she had rescheduled a shoot over the course of her career. Given the circumstances, postponing would be understandable. Or, she would miss the deadline, blow the campaign and millions of dollars would be lost. It would create a horrible problem. "Just two days. I want just two days away."

Marissa sent a message to her agent asking him to call her. Her lawyer would need to be involved, too. When she started thinking of the trouble, it almost made her want to forget the idea.

They arrived home and Jack parked in the garage. "Go inside. I'll check the perimeter and be in shortly."

Exhaustion and sadness weighed on her. Glancing at her phone, she still hadn't heard from her agent. The best message would be one letting her off the hook, giving her two days away.

Marissa opened the door from the garage leading into her home. She disabled the house alarm and flipped on the light in the small hallway leading into the house. Her breath caught in her throat and adrenaline rushed through her.

A tornado had whipped through the interior of her home. Couch cushions were slit open, bookshelves pulled down, vases and pictures frames smashed to the floor. She called to Jack, but her voice came out silent. She cleared her throat and tried again.

"Jack!"

She heard the heavy stomping of his shoes. He was at her side. His hands went to her shoulders.

"I'll call the police." His voice firm and solid.

She shouldn't do anything but she walked forward. She could hear Jack talking on the phone. Her home had been invaded again. This time, they had gotten around the alarm. She couldn't believe the destruction. Her feet crunched over glass and debris.

In her kitchen, the entire block of knives was empty. She spun, fear gripping her. The knives had been plunged into the wall, the handles sticking out. The action felt violent and angry.

"Marissa, we need to wait outside for the police." Jack's voice of reason. He sounded distant.

Marissa spun to face him. "Why? Why are they coming? What are the police going to do? Can they fix this? Can they put everything back?"

She felt her control slipping, fear taking over. The police had been looking for the person who had hurt Avery. The efforts had been fruitless.

"They might find the person who did this."

Marissa's temples throbbed. "They can't. They won't. But what about you? Your company is investigating, too. Why can't you tell me what you've found? Why all the secrecy? Why can't I be trusted? Why can't I know the details of why my life is being torn apart and the people around me dying?"

Jack seemed to be assessing her. "You are trustworthy."

Marissa threw her hands in the air. "You say that and yet no one wants to tell me anything. I'm kept in a glass house where I'm supposed to smile and look pretty. Does it dawn on anyone that I'm smart, too?

Of course not. My head is empty and I'm flighty and a prima donna." Fear was making her lash out.

"I know you're smart. I don't think you're a prima donna."

Her anger with him was misplaced, but she had to do something with the churning, ugly emotions. They were too strong, too much and taking her to a dark place. The place where criticisms and negativity shadowed the positives, darkening them into invisibility.

Marissa walked through the house, surveying the damage. This had been her sanctuary. She felt violated and angry and she had no one to lash out at. Bitterness seeped into her, amplified by her grief for Avery and Clarice. "I don't know who is doing this or why. I'm not hiding drugs here. I don't keep expensive jewelry here. The items in my jewelry box are costume." Her safe. She hadn't accessed it in months and at times, she didn't think of it. Had the intruder gotten to her safe?

She ran to her guest bedroom, trying not to think about the destruction around her and wondering if this was financially motivated.

Her pearls, a gift from her father, passed to her through Father Franklin on the occasion of her first Holy Communion. They meant everything to her. Her mother didn't know she had them. While her anger for her father was white-hot and she rarely wore the pearls, she hadn't thrown the necklace away.

The trunk at the end of the guest bed where she stored extra linens was overturned, the blankets torn out.

It must have taken hours for this much destruction. Or had it been a team of people? Hadn't anyone noticed something was amiss? Heard the racket and called the police? Apparently not.

She slid her pinky into the notch in the wood and pulled the release. The board lifted and the lock disengaged.

The safe remained untouched. She sat back on her haunches.

"Oh, thank you," she said. She needed to see the pearls. Needed to know they were okay. With the wreck her house had become, she doubted the vandals would have stolen from her safe and taken the time to close it, lock it and place the floorboard carefully over it.

Jack entered the room. "You have a safe?"

"I had this installed when I moved in."

"Odd place for it," he said. "Smart."

"Office or master bedroom too obvious."

She dialed the combination and opened the door. The pearl necklace, copies of her important paperwork, a hard drive containing pictures and a few miscellaneous trinkets that were priceless to her.

She held up the string of pearls. "They're safe."

"The intruders might have taken something else not stored in the safe."

They may have. She had some cash lying around for convenience. She had gifts from designers and artists that were worth a good amount of money. "It doesn't seem like they were here to steal. If they were, there are a dozen items on the main floor easily worth a few thousand dollars each. They didn't take those. They threw them to the floor and destroyed them. They were after something specific. And before you ask, I have no idea what."

"What's the significance of the pearls?" Jack asked.

Marissa touched the beads, loving the way the light glinted off them. "They were a gift from my father."

"They're beautiful."

The police called out from the main floor.

"Why don't you put those away and secure the safe? You'll need to do a walk-through inventory."

Marissa did as he asked, placing the pearls in the safe. She had been worried about the pearls almost above any of her other possessions. Almost no one knew she had them. But in this moment, they had been all-important.

She joined Jack and the police on the main floor, contemplating the bigger meaning of her concern for the pearls.

Marissa's plans for taking two days away were shot.

An insurance agent was in her home now, reviewing her policy and cataloguing what needed to be replaced. The West Company had sent an artwork expert to assist with the process.

Marissa had called a cleanup service and repairman to help put her home back in order. Their services were on hold pending the insurance agent's assessment. In a few weeks, if she was lucky, she could return home.

In the meantime, she was living in a hotel.

Her photo shoot in Boston had been pushed one day. Not enough time for a trip out of town. There had been some squawking from the photographer and talent involved, but Marissa hadn't slept and she was exhausted and frayed. Exhausted and frayed wouldn't photograph well.

She was by the open doors leading to her balcony at the Westside Hotel. A cup of hot tea chased off the cold. The day was overcast, her tea was black and her mood was dark. The one upside was that she had always wanted to stay at the Westside Hotel, but because it was located close to her home, she hadn't had the opportunity.

Jack had arranged for new clothes and personal items to be brought to the hotel. He had even found paints, brushes, an easel and canvas. Painting was a wonderful distraction and it relaxed her.

Sitting on the edge of her chair, she had tilted her canvas toward her. Jack watched her from across the hotel room. Matching colors came fluidly to her.

She was painting him. What captured her full attention was his eyes. They were gray with green flecks.

"Are you going to stare or are you going to come sit for me?" Marissa asked.

Jack walked to her side and looked at her canvas. "What inspired this?"

"You gave me the paints and this is like therapy. I needed to do something with my hands. I didn't have a plan when I sat down. I guess you're taking a leading role in my thoughts. If you'd sit behind my canvas, it would help," Marissa said.

Jack sat on the black chair across from her, turning to face her. "Want to talk about what's been going on?"

Marissa dipped her paintbrush into the paint. Those gray eyes were mesmerizing. Her fascination with Jack pointed to falling for him. Hard. "Can't get my head around it."

"My company is working with the insurance adjuster and repair staff to get a handle on the damages and get you an estimate of how long it will be before things are cleaned up," Jack said.

He was speaking about what was going on with the case, not between them. A spear of disappointment pierced her. "I've lived in hotels for months at a time. Not recently. But I've done it when I was younger and busier. I can do it again," Marissa said.

"Would you prefer other arrangements? Are you happy with this hotel?" Jack asked.

She kept painting, knowing if she didn't have the distraction of the canvas, she would launch into a conversation Jack didn't want to have and she wasn't sure she was ready to have. Given how emotionally fragile she felt, she should tread on safer ground. "It's fine."

"I don't think it is." He shifted his chair.

Marissa set down her brush, stood and took the two steps toward him. She angled his head, turning it to catch the light and returned to her chair. "It would be best if I moved up my retirement plans. Drop out of the spotlight. See if this stops." When Jack had suggested it before, she had thought it was the coward's way out and it would make this drag on infinitely. Now, she wanted to escape.

"We don't know how Clarice and Avery are connected beyond professionally. Were Clarice and Avery friends?"

Marissa didn't think so. "I wouldn't call them friends. They were *friendly*. They worked together. They were sometimes at the same parties or spent time at the same restaurants. But I don't think they were close. Avery was famous for her face. Clarice was well-known and well liked because she was good at her job. Most sets wanted her. Photographers and designers were willing to pay extra for her services."

"Did Avery and Clarice ever date the same man?"

"Not that I know of, but Clarice and I weren't close enough to talk about her personal relationships. Since they moved in the same social circles, it's possible," Marissa said. She turned the canvas toward Jack. "It needs work, but the face is right."

"My eyes are not that bright."

Perhaps she had exaggerated the color, pulling from her memory and from observation. "They are after sex," Marissa said.

He seemed unsure what to say about that.

Marissa dipped her paintbrush into the paint and stepped toward him. She ran the brush along his hand. He looked at the gray paint. Taking his hand, she held it up to his face. "Not after-sex gray, but close."

Then she swiped the brush across his cheek smearing the paint.

"That's one way to match a color," he said.

Marissa reached for her palette of colors. "If you had to pick a color for me, which would you pick?"

"Just one color?" he asked looking at the tray of paints, some pure, some blended.

"Or a mix of colors," she said. "One is so boring."

He looked at the palette. "Could be an array of colors. You're a free spirit. Light blue with white, like clouds floating in the sky." He dipped his finger in the white paint.

He held his finger close to her face. "I feel like I'm about to deface the Mona Lisa."

She leaned into his hand, letting the paint smear across her cheek. "I'm just a person. Not a work of art."

Their eyes connected and that sense of rightness amplified between them. Jack stepped forward and pulled her into his arms. He was strong and handsome and when she was with him, she felt wanted and precious.

"You seem sad," he said.

She set her hands on his arms. "I'm happy about this. This right now. But the big picture is a mess. My world is falling apart and there's nothing I can do to stop it." Her voice broke at the end of her statement.

"We should have found the person doing this. We need better leads. More leads. The police still have Rob as their prime suspect. Rob is either a fantastic actor at playing stupid or he isn't involved."

"Look what I did." The paint on her hand had smeared into his shirt.

"I'm not worried about my clothes. I'm just worried about you."

She reached to the hem of his navy T-shirt. "Let's take this off and rinse it out before the paint sets."

He lifted his arms and she pulled the shirt over his head. Bare-chested he was something worth looking at. Broad shoulders and rippled abdominals. Setting her hands on his chest, she leaned against him and kissed him.

"Let's close the doors so we're not cold," he said.

She snagged his T-shirt from the chair where it had slipped through her fingers. He closed and locked the door to the balcony and drew the curtains.

Ten steps to the bed and Marissa fell into his arms.

* * *

Marissa checked her outfit once more in the mirror. The Boston photo shoot had been delayed because of her and the juggling of schedules. Marissa sensed tension as soon as she walked onto the set.

The staff and talent were either angry that she had disrupted their scheduled or they were whispering in her direction, likely gossiping about what had happened to Avery and Clarice and not bothering to hide it. She had never been in a room with so many people avoiding eye contact with her.

Jack was with her. His unwavering strength and reassurance would get her through this. He waited outside the door for appearances. Though Marissa didn't care who knew she was involved with Jack, he wanted to keep boundaries when they were working.

She admired the fabric and the shoes she'd been provided for the shoot. The jumpsuit was similar to designs she had seen on the runway, but more suitable for everyday wear. It was constructed of soft and stretchy jean material and the slim orange belt around the middle provided the color and focal point. Her heeled orange shoes were comfortable. The ad they were shooting today would appear in women's magazines.

She exited her dressing room.

"That's a nice outfit," Jack said.

Was that sarcasm? He didn't seem to care about fashion. His wardrobe consisted of jeans, T-shirts and, depending on the weather, a simple tailored jacket. "Do you really like it?"

He nodded. "Looks good on you. But everything

looks good on you. That's why they hire you to show off the clothes."

She did a spin for his benefit. "Now my favorite part. Hair and makeup." She guessed, based on the style of the clothing, it would be big hair and heavy makeup. She wasn't opposed to that. When she stopped modeling, she would like to experiment with her hair color, like stripes of purple or darker shades of brown. Doing that now would be a problem with her contracts.

"Hey, Marissa."

Marissa turned at the sound of her name and recognized the woman approaching, but couldn't place her face with a name.

"Hi." Marissa waited.

The other woman, a brunette with long hair to her elbows, probably a model from her build and facial features looked irritated. Was she put out by the schedule change? "You must think you're Queen of Everything."

Jack tensed beside her, but Marissa shot him a look. She had to handle this herself. Marissa heard the venom. She was too tired and emotionally wrung to engage in a debate. "I'm here to work this photo shoot. That's it."

The brunette crossed her arms. "I was supposed to be skiing today in Aspen with my boyfriend. But because you had a break-in at your house, I'm here instead."

It wasn't just about the break-in. Avery and Clarice's deaths weighed heavily on her and the threats against Marissa were serious. She'd needed time to recover. "I'm sorry about that. I've had some ongoing issues in my life. Rescheduling was unavoidable." Unless this woman lived under a rock, she would know that Avery and Clarice were dead.

In response, the other woman huffed. As if that meant anything. Marissa brushed past her on the way to the set.

"What was that about?" Jack asked.

"Another day, another angry rising star trying to mark her territory," Marissa said.

"Does that happen often?" Jack asked.

"Models getting catty? The competition goes to their heads. Jobs and money are at stake. And maybe sometimes it's hunger. You've seen what models have to wear."

"I've seen you eat," Jack said.

"I eat. I work out. Some just don't eat. When I retire, I'm going to eat hamburgers with all the fixings and pizzas with every topping," Marissa said. She hadn't gorged herself on food in years.

"Count me in," Jack said.

Her heart lightened at the suggestion of a friendship that would persist between them. "I'll need fast food because I'll be up all night painting. If I invite you over for pizza on a Friday night, what are the chances you'll come?" Marissa asked.

"Pizza loaded with all the good stuff? Pretty high. Pepperoni, extra cheese, ham—"

"Okay, okay, stop. You're making me hungry." She couldn't eat now, right before a shoot.

"All right, but I think you should be very, very bad and Friday night, we eat pizza."

Looking at him, at the twinkling in his gray eyes, she felt like she was in high school again. That rush of emotion and endorphins and the absolute willingness to fall under the spell of the handsome guy with great smile.

Marissa was on the set, posing for pictures. Jack had seen her work several times and today, something was off. She seemed on edge. The longer the shoot, the tension in the room escalating, Marissa's agitation was clear. When Niles, the photographer, called for a break, she walked to him. They talked briefly and then she strode to Jack's side. She appeared drained.

"Want to talk about it?" Jack asked.

"Niles wants to do another shoot tomorrow. To give me time to get it together," Marissa said.

"He didn't say that," Jack said.

"He didn't say it, but I know it's what he meant. I'm trying to think of the shoes and pizza and fun, but Avery and Clarice are on my mind. If I were new to the job and hadn't worked with Niles on this campaign before, I would have been fired today. I was a mess. I am a mess."

"Why don't we hit the gym? Blow off some steam," Jack said. If it wasn't clicking today, she'd get it together another day.

Marissa gestured at him to follow her. They entered her private dressing room. In the middle of the room was a large sink and mirror. Lining the sink were a dozen beauty products. Marissa brushed her hair and then tied it back. Then she turned on the sink and started taking off her makeup. She moved quickly, picking up the little bottles, pouring the contents on a cotton ball or a small square pad and wiping at her face.

When she was finished and she turned around, her face bare, Jack's breath backed up in his lungs. Without the makeup, she was more beautiful. She patted her face with a white towel.

"What's wrong? You look…something," she said.

"Niles should take your picture right now. The shoot would be done," Jack said.

Marissa glanced in the mirror. "Without makeup? I'd shock people. I can see the tabloids now."

"You don't see what I do. That's too bad. It's not the hairdos and the makeup and the clothes. Your expressions and your eyes and your confidence. That's what sells products. That's what everyone wants a piece of."

Marissa inclined her head. "Thank you. That's kind of you to say." She set the towel on the side of the sink. "Instead of the gym, why don't we go to a shooting range?"

Jack was up for it. Was this a regular thing for Marissa? He hadn't seen it on her schedule. "Have you ever been?"

She shook her head. "It's time I learn."

It might empower her. Given what she had been through in the last several weeks, knowing how to use a firearm could help. She wouldn't learn everything she needed to know in one session, but it was a place to start. "It can't hurt to know how to handle yourself in various situations."

"I thought you would say no," Marissa said.

"Then this was for shock value?" Jack asked.

Marissa shook her head. "I want to learn. I was bracing for the argument."

The nearest range was thirty minutes from them.

After confirming the change in their plans with the rest of the security team, driving to the range, registering and paying their fee, Jack led Marissa to the stall. They put on their ear and eye protection.

She removed the green ball cap she had been wearing. Jack glanced around. No one was paying attention to them. Even the employee who had done their paperwork and checked their identifications hadn't mentioned Marissa's profession or looked at her twice.

Jack demonstrated basic safety on the gun and he showed her how to use the weapon. It was a small gun, good for beginners. He aimed and fired, making his target within a few inches.

Marissa appeared impressed. "How long did it take you to learn to shoot that way?"

Years of practice and drilling and lessons and training. "My entire career."

She stepped up to the stall. Jack placed the gun in her hands and she leveled it at the target. The shot went wide.

She tried again. Missed. Tried several more times. Missed each time.

"This is harder than it looks," Marissa said.

"It takes practice. Don't get discouraged. We can make this a regular thing if you have an interest in learning."

Marissa furrowed her brow in concentration. "I want to do this. I can do this."

He was getting the sense this was about more than hitting the target. She was looking for a sense of safety that had been taken from her. Knowing she could protect herself might give her a boost.

Several more attempts and after discussing technique, Marissa hit the target. Not anywhere near the center, but a hit. Her shoulders relaxed and she seemed pleased.

They left the gun range an hour later. Marissa's steps seemed lighter. In her hat and sunglasses, she was almost unrecognizable.

She slid into the passenger seat. "I feel better. That was stress relieving."

"I'm glad you feel that way," Jack said. He was starting to think this might go on for months. He couldn't stay for months. His relationship with her was escalating and it would cause him to make a mistake. Having been down this road with Bianca, he wasn't willing to travel it with Marissa. His best focus came from being emotionally distant.

She should know how to defend and protect herself. In the immediate term, he was the right choice to protect her. But in the long run, he couldn't commit. How would she feel when he left?

Avoiding hurt when he left was impossible and Jack didn't know where that left them or where to go with that sentiment.

In high spirits, Marissa was ready to face the photo shoot again. She wouldn't allow her grief or worry or anxiety to play on her face today. She was a professional and she'd act like it. It wouldn't be the first time in her life she'd masked her emotions for the sake of a job.

Yesterday was behind her. Negative thoughts and disparaging looks from her coworkers wouldn't bother her. A night of sleep—with Jack in her bed—had been restorative. Her workout that morning had been intense and she'd eaten well. She was physically and mentally prepared.

"You ready to do this?" Niles asked. He was a great photographer, experienced and well-known, having had his photographs in every major fashion magazine and website over the last decade. He was also a friend. She appreciated that he'd recognized she'd needed time and had been willing to adjust his schedule to give it to her.

"I'm great. I'm sorry about yesterday. I got this now," Marissa said.

"If it helps, you look fierce today. Much higher energy. Does your good mood have anything to do with the sexy man escorting you around town?" Niles asked, holding up his camera and snapping a picture of her, while inclining his head at Jack.

Marissa glanced in Jack's direction. He had centered her. Helped her put her life into perspective. "He's my bodyguard. With everything that's been going on, he's been working extra hard. We've gotten close."

Niles snapped another picture. "Close. That's a good way to put it. When you're working today, think about him. Your expression when you looked at him is radiant."

Marissa tossed her hair over her shoulder. "Thank you for understanding."

Niles turned to check the lighting again. The model who had mouthed off the day before stepped onto the set. "You ready today? Or will you blow this whole thing? Some of us need to work new jobs, not spend days on this."

Marissa had tried to be kind and understanding

and sweet. But this woman was pressing her beyond her patience level. She had held her tongue before. Being pushed around wasn't in the cards today. "I've lost two good friends in the last month. Your comments are uncalled for. Delays happen. I didn't intentionally screw with your plans. Instead of attacking me, why don't you consider that I have a lot going on in my life and show some compassion? Perhaps if you were nicer to work with, I'd recommend you for another campaign. If you hadn't realized it, I'm principal on some campaigns and you wouldn't be the first model I've helped. So get down off your self-righteous horse because maybe next time, you'll need some compassion. I only hope that you aren't given the same that you've shown me because you'd come up empty."

Unloading felt great like a weight lifting. It was rare for her to fire back at anyone and it felt good.

"Michael said you were self-centered," the model said.

Marissa blinked at her. *Michael?* "Michael who?" She knew dozens of Michaels.

"Michael Langer?" The attitude on the model's face made Marissa want to slap her.

Marissa's ex-husband and lead singer of Silver Sundays. Surprise and hurt sliced through her. Michael had acted fine toward her at Avery's funeral. Perhaps that had been a pass given the circumstances, and he was still harboring anger. "I'm sorry Michael feels that way. But maybe you should give me a chance before you believe one side of a story. Marriages are complicated."

Marissa whirled away. She was finished with the

dirty looks and arguing. She was here to do a job and she would do it. If she didn't leave the negativity behind, it would pull her under.

Determined to prove she could ignore her personal life and focus on the job, Marissa was all in.

Screaming filled the air.

Jack's adrenaline fired. He was looking at Marissa and she was fine. Primary objective met. But someone was in trouble.

"Stay where you are!" he shouted to Marissa. He pointed to one of the bodyguards on set. "Watch her!" In the case this was a careful distraction, he wanted Marissa protected.

Jack raced in the direction of the noise. A brunette stumbled toward him, her hand over her cheek. One of the models. Her long brown hair was hanging over her face as she hunched over, screaming.

Jack rushed to her. He had to calm her and assess the problem. She was wailing. He knelt next to her. His knee twitched, reminding him of his injury and the mistakes of the past. Focusing on the screaming woman, he ignored it.

"Call for an ambulance," he yelled to another model standing close and watching slack-jawed.

He sensed Marissa next to him. "What happened?" She extended a first aid kit to him.

He hadn't figured that out. He moved the screaming woman's hands away from her face. The wailing has stopped, but she was whimpering. He didn't see an injury. Bruise? Broken bone?

"You need to tell me where you are hurt," Jack

said. He repeated himself three times before the woman was composed enough to speak.

"I went outside for a smoke. A man grabbed me!"

"Are you injured?" Jack asked.

She touched her face again. "I hit my face on the doorjamb when I ran."

Jack opened the first aid kit and withdrew a cold pack. He broke it and set it over her face. She started crying again. Jack suspected she was more scared than hurt.

"I screamed and kicked and they let me go. He said I was the wrong one."

Fear twisted in Jack's stomach. He exchanged glances with Marissa. The wrong one, a kidnapping gone awry. Jack formed a hypothesis from the few facts. The would-be kidnappers had been targeting Marissa. With the brown hair and at a certain angle, the two models had similar appearances. Having realized their mistake, the kidnappers had let this woman go.

"Do you remember anything about them?" Jack asked.

The woman moved the cold pack from her face. "Their van. It was black with a sliding side door."

"What about the men themselves?" Jack asked. He was hesitant to use the word kidnappers out loud, afraid it would set her off again.

The model narrowed her eyes in thought and brought her hands to her head. "I can't remember. It happened so fast. They grabbed me and I started screaming. Then they threw me against the building and raced away."

A few minutes later, the ambulance arrived on

scene. Jack took a step back to allow them to do their assessment.

Marissa was upset, too. Her mouth was pinched and her eyes narrowed in thought. Jack led Marissa away.

"You know they were after me, right?" she asked.

"I had the same thought," Jack said.

"If it had been me out there, they would have kidnapped or killed me."

It was his fear that was their plan. "It's a persistent mission, but they are sloppy. And they wouldn't have kidnapped you or harmed you because I would have been there. Right there."

Marissa wrapped her arms around his waist and rested her head on his shoulder. He considered the inappropriateness of touching her this way and what it meant about their relationship, but the need to comfort her outweighed it.

Chapter 10

Jack couldn't postpone returning to Washington, DC, to testify about the incident with Bianca any further. He wasn't eager to spell out his mistakes and review the circumstances leading to his being shot, but he didn't have a choice.

Marissa was in the kitchenette of the hotel, leaning against thc countertop, bottle of water in one hand and her phone in the other.

She looked up when he entered the room. She had been in the hotel's VIP gym for the two hours before while Jack had guarded the room and made his travel plans. He hated to leave her under the difficult circumstances, but he had arranged for the best in the business to fill in.

"Your sister and Griffin are flying in tomorrow. They're planning to stay with you for the next couple of days."

Marissa looked at him. "You're leaving?"

"I have something I need to take care of. Two days max." He didn't want to elaborate. It was a mess and that it had happened at all embarrassed him. He considered himself a better operative; he should see betrayal coming.

Marissa set her water bottle on the granite countertop. "You've been working around the clock for weeks. Are you burned out?"

He wasn't interested in a vacation. "I'm not taking a break."

Marissa stared at him. "Don't make me drag it out of you. What's going on?"

He had known she wouldn't let this go. It was one of the reasons he had delayed telling her about it. "I have a work-related issue to resolve."

Marissa moved closer to him. She set her hands on his upper arm. "Tell me what's bothering you so I don't worry."

She was hard to resist. He wanted to wave it off, but that felt like a lie. "I was involved in an incident a few months ago."

"An incident that's the reason you were injured?"

She was intuitive. He liked that about her. "That's the one. My partner was involved. Was the reason for it." He hadn't meant to tell her that much.

"Are you meeting with your partner?" Marissa asked.

"I'm testifying against her."

"A court appearance," Marissa said.

"Not a court issue." What Bianca had done was beyond the American court system. She was a traitor to the flag and in his field, there was no worse crime. Given how much she had been trusted and how many people she had hurt, she wasn't getting a trial. She would be spending the rest of her life in a secret government-run prison for traitors and spies. His testimony was to complete the classified documentation on the matter.

Marissa inclined her head, her long ponytail swinging to the side. "Tell me about it. I know you can't tell me everything. But tell me how you're feeling. Tell me what's most upsetting to you."

Jack needed to be careful to confide only parts of the story that didn't involve classified information. "I was undercover for over a year on a job." He checked each word as it left his mouth. Going over the incident too many times, it came easily to him. "She was my partner. My friend. I trusted her. She decided she didn't want to work with me anymore. She sold me out." Bianca had fallen in love with the head of the criminal group they were supposed to be taking down. She had gotten too close to François. She had spent time alone with him. Jack had questioned her about her behavior and she had claimed to be fine. She had said that her relationship with François was aboveboard and she was simply playing a part.

Jack didn't know when Bianca had crossed the line, but she had lied for months. She had blown their cover and then allowed Jack to walk into a trap. He almost didn't get out. "She was recently captured by the United States government," Jack said. He didn't know the details of the operation, only that when François and his network were taken down, Bianca was apprehended and extradited to the United States.

"You're planning to face her?" Marissa asked

He didn't know if he would have to look Bianca in the eye or if his testimony would be recorded. "If I need to."

Her brows furrowed with concern. "Let me come with you for support."

That wasn't their arrangement. She wasn't supposed to support him. He was watching out for her. "That's not necessary." The tightening in his gut indicated he wanted her with him and that surprised him. He had been alone for as long as he could recall. His last serious relationship had ended years before. His preference was to be by himself. Yet Marisa's offer stirred him. Saying no was his impulse, while his true desire was to answer with a firm yes.

"I know you can handle it alone. I want to be there for you. I want to be a friend when you might need one. If it's bad, you'll want a drinking buddy after."

"We're not going anywhere glamorous," Jack said. To the capital where his lawyer from the West Company would meet him and walk him through his testimony.

"I don't need glamour. I need a bed and a shower and food and I'm set. I can't go home. A hotel is a hotel. A change of scenery will be therapeutic."

"I'd like it if you came." The admission was hard to speak. It disclosed a weakness and Jack had built his career around his strengths.

She kissed his cheek. "Thank you so much. I'll pack. And thank you for letting me in just a little."

He had let her in more than a little and it scared him a great deal.

Jack had experienced a range of emotions in the months since he had been shot. It had taken time to accept what Bianca had done. Anger, guilt and depression had been his constant companions through his physical therapy. He had been to countless meetings, responded to hundreds of questions and had written about the incident several times.

Going over the events didn't make them easier to understand. He wanted to find that one moment in time when he could have seen what Bianca was doing and persuaded her to make a better decision.

He would watch someone he loved and cared about be taken to jail. Worst still, he had a hand in putting her there. Despite what she had done, he wasn't happy about it.

He and Marissa drove from New York to DC. Traffic was heavy on I-95, but her company made the miles roll by. Marissa was helping more than he would have believed. Her being beside him was a new dynamic and he was surprised at how comforting he found her presence.

"You won't be allowed to be part of the proceeding, but my boss is aware of our situation and will make sure you're safe while I testify," Jack said.

"I'm here for you. Don't worry about me. I brought my e-reader and computer. I have thousands of unread emails and ten years' worth of unread books," Marissa said.

Jack reached across the car's console and grabbed her hand. "Thank you for coming with me. This is unexpected and it means a lot to me."

Her smile bowled him over. "You should expect more from your friends."

Is that what they were? Friends? "It's better to have low expectations." As a great example, Bianca, whom he had trusted and cared for, had betrayed him. He should have anticipated it.

"Do you have family coming to meet you?" Marissa asked.

"I'm not from Washington, DC," he said.

"Where are you from?"

"Born in Idaho. Grew up in Springfield, Missouri."

"I wouldn't have guessed," Marissa said.

He had worked to ditch his accent. It was too noticeable and as a special operative, he put a high value on every scrap of information about himself. "I try not to advertise too much about my life."

"Why?"

For a woman who was in the public eye every day, he understood her confusion. "I'm a private person."

"What did your family do in Missouri?" she asked.

"Farmers," Jack said. "Corn and soybeans. My mom kept turkeys for a while, but they were more trouble than they were worth."

"Does your family still live in Missouri?" she asked.

"Nope. My dad died ten years ago and my mother the year after that."

"I'm sorry," Marissa said.

"It's okay. I've been leasing my quarter of the land to my brother and two sisters. One day, I plan to retire in Springfield."

"You want to be a farmer?" Marissa asked.

Difficult for him to explain why that was the next logical step for his career. He couldn't work international operations for the rest of his life. His body would break down. The job required skills and physical acuity that would fade with age. Being a farmer was going home. He'd acquired a great deal of savings in his line of work. "When I'm finished in this line of work."

"Finished being a bodyguard." She let the word bodyguard hang in the air between them. He sensed what she was really asking, but he wasn't ready to discuss it. He thought of Bianca, of her betrayal and the testimony he was giving against her. Trusting easily had never been in his repertoire, but on the heels of stinging disloyalty, it was especially difficult.

The three-story brick town house built in the 1800s had been restored and was the West Company's remote office location in Washington, DC. Polished wood floors and sparkling white trim, the space wasn't what Jack had expected. The house was a twist of historic and contemporary, fresh and inviting.

He had been in communication with Kelly St. John, his lawyer, over the last several months. She was wearing a navy blue skirt suit and greeted him cordially at the front door. Marissa was welcomed inside and escorted to the reception area.

"If you don't mind waiting, we'll be across the hall," Kelly said, ushering Marissa into a room that smelled of fresh coffee and spices. A television was turned on to a national news station and the coffee table was covered with magazines and books.

"You don't have to wait here. You could explore DC," Jack said. "This is supposed to take anywhere from one to three days."

Marissa shook her head and patted her bag. "I have my laptop. I have work to catch up on. But if I need to go out, I know how to call for backup. I want to be here in case you need me."

Her last sentence wrapped around him and his uneasiness about this process lessened.

The West Company had arranged for another bodyguard to be available to protect Marissa, if she wanted to sightsee. She was sticking around for him. If Kelly thought their relationship was unusual, she didn't indicate as such.

Kelly and Jack entered the room across the hall.

Two FBI agents, a contact from the CIA and a representative from the West Company were waiting in the meeting room. The long wood-topped table sat twelve. The fireplace was unlit, the sun from the front windows warming the room. Jack removed his suit jacket and placed it over the back of his chair.

"Is Bianca coming to the meeting?" he asked. Better to brace himself for impact and not leave the question looming over him.

No one answered. In the room filled with special operatives, no one was quick to volunteer information.

Kelly cleared her throat. "She will not. Her lawyer will be here this afternoon in her stead."

Jack loosened his tie and unfastened the first button. This didn't need to be an ordeal, but it would be.

More questions, more review of the information he had submitted. He was forced to relive the time he and Bianca were undercover. Each agency had their bases to cover and ultimately, Bianca's fate would be known to few people outside the room. Jack wasn't sure he would be told what exactly would happen to his former partner.

When they asked him questions he couldn't answer, Jack told them as much. He hadn't been aware that Bianca was intimately involved with the target. He didn't know why he'd missed it. No, it wasn't that he'd had feelings for Bianca that had blinded him to her deception. He didn't have feelings for her now. He wasn't holding back to protect her.

Their questions ended around five in the evening. Jack had spoken more today than he had in the last week. On the plus side, they had covered everything that was needed. He was free to return to New York. Stepping out of the office, he half expected Marissa to be gone.

She was still in the reception area. She was watching television and had removed her shoes. She looked like she was at home, relaxing. Looking up, she smiled when she saw him.

"How did it go?" she asked.

"Great." Terrible. Going over the events had made him feel ill and tired. His brain was fogged, as if half-awake. "We're done. I don't need to return tomorrow."

Marissa frowned. "You seem upset. I realize you were doing something difficult, but I'm still worried. Don't box me out."

"I'll be fine. I need to eat."

"I have a great idea," Marissa said. She seemed excited, her eyes sparkling and she rose on her toes slightly. "Since you had planned to be here for a couple more days, let's fly to Springfield and see your family. It will be therapeutic for you."

He liked the idea. Being around his siblings would help take the edge off and no one looking to hurt Marissa could anticipate the trip. "Okay."

She clapped her hands together. "That easy? You want me to meet your family?"

His thoughts stuttered. He hadn't considered that angle. His sisters would be like foxes who'd caught the hen. They were after him often enough about his personal relationships. But he'd agreed and he couldn't back out. "That sounds fun."

"I have more good news. I got in touch with a friend and we have a table, if we want it, at Donahue's, a cool, new restaurant. Any interest?" she asked.

He wanted to check into their hotel and flop face first into the mattress. But she seemed excited about eating out and she had waited for him all day. "We can do that. You must have been bored today."

"Not at all," Marissa said. "I was worried about you, but I had work to distract me."

She slipped on her shoes and stood. They came together and when her arms went around him, he enjoyed the closeness of her skin, the scent of her hair and the warmth in her embrace. He couldn't recall the last intimate relationship he'd had with a woman that extended beyond the bedroom. But he had it with Marissa, genuine affection and deep caring for her.

It scared him a little, but he enjoyed it much more.

He and Marissa took a private car to Donahue's. After Marissa gave her name, they were seated within minutes, strolling past a crowded bar of people waiting for a table.

Their table was in a quiet part of the restaurant. They took their seats and Marissa reached across the table and covered his hands with hers. "You look like you could use a drink."

Jack could have used ten drinks. It would be a while before he could shake loose the emotions surrounding the day. "It was a long day."

Marissa squeezed his hands. "I'm sorry. Want to talk about it?"

Jack wanted to forget about the crushing sense of defeat that dogged him. "It was almost like I was being blamed for what happened. Like it was my fault things went down the way they did."

"I'm sure no one thinks that," Marissa said.

"I was in the meeting with some heavy hitters. I was getting looks. Like I missed something important and turned a blind eye to obvious problems."

The waitress appeared and Marissa ordered drinks and appetizers. Neither sounded appealing, but he had to eat.

As they talked, he realized he was doing most of the talking. She was a good listener. Asking the right questions without prying. It wasn't like him to ramble, but he was doing just that and it was helping, unburdening some of the emotions surrounding the day.

Marissa wasn't who he'd expected when he'd taken this job, but she was becoming someone he could trust and could count on. He decided he would tell her what he did for a living. Not name names or give specifics, but he wanted her to know who he was. The urgency and need felt pressing. But not in public where he could be overheard.

A couple hours later, after a decadent dinner and shared dessert, they checked into their hotel. It was a basic room with two double beds, flowered wallpaper and heavy green curtains over the windows. The bathroom was serviceable, rather than luxurious.

Marissa propped open her suitcase on a small table in the corner of the room.

He watched her, insecurity forcing him to hold back. Scaring her away wasn't his intention. His career was as important to him as was Marissa. He took a deep breath. The truth wasn't something to fear. "I haven't elaborated on what I do for a living because it invites questions. But I want you to know. I want you to understand that my work is important."

Marissa faced him. "I know your work is important without you telling me the details. Although if you are willing to tell me, I am more than willing to listen." Her voice was practically a purr and she crossed the room to him, taking his suit lapels in her hands.

The truth as an aphrodisiac. Interesting concept. "I work secret, special operations for the United States government."

He waited for her to react. She blinked at him. "You're letting me in and I'm afraid to jinx it with questions, but what does that mean exactly?"

"I usually work internationally and on jobs that the public doesn't know about. They are jobs that others won't do. Too dangerous or too risky. But I do them."

"My sister does this?"

He didn't want to give away what Kit did. It wasn't his place. "I don't work with your sister directly. I've worked with Griffin in the past."

"Okay. Tell me more," Marissa said.

"My work keeps me out of the country. Sometimes I can't call home. When I am home, I'm usually training."

"Your injury kept you in the States and that's why you're with me," she said.

She had put the pieces together. "Once I'm back to a hundred percent, I'll be wheels-up again."

He expected her to retreat. With the bluntness of the truth, he wasn't looking to drive a wedge, but he knew she wouldn't like it. Instead, she slipped her arms around his neck. "Then I'm lucky that you're in my life and our paths crossed when they did."

"That's one way to think of it." She was handling this better than he could have expected. Showing interest without prying. Not put off by his description, but reasonably curious.

"I put a lot of this together," Marissa said. "Even though it's only been a short time, you have been a constant in my life when I've needed it. If not your international work, I knew you would have other clients one day. Thank you for telling me. I know it's a big deal for you and that means a lot to me."

Marissa pressed her lips to his. Jack slid his hands down her sides and to her shapely hips. Reaching under her rear, he lifted her and she wrapped her long, slim legs around him. Carrying her to the bed, he covered her with his body. They fell into the mattress, a tangle of arms and legs, locked in each other's embrace.

Traveling as often as she did, it wasn't the trip making Marissa nervous. It was meeting Jack's sisters. Unsure what to expect her first time in Springfield, Marissa stayed calm as she walked to the front door of the ranch-style house.

"Beatrice is great. She'll love you," Jack said, lifting his hand and tapping the brass knocker.

A petite woman with red hair cut into a pixie style opened the door. "You must have made great time. Less than an hour ago, I found out you were coming and here you are. Hi, there. I'm Bea."

Another woman appeared behind her. She was taller, her hair long and woven into a braid over her shoulder.

"Come in, please. You must be Marissa. I'm Rachel. I made peach iced tea and I have Jack's favorite cookies," Rachel said. She hugged her brother.

Jack was silent.

"I didn't mean to surprise you. The trip was spur of the moment," Marissa said.

"I'm glad to have you," Bea said. "Welcome to my home. Rachel lives on the other side of the pond. Travis is out of town and he'll be sorry he missed you."

Jack would miss seeing his only brother. "Travis and I will catch up," Jack said.

The foursome settled in Beatrice's kitchen. The back windows were open to the farm, providing a view of the rolling pastures, a small pond and fields.

"Tell us how you met," Rachel said. She set a tray of iced teas on the table and set a glass in front of Marissa.

Jack took another glass from the tray and set it on the blue-and-white-checkered tablecloth. "She doesn't want to be questioned."

"If we don't question her, we won't get to know her because you won't tell us anything," Rachel said.

"No one can know she's here," Jack said. "No pictures." He sounded grumpy about it.

Rachel rolled her eyes. "He is so surly."

"I agree." Marissa chuckled, amused to find two people who didn't take Jack too seriously. The sisters were friendly and warmth rolled off them. She liked them immediately. She sipped her tea. It was good and sweet.

Conversation flowed easily. Rachel and Beatrice seemed interested in what she did for a living and she felt likewise.

"I promised Marissa a tour," Jack said.

Marissa glanced at the clock on the wall. Two hours had passed. She'd been having such a good time, she had lost track. Marissa wanted to see the farm, but was disappointed to leave the sisters. She stood from the table. "It was great meeting you. Thank you for the tea."

They said their goodbyes, put on their coats, gloves and hats, and she followed Jack out of the house.

"I'm sorry if they were too much," Jack said. They stepped onto the porch. The air was crisp, fresh and cool.

They had told stories about the farm and their brothers. It was plain to see they loved and missed their brother. "They're great. Easy to talk with," Marissa said. She inhaled deeply. "I could stay here for another month. It's quiet here."

"Off season," Jack said.

"I'd spend the day painting," Marissa said.

Jack looked around. "This is one of the most beautiful places in the world. I love it here."

As they walked, Jack told her about the land and their crops and Marissa felt his love for his family and the farm. He had been quiet while his sisters had talked, but now he seemed to have much to say, too.

"This place is great, Jack. Thank you for sharing it with me."

Jack slung his arm around her shoulder. It was rare for him to show affection when they were outside and she reveled in this. Maybe it was because the farm was his home and that familiarity and comfort was rolling off him in waves, but in the warmth of his embrace, she felt like she was where she belonged.

In her office in New York, Marissa was paging through a document of fashion designs Ambrose had emailed to her. He wanted feedback and she hoped to provide worthwhile advice and suggestions. She was coming up empty. Having gone through so much in the last few weeks, she was running on fumes and her creativity was low.

Her phone rang with Clarice's number on the display. The name jolted her. Clarice couldn't be calling. Had to be one of her family members using Clarice's phone. Or maybe the police. With a shaking hand, Marissa answered.

"Marissa? I'm sorry to bother you. This is Jeanne, Clarice's mom. I hope I'm not catching you at a bad time."

Sympathy swamped her and fresh grief bloomed through her. "Hello, Jeanne. Now is a fine time. I am so sorry for your loss. What can I do for you?"

Jeanne cleared her throat. "I wanted to know if you'd come to Clarice's apartment. There's something I need you to see."

Suspicion and wariness crept over her. "Can you tell me over the phone?"

A pregnant pause. "It would be better if you came over."

Marissa felt bad saying no to a woman who had lost her daughter. She couldn't imagine how going to Clarice's would change anything. "All right. I can stop by."

"Thank you," Jeanne said. She provided the address and then disconnected the call.

Uneasiness swept over Marissa. Visiting Clarice's apartment felt strange and she wasn't clear why Jeanne wanted her there. Clarice could have work items that Jeanne wanted to know about or perhaps Jeanne needed closure or wanted to talk about her daughter.

After explaining the situation to Jack, thirty minutes later, she and Jack were walking up the five flights of metal stairs leading to Clarice's apartment. The stairs split the complex into two sides. The building was constructed of brick that had been painted red. Clarice's apartment was on the top floor, the door bright green. Made the whole building seem like it belonged in a Christmas movie.

Jack knocked and Jeanne answered the door. She opened it to allow them to enter.

"Is anyone else here?" Jack asked, looking around.

Jeanne shook her head. "Can I get you some tea? I put on a pot of water."

The kitchen was small, but modern with dark brown cabinets and granite countertops in brown, beige and black swirls. Not big enough for a kitchen table, a breakfast bar divided the kitchen and the living room. The short hallway leading to the only bedroom was painted bright white, giving the small space better lighting.

"No tea, thank you. Jeanne, you sounded upset on the phone. Can you tell me what's going on?" Marissa asked.

Jeanne wrung her hands. "It's better if I show you. This is why I couldn't explain it on the phone." She walked into Clarice's bedroom. Marissa and Jack followed.

On the wall of Clarice's bedroom were pictures of Marissa, Avery, Ambrose and a few other models who had walked in Ambrose's fashion week show. Below them were printouts from internet news sites and newspaper stories regarding Avery's death and Ambrose's show. Sadness pressed on Marissa, making her feel like she was underwater. Seeing the details laid out in this way was hard to handle. The photos and accompanying articles were lined up neatly in date order.

Struggling to take deep breaths, Marissa couldn't look away. Upsetting to see her and Ambrose's pictures posted next to Avery's.

"What is this?" Marissa asked.

"I found it when I came over to start cleaning out her apartment. I can't afford to pay the rent and the landlord gave me three days to vacate. I thought about taking this down and throwing it away, but I got to thinking it might have something to do with what happened to her," Jeanne said. Her voice broke and she brought her hand over her mouth.

Marissa hugged Jeanne, wishing she could help ease the woman's hurt.

Clarice may have been looking into Avery's murder herself. Had she seen something backstage at Ambrose's show? Noticed something in the articles tying the murderer to the crime?

"Did Clarice keep a journal or notes?" Jack asked.

"I don't know. I've been hurrying to pack and I haven't gone through her personal things yet," Jeanne said.

"I will speak to Clarice's landlord and ask him to give you time." Even if she paid a month's rent to take the pressure off Clarice's mother and give her time to go through her daughter's things with care, it was worth it. "We need to bring this to the attention of the police. Clarice may have known something about Avery's murder. She might have stumbled onto something that made the killer nervous."

Jeanne sat on the edge of the bed. "Clarice talked about you." She looked at Marissa with haunted eyes. "And about Avery. She wasn't pretty like you are. In high school, she was teased for being poor and wearing the wrong clothes. That wasn't her fault. That was mine. She said that you and Avery treated her nice."

Marissa's heart ached for Jeanne. "Clarice was good at her job, the best in the business. Everyone who worked with her respected her. She is deeply missed."

Jeanne put her head in her hands and started to cry. Marissa sat next to her on the bed and patted her back gently. No words could make this right.

Jack was staring at the photos on the wall. After Jeanne composed herself, she stood from the bed.

Jack took out his cell phone. "Do you mind if I take pictures? Clarice was a smart lady. She may have been onto something important. I'm not seeing it now, but maybe it will come to me."

"Jeanne, let's you and I fix a cup of tea and let Jack get what he needs. I can tell you some stories about Clarice that will make you proud." Marissa steered Jeanne out of the bedroom and into the kitchen, leaving Jack to look around.

Museums relaxed Marissa. Her love of art was well fed there. The Metropolitan Museum of Art was one of her favorites. It had on display a collection of artwork and furniture from the Gilded Age. Marissa planned to meet Kit at the museum to peruse the exhibit and then have lunch together in the city.

Kit was waiting near the front doors inside the main lobby of the museum. The vaulted ceilings, pillars and arches never failed to take Marissa's breath away. The lobby itself was a work of art. Marissa hugged her sister, happy to be with her. They didn't see each other as often as Marissa would have liked. She had sold her apartment in Los Angeles the year before and had moved to New York. It had been a change she'd needed and had made travel easier, having more jobs on the East Coast.

Griffin and Jack exchanged greetings and followed them into the museum.

"I've been worried about you," Kit said.

"Even with Jack with me?" Marissa asked.

"Even with Jack. I've followed the case through his reports. He's detailed, which means I know what's been going on," Kit said.

Marissa and Kit stopped in front of a portrait of a man in a beige suit and red sweater vest, his hand propped on his hip. His arm was resting on a stairwell bannister and he looked a mix of angry and bored.

"I'm sorry I've been out of touch. Griffin and I were working a project that required our full attention. Going forward, I'll check in more. We're thinking about staying in New York for a few weeks," Kit said.

"Staying to sightsee or to keep an eye on me?" Marissa asked.

"Not just you. Mom. Luke and Zoe Ann. Mom's called a few times. I feel disconnected not living close to you all," Kit said.

Her mother and brother had moved back to New York around the time Marissa had. Kit, true to form, had followed her own path.

"Do you feel like New York is home?" Marissa asked. They had grown up in Queens and it was Marissa's career that had sent them across the country and her work that had brought her back.

Kit looked over her shoulder at Griffin and Jack. They were standing near a cluster of benches speaking in hushed tones. Their arms were folded and they were watching her and Kit.

"Home is where I am with Griffin."

The warm sentiment made Marissa jealous. She had never felt that way about a man as if being near him brought a sense of peace or security. "I have so much to tell you."

Kit nodded, encouraging Marissa to continue.

"First, Mom wants me to let Luke and Zoe Ann move in with me because she's pregnant and neither of them has a stable, safe place to live."

Kit rolled her eyes. "Mom is crazy. That would

never work. Luke needs to get up off his rear end, dust off his ego and get a job."

"He claims he can't find one," Marissa said.

"He's had job offers. He just wants a job that's as good as his last one. That doesn't exist. It's a different world. He won't find a six-figure job with an expense account."

"He could move back to LA, but Zoe Ann wants to stay in the city. She's hoping to get a lead in a play." It was a good reason to stay in the area. "Do you think I'm selfish for not letting them move in with me?" Marissa asked.

Kit considered it. Marissa could expect the truth from her sister.

"In this case, no. I think you should talk to Luke directly. If Mom gets involved, it will be complicated and over-the-top dramatic. Spell it out for Luke. You will be happy to help him, but he needs to do the heavy lifting."

Hearing Kit reaffirm what she'd thought, Marissa felt better. "The second news is that I'm falling for Jack."

Kit's eyes went wide. "You should have led with that! What do you mean? Are you in love with him?"

Marissa brushed her hair out of her eyes. She wouldn't call what she and Jack had love. He was sexy and smart and had a fine body, but love was a huge step. "Not love. At least, I don't think so. I have feelings for him. I have a terrible track record with men. I fall in lust easily. I feel it strongly and I think it's love, but I don't know for sure."

"If you were in love with him, you'd know for sure."

"I married twice, because each time I thought I was in love. When I look back, I don't know," Marissa said. Love, excitement, lust, adventure and a challenge produced similar highs in her psyche.

"Have you told him? Has anything happened between you two?" Kit asked.

"Is this between us as sisters, not you being his colleague?"

"Of course. Just sister stuff. None of this gets back to work."

Marissa tried to find the words to explain what had happened between her and Jack. It was simultaneously magic and real and wonderful and inspiring. "When we're out, and he's on duty, he is totally professional. He misses nothing. He is careful and watchful. But when we're home and I make it clear that he is off the clock, he's warm and tender and sweet. And my goodness, he is the sexiest man I have ever seen."

They walked to the next portrait on the wall. This one featured a woman with almost ceramic skin wearing a cylinder-shaped hat and staring blandly.

"I think you're a catch, Marissa, but I'm surprised. You're not his type."

Marissa felt like her feathers had been ruffled. "Not his type?" Her sister didn't underestimate her the way most others did and her words felt like a slight.

"Has Jack told you about his past relationships?" Kit asked.

"We haven't talked about exes. I like to avoid that conversation whenever possible because it's not an area that I'm proud of," Marissa said.

"You'd have to get the details from Jack, but he

dated someone in college. Jack wanted to marry her, but she broke up with him to move to LA to become an actress. Never got a part, but she didn't come back to him. She married some ad executive. Broke and stomped Jack's heart."

"He's still pining for her?" Marissa asked.

"I didn't say he was pining for her. He was hurt and according to Griffin, he's got a thing against women in show biz."

"He never mentioned it," Marissa said. The former relationship could explain some of his hesitation to get involved with her.

"Did you mention your ex-husbands?" Kit asked.

"Maybe once or twice. Only as it related to the case."

"Has he told you about how he was injured?" Kit asked.

"He did," Marissa said.

Kit's eyes went wide with surprise. "You're not dealing with a trusting man eager to jump into a relationship."

Though Marissa sensed him holding back at times, he had also showed her a side of him that was open and warm. "Why are you telling me this? Do you not want me to be with Jack?"

"I don't want you to get hurt," Kit said. "And men like Griffin and Jack come with baggage. They've seen dark things and have been to dark places."

"Isn't it our role then to make sure they see and feel the light?"

"You slept with her," Griffin said.

A statement of a fact, not a question. Jack didn't

deny it. They were operatives, trained to see the truth written between the lines. "Yes." He felt a twinge of guilt, knowing Griffin had asked him to look after Marissa and this wasn't what he had in mind.

"I know you well enough to say that you're not sleeping with her for sport."

"I don't sleep with women for sport. I respect them too much," Jack said.

"Good answer. But you have a lot going on. How does Marissa figure into your long-term plans?" Griffin asked.

Jack didn't have a plan. He had been moving from operation to operation for years. When he was seriously injured and betrayed by Bianca, his life slid off the skids. He was trying to put it back together. "I'll be retested for fitness in the field when my knee is better. I'll know more then."

Griffin rocked back on his heels. "You plan to leave Marissa and end it when your knee heals."

"What's the alternative?" Jack asked. To stay her bodyguard forever was unrealistic. The person targeting her would be caught and following her around the country would get old. He needed a life of his own. Following her when she didn't need him wasn't appealing.

"Kit and I make it work. I travel. She sometimes comes with me."

Kit and Marissa were opposites. Kit worked for the West Company. She was involved in difficult operations and she understood the restrictions of the job. "I told Marissa about what I do for a living. Nothing too detailed. She won't understand the traveling and the pressure." He didn't understand it at times. Doing those jobs no one else was willing to do had cost him.

"What did she say when you told her?"

"She was chill about it. She had already guessed most of it. I filled in a few details."

"You're not giving her the benefit of the doubt," Griffin said.

"Being photographed with her too often could become a problem for my work. What if I'm on an undercover op and someone recognizes me from a tabloid picture?"

"I can see how that would be a problem," Griffin said. "I've been where you are. It sounds like you're burned out. Maybe you need a break."

"This job was supposed to be my break. But it has me thinking about work and if I want to return."

"Does your reluctance to return to work have anything to do with Bianca?" Griffin asked.

The familiar sensation of sadness slid over him. "I've considered it. It was hard to testify against her. Hard to know she would spend the rest of her life in prison."

"She made her choices," Griffin said.

"But I was her partner and I should have seen it and stopped her. Maybe I'm getting rusty. Maybe it's time for me to be put out to pasture."

"Don't talk like that. If you're ready to retire, then you've earned it. But no one will force you out," Griffin said.

Griffin had helped him out of a tough spot a few years prior. Jack had needed shelter during an operation and Griffin had been working an op in the area.

He had hid Jack and lied to the people pursuing him to protect him.

"I feel burned out," Jack said.

"That's the injury talking," Griffin said.

Jack wasn't sure. He had been hurt before. Never shot; that was a first. But he had never felt mentally and emotionally exhausted by the job.

Chapter 11

Marissa hated the dress she was wearing for this live television interview. It was blue and white, like something Dorothy from *The Wizard of Oz* would wear. The shoes she'd been handed were great. She was running late and she didn't have time to argue about the wardrobe.

A clothing guard was draped around her shoulders and her hair and makeup were done in a hurry. Being a guest on the morning news program was an honor. Ambrose had been invited as well and he would be coming on after her interview. They'd be on the set together, which Marissa hoped would play well. Her genuine affection and friendship with Ambrose would come through to the audience.

Marissa's name had been in the headlines lately and the interviewer had agreed that any questions about Avery were off-limits. Marissa didn't know the host, Sarah Chasen, well enough to know if she would abide by their agreement.

Marissa had half a mind to walk out of the interview if it went sideways. But doing that would show badly on television. She tried to keep her hands steady and not show how nervous she was.

Sarah was introducing Marissa and then the stage assistant was cueing her to walk into the set. Marissa couldn't see the audience with the blinding lights. That might be better. It was easier for her to imagine she was speaking with Sarah without several thousand eyes watching her. One of those eyes could be Avery's killer. Marissa focused on appearing relaxed and happy as she strode across the polished hardwood floors.

She took her seat in the purple chair across from Sarah's pale pink couch. The white coffee table was set with coffee mugs; Marissa's was filled with water. She and Sarah greeted each other.

"I know you are very busy. Thank you for coming out to talk with me today," Sarah said.

"My pleasure to be here," Marissa said. Did that sound fake? She wished she was anywhere else.

Jack was standing off the sound stage. She could see him ten yards behind Sarah, out of sight of the audience, watching.

"Declan Ambrose says that you're a huge inspiration for his latest line of clothing. How did you two meet?"

Her nerves touched down. No mention of Avery. "Ambrose was working for another designer, who is a friend of mine and he made the introduction. Ambrose was also teaching fashion design classes at the community college. His talent was obvious from the first time I saw his designs," Marissa said.

"How much influence have you had over Ambrose's designs?" Sarah asked.

Another work-related question. Still in the clear. "Ambrose could better answer that question. I weighed in on fabrics and Ambrose has asked me when he's trying to choose between two similar designs, but the genius and the freshness is him." She wouldn't take credit for Ambrose's success.

"Tell us what you have planned over the next year," Sarah said.

Marissa hated that question. She had made the mistake before of mentioning her husband and their plans, which was inevitably rehashed in the media after her divorce. Her career continued to move forward, more contracts, more work, but she wanted to have a significant life event to share. "I've been working, but I'd like to take some classes to pursue my interests."

"Modeling classes? Surely, you don't need those," Sarah said and laughed.

"Nothing related to modeling."

"Are you retiring from modeling?" Sarah asked.

Marissa could imagine her agent and press relations manager's faces if she answered that question honestly. She hadn't constructed a game plan for how and when she would retire and announce it. "I'm considering taking a break."

Sarah's eyes lit. Marissa had just given her the

scoop on a story she hadn't planned to reveal. "Does the break have anything to do with the man you've been seen with around town? There's been speculation that your marriages struggled because you're in the spotlight."

Marissa kept her expression neutral though she was incensed. Talking about her previous marriages was a sore spot and she had practiced her response in the mirror. Discussing Jack and his reason for being in her life would open the door to a conversation about Avery. And while Sarah probably wouldn't ask about Avery directly given their arrangement, most of the audience knew what had happened to her and the conversation could swirl around it. "I'm not dating anyone."

Sarah crossed her legs. "That can't be true."

"Not looking for ex-husband number three," she said. She had intended the comment to be humorous, but her own words were like a knife between the ribs.

Sarah laughed, seemingly unaware how uncomfortable she was making Marissa. They talked for a few minutes about a recent jewelry campaign Marissa had modeled for and Sarah went to break.

"Cameras not rolling, if you aren't with that handsome man who escorted you here, who is he?" Sarah asked.

Marissa was smart enough to know nothing was off the record. "My security," Marissa said.

Sarah looked over her shoulder at him. "He's cute."

Jack was a handsome man, no denying it. "You are not the first woman to tell me that. I didn't select him because of how he looked. In fact, I didn't select him at all. I needed a security detail, and Jack fit the bill." Cameras on or not, speaking to Sarah meant edging around topics she didn't want to discuss: Kit, Avery or Jack. She strove to keep her tone light.

"Then tell me, is it hard to have a personal life with security circling you all the time?" Sarah asked.

Marissa didn't like how close to the truth the questions were hitting. "My work and the travel are what make having a personal life hard." She was proud of herself for thinking of that answer quickly and skirting around more probing questions about her lack of a love life.

Sarah asked more questions about her ad campaigns and a few about her beauty routine, and then the commercial break was over.

Marissa was relieved. She would be on the set for a short time with Ambrose and then she was home free.

Marissa had poise and confidence. Jack admired the skillful manner she answered questions, not sounding hostile or surprised and keeping the interviewer away from conversational landmines.

Marissa exited the stage and they walked together to her dressing room. The room was ten by ten, with a white leather couch, white fixture and light blue walls. The flooring was beige tile. It reminded Jack of decor for a beach house. Hung on the walls were copies of the awards the show had won mounted in dark wood plaques.

At the sink inside the room, Jack watched Marissa remove her makeup. He'd observed her doing that before. He had come to like it better when her face was bare except for a genuine smile.

"I lied to Sarah," Marissa said as she applied lotion to her face.

"About what?" Jack asked. He had heard the interview. He hadn't caught a lie.

"About you."

He felt his chest grow tight. "Which part in particular?" She had kept him out of the center of attention. He appreciated it.

"I told her that I didn't have a love life. That's not true. I didn't want to discuss you. I didn't want to discuss what we have." She tossed a cotton square into the trash and reached for another one. "I didn't want to admit how much I like you. I want to fire you so that we can date in the open. That would get you into trouble and I am not sure you would accept it."

Stunned into silence, he hadn't considered not being her bodyguard and filling another role in her life: boyfriend.

"I've been thinking about what you'll do when you can't be my bodyguard anymore. I know your work is important and I would like for you to believe that I could handle being in a relationship with someone who wasn't next to me every day."

She deserved better. It wasn't that he would be unavailable to her most of the year. Physical distance created an emotional one. Jack struggled with nagging doubts. Bianca had betrayed him and he hadn't seen it coming. He questioned whether he would be able to navigate a relationship with Marissa. "It's not just the time. History would indicate I can't make a relationship work."

"Because you're single? You think that worries

me? I've been married twice. Twice before I turned forty. I've learned from my relationships. I know what's real and I know what's smoke and mirrors. What you and I have, it's real, but you're holding back."

Of course he was. Focus on the job was most important. He wasn't a man who lost his head in a relationship. He could lose his heart to Marissa easily. Preventing that was at the top of his list. "I don't want you to be hurt." Emotionally, because he did something stupid to torpedo the relationship or physically, because he let his guard down and the person who was targeting her succeeded.

Returning home, Marissa felt like her life was moving in the right direction for the first time in a month. The insurance company had worked with the restoration company to make the necessary repairs. Many items had been irreplaceable, but at least she could live in her home. After the fiasco with Rob, her doubts about her career, Avery's death, meeting Jack and Clarice's death, her world had been shaken. It would be years before she could go a day without thinking of Clarice and Avery.

"We've upgraded your security system," Jack said. "Bulletproof windows have been installed. The doors and door jams have been reinforced. We have alarms in place and backup alarms for any type of failure, mechanical or electrical."

"But my sense of peace. That can't be fixed as easily," Marissa said. She was grateful for how quickly the restoration team had worked and the efforts Jack had put in to ensure her home was safe. But she wondered if she would ever feel safe again.

She opened the front door and Jack showed her how to disable the alarm.

She turned around and her breath caught in her throat. The rainbow chandelier she had seen at the flea market was hanging in the lobby. "Did you do this?" she asked, pointing to it.

His cheeks turned light pink. "You liked it. I wanted you to have it."

She circled it, looking at the colorful lights. It was a bright white light at the center, but also threw colors against the wall. Better than she had anticipated. "It's beautiful. Thank you so much. I love it."

"I want you to take your time walking through the house. If you notice anything out of place, let me know and I'll contact the restoration company. It might be a few weeks before you've gone over all the details, but the project manager is waiting for your call. He expects it and he's ready to come quickly to make you feel at home." Jack took her hands in his and kissed her knuckles. "I want you to feel safe in this space. This is your home and no one can take that from you."

Marissa pulled her left hand away and ran it through Jack's hair. "You are a sweet man." He was doing everything he could to right her world.

"The breach was unacceptable and we want to do everything we can."

"Stop saying we. You don't need to give credit to anyone else. I know much of this, the speed and the details, was you. I know you led the charge," she said.

Jack had gone above and beyond anything she would have expected. He had pushed hard to get the repairs completed in the short time frame.

"I had pictures from your home. We used those to match paint and find replacement items. Some of your artwork is at a specialist being evaluated for repairs and we'll know more about that later." He stroked the side of her face with his fingertips. "I want you to be happy."

"I am happy. Right now, here with you. I am very happy." She wrapped her arms around his neck and kissed him.

Slipping his arms around her waist, Jack drew her against him and Marissa lost herself in his touch.

The information Jack had requested was waiting for him in a stack of manila folders, each tab labeled. One hundred and fifty people had been backstage at Declan Ambrose's show. Security had been tight, but not impossible to break. Someone could have gotten backstage. After Jack read these documents, round two would include every person who had purchased a ticket to the fashion show or had been given tickets. That list would be longer and more tedious.

The West Company had provided profiles of the individuals in question: pictures, psychological assessments and anything they could assemble. Wading through the material would take hundreds of man hours. Jack started with the most prominent staffers, those who could move around backstage without being questioned.

He was interested in knowing more about the rumors Marissa had heard at Ambrose's award show after party about Avery and Rob gambling. There was truth in the rumors. Avery's net worth was fifty times higher than Rob's, so while she had a long history of gambling, throwing big money into a game and losing, her finances could tolerate it. Rob's couldn't. He gambled more frequently than Avery. A notation in his file indicated several large withdrawals and loans from his bank and investment accounts. The withdrawals hadn't all been tied to a legal gambling organization. He could be placing illegal bets on sports with a local bookie.

Marissa was outside in her private lap pool. The eight-foot white vinyl fence encircling the yard provided her privacy. The pool was enclosed in glass and the windows were steamed. He entered and the heat and humidity in the room socked him. Her aqua lounge chair was empty, a cup of water, her sunglasses and bottle of sunscreen on a small table beside it.

She was in the pool, her kick even and her strokes smooth. Jack watched her and she must have sensed him because she stopped swimming and came to the side of the pool.

"Hey, Jack," she said, pushing her hair off her face.

Jack felt his blood rush to his lower half. She was his dream woman and the casual way she set her hands on the side of the pool with her wet hair pushed off her face, looking at him with big eyes, made his pulse pound. "Sorry to interrupt."

"It's okay. I was getting ready to take a break."

She lifted herself from the pool, the tone in her arms flexing, her abdominals tightening and water sliding down her long, slim, toned legs.

She took a sip of her water and picked up her towel, wrapping it around herself. “What can I do for you?”

He was staring. Just looking at her like a predator considering pouncing. He collected his thoughts. “Do you know if Rob had interest in gambling on sports?”

Marissa wrung out the end of her hair. “He’s watched games with buddies, but I don’t know if he gambled on the results. I have a friend who works for a professional basketball team. I had courtside tickets and Rob had no interest in going.”

“You had courtside seats and Rob didn’t want to go?” Jack asked. He didn’t know Rob well, but the more he learned, the less he understood him.

“He had no interest. I gave them to someone else,” Marissa said.

He was letting the conversation get off track. “I’m seeing a number of large withdrawals from various accounts and none can be tied to vacations or large purchases.”

Marissa rubbed her forehead. “About a year ago, Avery asked me to come with her to a new casino. She said it was underground and we needed a password and a key to get into it. It sounded fun, but at the last minute, my agent booked a commercial for me, so I flew out that night. She and Rob could have been going to underground casinos.”

“Avery and Rob could have gotten caught up with anything.” They could have gotten into debt, financial or metaphorical, with a criminal element.

It was a good theory, but Jack couldn't undisputedly tie it to Avery's murder.

"What are you thinking?" Marissa asked.

"I'm following every lead. We might have found a connection to an enemy that either Avery or Rob had."

Marissa shivered. "It's cold out here and this conversation is creeping me out. I need to take a shower. Come with me?"

The word no was on his tongue. He had more files to review. Calls to make.

Marissa pulled on furry boots and wrapped a thick robe around herself. "Come on. We need a break."

He followed her into the house and into the shower.

Marissa rang Ambrose's doorbell. She could hear the sound of the bells from the street, a small, familiar song she couldn't identify by name. Her fashion designer friend had invited her over for a drink. That was code for: I need to talk. Ambrose opened the red slatted wood door and it squeaked on its nickel hinges.

"Glad you could make it!" He hugged her and his gaze darted over her shoulder to Jack. "You brought backup?"

"He insisted. Jack wants to go everywhere I do for now," Marissa said. Jack wouldn't eavesdrop or weigh in on her and Ambrose's conversation, unless invited to do so.

Ambrose smiled. "Come on in. I made a pitcher of margaritas."

They entered the house. It wasn't her first time at Ambrose's place, but he had changed some of the art and decor since the last time she had visited. Detailed sketches of animals were hung on the wall, lions and giraffes and zebras. Previously, the walls had been covered with alligators and parrots and panthers and white-tailed deer. They had played a role in his designs and presumably the new sketches were meant to provide inspiration for his next collection.

Ambrose poured himself and her a drink. He offered one to Jack, who declined.

"I'll stay out of your way," Jack said. He had locked the front door and was looking around the space.

"Doesn't that bother you?" Ambrose asked, nodding in Jack's direction.

Jack didn't. He was doing his job and one that was needed. "Not really. I'm used to having him around. And I need him."

"Making any progress on the investigation?" Ambrose asked.

Marissa considered telling him about the gambling theory, then thought better of it. If their theory was wrong, she would be badmouthing Avery and Rob unfairly. "Nothing new."

"I'm sorry to hear that." He took a sip of his drink. "The reason I invited you over is because I'm going through a dry spell."

"Like in your relationships?" Marissa often had the most career success at times when her social and personal lives were the most dead.

Ambrose rolled his eyes. "No. I have plenty of dates and for now, that's all I want. I mean my designs. I have ideas. Lots of directions I want to move the collection, but everything comes out like the previous collection or I finish a design, and it looks blah."

He was being overly critical about his work, she was sure. "If that's true and you're not just being hard on yourself, you might be having a mental block. Going through a phase. I've had trouble shaking what happened to Avery and Clarice. I can't believe they're gone. It makes it hard to work and be upbeat and creative."

Ambrose took a long swallow from his glass. "I think of them every day."

The sadness in his voice was thick. "That's probably part of the mental fatigue. And what about the expectations? You impressed everyone who came to your show. Now they want more. And they want it to blow them away. That's a lot of pressure for you."

Ambrose stood and strode to the kitchen counter. Picking up the pitcher, he refilled his cup. At this rate, he would be hammered in the hour. "What if I can't do it? What if I'm a one trick pony? If I've peaked, then I'll never have a show as great as my first."

Marissa had seen his designs. They were fresh and inspired. "You can't let this go to your head. The stress alone will stunt you." She had felt stress at points in her career, worried an ad campaign may be her last, afraid she may not get hired for another.

"The stress. The demands. The long hours. I'm not sure I can do it." Ambrose's voice had grown quiet. He looked out the window and Marissa searched for the words to make him feel better. As he continued talking, Marissa stayed quiet, hoping listening was what Ambrose needed most.

* * *

Jack wasn't intentionally listening to Marissa and Ambrose's conversation. But it was otherwise quiet and hard to tune it out.

Jack didn't blame Ambrose for encountering trouble. He'd become famous overnight. It was a pressure-filled situation.

The apartment was nice, though it lacked the refinery and expensive finishes that Marissa's place had. Success was new to Ambrose. If he continued to do well in his field, he would move to a bigger place.

Jack needed to use the bathroom. Without interrupting Marissa and Ambrose, he found it in the hallway off the kitchen. Across from the bathroom was Ambrose's office. The door was open. He was curious and entered.

The space was tidy and unlike the rest of the apartment, lacked decor. The walls were white and bare. The small desk in the room was cherrywood and the chair behind it a simple four-legged plastic black chair. Perhaps blandness in his workspace helped Ambrose to focus on his work.

In piles across the top of the desk were fashion designs. Jack wasn't an expert and didn't know what he was looking at or for. He snapped a few pictures. Though undecorated, the room was quiet and serene, a nice place to focus.

After using the bathroom, washing his hands and drying them on alligator-printed towels, Jack returned to the family room.

His phone buzzed in his pocket. Taking the phone out, he glanced at the message. "Call home base. 911."

A brief message that he needed to contact the West Company immediately.

He pressed the button to call the secure line. Abby answered.

"Rob Travers was hospitalized this evening at Mount Sinai in Queens. I have his condition listed as serious but stable. Diagnoses not confirmed, but from the scraps of information I've collected, it sounds like either a drug overdose or alcohol poisoning."

"Do you know if he's conscious?" Jack asked.

Marissa glanced over at him, worry etched on her face.

"Accidental or intentional?" Jack asked.

"Unconfirmed to both questions," Abby said.

"Where was he before being brought to the hospital?" Jack asked.

"Again, not confirmed intel, but an illegal casino operating in Brooklyn."

It fit with the information he had theorized about Rob and his financial issues. "Do you have anything else on the casino?" Rob was in debt up to his eyeballs. If he was still gambling, whoever he owed money to would see that Rob got the message.

"It was raided by the police. I'm working to obtain the police records. I'll get them to you as soon as I can," Abby said.

They said their goodbyes and disconnected.

"I can see it on your face. Something bad has happened," Marissa said.

She wasn't speaking to Ambrose. Marissa and Ambrose were staring at Jack expectantly. Jack wasn't sure how Marissa would react. She and Rob weren't friends any longer, but she didn't wish him harm.

"Rob is in the hospital recovering from an overdose. He is in serious, but stable condition."

Marissa rose to her feet. "How? The same person who killed Avery hurt Rob?"

Jack didn't think so. "From what I've been told, it wasn't an attempted homicide."

"Rob overdosed." She spoke the words like she couldn't believe them.

"Do you want me to take you to the hospital?" Jack asked.

Marissa blinked and then shook her head as if trying to clear her thoughts. "I don't think he'd want to see me. Was it an accident? Or was Rob…"

Trying to kill himself? She didn't need to ask the rest of the question. "We don't know yet."

Marissa looked like she was coming apart at the seams. She wrapped her arms around her waist. Jack wanted to comfort her, draw her against him and tell her everything would be all right. This was something he hated about this position. On the job, he couldn't be her friend and now that was what she needed.

Ambrose looked between Jack and Marissa. "Have either of you considered the guilt of what he did to Avery and Clarice got the better of him and he tried to kill himself?"

Jack couldn't make the connection from Rob to Clarice's murder, but he was willing to consider the idea. "Could be."

"I'd put money on it," Ambrose said. Something in his words and his tone communicated confidence.

Jack's attention swerved to Ambrose. "Do you know something about Avery's death? Or Clarice's?"

Ambrose poured himself another margarita from the pitcher. "Rob was dating Avery. He was unfaithful to Marissa. Maybe he was unfaithful to Avery with Clarice. I can imagine a number of scenarios where Rob killed Avery, maybe jealousy or anger, and did the same to Clarice."

Rob had been the police's first suspect and while Jack had dismissed him due to the bungling nature of the attacks against Marissa, he considered it.

"Why would he kill them directly but hire others to kill Marissa?" Jack asked.

"He could have killed Avery and then hired someone to kill me and Clarice," Marissa said.

"It's possible," Jack said. The idea held weight, but he didn't have proof of anything yet. If Rob had done this, Jack would nail him for it.

Marissa enjoyed the heat and strength of Jack's body. Tucked in the comfort of his arms in the aftermath of great sex, her muscles were loose and exhaustion tugged at her. Except she couldn't sleep. She was thinking about Rob and about the overdose. Drugs and alcohol could be Rob's coping mechanism for handling Avery's death. Could be he was self-medicating his pain away. Whatever he was doing, the destructive behavior had almost killed him.

Or was Ambrose right and Rob had killed Avery?

"Want to talk about it?" Jack asked.

Marissa thought he had been sleeping. "Just thinking about Rob."

"He'll be okay," Jack said, rubbing her upper arm in a motion that was soothing.

Marissa rolled to face him and propped her arm and chin on his chest. The rise and fall of his breathing was comfortable and melodic. "We can't know. I've been blowing him off. I haven't wanted to deal with him. After Avery died, he needed a friend. I could have been a friend. Instead, I was dismissive and rude to him."

"He's an ex-boyfriend. Most people are not warm and welcoming to their ex-boyfriends especially after the way he treated you."

Marissa expected better of herself. "I could have been nicer."

"You'll have the opportunity again soon to be just that," Jack said.

"I think all of this is getting to Ambrose, too. He can't come up with new designs. He says he just keeps rehashing the old ones."

Jack reached to the bedside table and picked up his phone. He turned the screen to face her. "Does this look familiar?"

Marissa took the phone from his hand and studied the photograph. It was a picture of a fashion model. Beautiful lines and color. "The design looks familiar. What is this picture from?"

"Ambrose's office," Jack said.

Indignation rose inside her. "You can't just go into his office."

"Sure I can. I was bored."

Marissa made the design larger on the screen. "Violation of Ambrose's privacy aside, this looks like the designs we saw in Avery's closet."

"Could Ambrose have given her copies of his designs?" Jack asked.

"Maybe. He's shared designs with me. Not going as far as giving them to me, but I've been by his house, opened a bottle of wine with him and given him a critique," Marissa said.

Jack seemed lost in thought.

"What are you thinking?" Marissa asked.

"Just seems strange that he would give people access to his designs. If another designer got a copy of them, he could lose his edge," Jack said.

"Ambrose is a trusting man and he trusts me and he trusted Avery. His personality is open and warm, but I can see how that would get him into trouble in this industry. I can talk to him about being more careful. He's had a relatively easy time, to strike pay dirt in less than five years is a tribute to his talent and ingenuity."

Jack took the phone from her hands and set it on the bedside table. "You're too nice to your friends."

"It takes just as much effort to be nice as is does to be mean," Marissa said.

"Really? Let's see if I can be nice to you," Jack said. He kissed her and shifted her body beneath his.

His hand moved down her side and cupped her hip. Marissa stroked the back of his calf with her foot and wrapped her arms around his back, enjoying his every touch completely.

Jack hated to leave Marissa alone. Though the rate of attacks had slowed, his absence from her side might give the man after her an opening. But he was due at the West Company's training facility in Burlington, Vermont.

Following his injury, he needed to be retested and recertified to be approved to return to undercover operations. It was for his protection, as well as his clients and partners.

The flight from New York took about an hour and a half. Jack's plane touched down at 4:00 a.m., and too tired to sleep, he drove straight to the training facility. Parts of the test would be easy for him. His aim and marksmanship with a gun were as strong as ever, he was mentally competent, but he was concerned about his speed and agility. He'd been training in the gym and running outdoors when possible, but the West Company certification course was meant to simulate obstacles he could encounter in the world.

Though he couldn't be shot, trainers could attack him to test his reaction and speed.

He approached the sign-in desk. A man in dark sunglasses with the build of a linebacker handed him an armband. "Jack Larson. You're early. I like that. I'm Oliver. Put this on your right arm." Oliver extended a black arm band with a device sewn in the middle.

"What's this?" Jack asked. The last time he had completed the obstacle course, he hadn't worn anything similar.

"We had a guy stroke out last month. Couldn't handle it. Now Connor insists everyone recertifying wear this. It's from the medical department. Has a GPS in case you get lost and we need to pull you out. It monitors your heart rate and oxygen levels and makes sure you're doing okay. Anything gets crazy and I'll get you. But if I have to rescue you, you fail."

Not comforting, but Jack wasn't worried. He was ready. Cold weather gear, fleece lined pants, his subzero temp jacket and fingerless gloves.

Jack gave Oliver his personal affects and was handed a small pack in return. Jack checked the contents. Water. Rope. Matches. Compass. Protein bar. The test was three hours.

Jack heard a helicopter overhead. Linebacker pointed to it. "Get in. You're being air-dropped into the course."

Jack went with the flow. Surviving this was a mental game.

For the first time in over a year, Marissa attended a church service. She had been drawn to the church and felt compelled to go. Attendance at the 7:00 a.m. service was less than twenty people in the cherrywood pews, almost all of them over the age of sixty. She was completely unnoticed and she loved that.

Her bodyguards waited outside. Jack had needed to fly out that morning for training. He hadn't wanted to discuss the details. She was in church for him, for Avery and because she needed to talk to an old friend.

After the service, Marissa waited in the pew. Once Father Franklin had finished shaking hands with the other congregants, he walked toward her. The lights in the church were dim except for the ones over the altar. Those were bright and white and crisp. A collection of candles in red containers along the left wall flickered with the prayers they were meant to answer. It wasn't too late to leave. She and Father Franklin had had some great conversations on the heels of a strange connection.

He sat in the pew. "I wondered if you would be by to see me after Avery's memorial service."

Guilt sliced through her. She touched the pearls at

her neck. Father Franklin may not remember them. Marissa had needed to wear them. "I've been busy."

"I see your picture most every day. Hard to avoid in the city. I know you do things in your own time," Father said.

"It's not really an excuse."

Father shrugged. "We're here. We're always here. I don't require an explanation. Even a long bout of absence doesn't mean you can't come back when you need to."

She appreciated the non-judgment. "Kit's engaged."

"That's great news. I hope to someone who is deserving of her. Someone who challenges her."

Kit was happy. It was enough for her. "Seems to be. They're good together."

"And your brother?" Father asked.

Marissa felt strange telling Father Franklin about it. "Luke and his girlfriend Zoe Ann are having a baby."

Father Franklin inclined his head. "You sound worried."

"They aren't the most stable parents. They don't have a place of their own and neither have steady jobs."

"That may change. Luke hit a bump in the road when he lost his job and he hasn't recovered. But he will. He's strong."

"Or he'll walk out on his child," Marisa said. Subtext, just as her father had done to her and her siblings. Until she spoke the words, she hadn't realized she'd been thinking about it.

"He may. But he was hurt when your father left. I don't think he would pass that hurt to another child."

Maybe those age-old hurts were why she was here. Her father's connection to Father Franklin and Father Franklin's surrogate role of father in her life over the years made her seek him out. Marissa's disastrous marriages were centered around her terrible connection to men, starting with her father.

Marissa picked men for the worst reasons. They inevitably lost her trust and she was left in a broken relationship she didn't know how to fix. "I met someone."

"A new man in your life?" Father Franklin asked.

"A good man. Different from the others. Not interested in how I look."

Father Franklin gestured for her to continue.

"But the one thing he has in common with the others is that I don't trust that he'll stay. I don't know what he wants from me or why he's in the relationship. He seems to like me and enjoy my company. But how will I know if it's real? I've made terrible relationship mistakes. I am a horrible judge of character. I could fall in love with him. Maybe I already have. But I'm scared to give my heart away when I don't know if he wants it."

Father Franklin folded his hands in his lap. "You're a good woman with a good heart. You deserve happiness. Relationships don't need drama or grand gestures to be real and good. If you've fallen in love with him, that's the first step. You have to keep falling in love with him. Over and over, every day."

"He might leave me," Marissa said.

"He might. He could walk out of your life. But would he have left you with something good?"

Marissa thought of Jack and her chest warmed. The way he looked at her, listened to her and supported her dreams. He protected her. He was interested in seeing her happy. "He has every confidence in me and that makes me feel like I can do anything."

"A loving, supportive partner makes you feel like you can fly."

Father Franklin had never married and Marissa knew it had something to do with her father. It was a subject they had skated around over the years and never openly discussed. "You've not had that for yourself?"

"I've made mistakes in my life," Father Franklin said. "Now my life is the church and the congregation here."

"Have you heard from my father lately?" Marissa asked.

Father Franklin shook his head. "It's been over a decade. Since he left the city, I've seen him only a couple of times. I'm not sure I'd recognize him if he walked through those doors."

Marissa had a picture of her father from his wedding day to their mother. She had no childhood memories of him. Looking at the picture brought back nothing. "You married them. My parents."

Father Franklin nodded. "Yes."

"Did you know they were wrong for each other?"

Father Franklin rubbed his forehead. "That's a complex question."

"There are questions I've pondered and I've been too afraid to ask. You and my mother have seemed awkward with each other. I thought maybe it was because you were my father's friend in seminary school and so my mother didn't want anything to do with my father or his friends when he left. But that wasn't the whole truth."

"That was part of the story. Lenore has good reasons for why she keeps her distance from me."

"Please tell me. I know it might seem like ancient history. But it's important that I know."

Father Franklin adjusted his glasses. "Your sister visited me a few years ago. She had the same questions. I thought she was too young to know."

"To know what?" Marissa asked.

For several long moments, Marissa was sure that Father Franklin wouldn't tell her.

"I was in love with your mother. Couldn't see anything clearly about her or your father. My feelings for her shaped how I viewed their relationship. I didn't express my misgivings about their relationship, thinking they were born of my jealousy."

In love with her mother. It fit. A dozen childhood memories snapped into place. She should have seen it. "And now? How do you feel about my mother?" Marissa asked.

"We exchange holiday cards. I don't seek her out. She has a different life, one involved with your successes. I wish her the best, but I don't belong with her."

Marissa sat in the pew contemplating his words. "Did she know?"

"I never told her, but I suspect she knew I had feelings for her beyond friendship."

"Do you wish you had told her?" Marissa asked.

Father Franklin looked at her. "Not telling your mother how I felt was one of the biggest mistakes of my life. If I could go back in time, I would tell her and hope for the best."

Marissa had been holding back. Was it was worth it to take a chance and tell Jack how she felt? Putting it all on the line and risking her heart seemed like a big step, but without it, she might lose Jack forever.

Chapter 12

Jack jumped out of the chopper. The short drop meant opening his chute earlier. The place he was to land was clearly marked, a large white X spray-painted on the green grass. The wind made it difficult to hit it, but Jack was close, landing on the perimeter of the mark. He removed his chute and disconnected from the harness. His knee felt good even after the impact against the ground and that bolstered his confidence.

He had been given brief instructions regarding the path to take. He wasn't told what obstacles he would face and it was a timed course. Gathering the parachute, he cut the ropes and stuffed them into his pack. Ropes could be helpful. Given the length of the test, he paced himself, but would need to keep to a quick clip not knowing how far he needed to travel.

Jack checked his compass and started along the

path due west. He scaled an eight-foot wall, then a ten-foot wall using the ropes swinging from the top. His knee held. This was too easy. Worse was coming.

He maneuvered over rocks and fallen trees. Then he reached a river. Snowdrifts lined the woods and the ground was frozen solid. Looking around for a canoe or a raft, he came up short. Hard to judge the depth of the river. He would have liked to wade across it holding his clothes and supplies overhead. But that was shortsighted. Getting in the water without the ability to dry himself quickly would lead to hypothermia. If he reached the middle of the river and it was too deep, he'd need to return and come up with another plan.

He looked around for some wood. Locating a couple of pieces, he lashed them together with his parachute ropes. A third piece served as a paddle and guide. His shoes, socks, gloves and pants went into the pack. He was cold, but being wet was worse. He shoved his small raft into the water. The river carried him and he used his paddle to move toward the opposite bank. When he was close enough, he hopped off his raft, letting it float away. He pulled on his pants, gloves, socks and shoes. His paddle became his walking stick. If he had time, he would like to bring Marissa to the woods in Vermont and take a long, leisurely hike to enjoy nature. Nothing about this felt leisurely. The crisp air kept him alert. The trail was passable, even with the snowfall, which was lucky. Wading through waist deep snow and ice would take hours.

The bank was covered with ice. He slid as if on ice skates, using the hiking stick to help keep his balance. When he reached a place where he could rest, he stopped to get a drink of water from his pack. He checked his compass again to ensure he was moving in the correct direction. Adjusting his position, he mentally redirected himself.

He reached a clearing and a bow and arrows were set out. Picking up the bow, he slid an arrow into the quiver. A target dropped from a tree. He aimed and let the arrow fly. Direct hit. Six more targets appeared in the trees and he struck each one with an arrow. He thought of Marissa and the training he had given her at the firing range. She had been intent and interested in learning how to shoot a gun, but also in awe of its power. A remarkable, unique woman and he missed her.

When no more targets appeared, he continued. He reached a cliff with a rope tied to a tree trunk and dangling over the side. Rapelling would put a lot pressure on his knee. That was likely the point. Connor West didn't shy away from testing weaknesses. Checking that the rope was secure, he wrapped it around himself for safety and moved over the edge of the cliff. Halfway down, his knee burned, but didn't give out. Reaching the bottom, his knee ached and Jack mustered his resolve. He imagined Marissa strutting in five-inch heels through the woods and was amused and distracted by the image. It couldn't be comfortable to wear the shoes she did, but she never let it show.

Jack checked the time. Two hours and forty minutes had passed. Despite the crispness in the air, beneath his jacket, his shirt was wet with sweat and he was beginning to feel fatigued. Twenty minutes remained to reach the end post. He wasn't certain if he had covered enough ground. He ran along the trail, moving across a narrow bridge with wide gaps between the footboards and trying to avoid the iciest spots. His destination was ahead, the yellow roof half covered in snow visible through the trees. Relief passed through him. A little more hustle and he could make it.

He wished Marissa was waiting at the end, but she was in New York. His desire to see her amplified his feelings for her. She was more than a client. Much more. It took being away from her to realize it.

The last ten yards, Jack jogged. Though he was tired, hungry and thirsty, a sense of accomplishment carried him farther. Jack arrived at the yellow roofed house. He was breathing heavy, his muscles were tight and tiredness tugged at him.

Oliver opened the front door. "One minute and forty seconds remaining."

Awareness of time passing had stayed with him, but Jack hadn't obsessed about it.

"I have lunch for you." Oliver looked at his watch. "Or breakfast. A committee will review the footage of your work and we'll be in touch in an hour."

Other physical tests had brought a level of stress. Though his career was riding on this, he wasn't worried. He wanted to call Marissa and share the good news.

Inside the training shack, the space was open with plush, brown couches set around an oversize stone fireplace. The hearth was stacked with wood and a fire blazed within. A cedar table extended almost the length of the building along the back wall. On his left was a small kitchen with a sink, refrigerator, cabinets, a cooktop and oven and a long row of closets.

A brown bagged lunch with his name on it was at the head of the long table. Next to the lunch was his cell phone and other personal affects he had given Oliver. He had no signal. Disappointment streaked through him. He couldn't call Marissa and all he could think about was talking to her and giving her the news. Whether he passed or not, and regardless of what criticism he would receive from the review committee, he had finished the course and he was still standing.

"Cleared for duty."

The words echoed through his mind. Oliver had delivered the news with a mask of indifference. Jack hadn't expected anything else. Oliver would have likely spoken in the same unemotional tone if Jack had failed.

On the return flight to New York, Jack wrestled with his thoughts. He wasn't as happy to be approved to be back in the field as he had expected to be. It was his option to return immediately or when his assignment with Marissa was completed. Staying with Marissa was the obvious answer. Admitting that to himself meant admitting he was thinking about her in the long run and putting her ahead of his career goals. Knowing it, acknowledging it, made him feel like a fool.

What he and Marissa had wouldn't last. It had burned too hot and would flame itself out. Marissa's world was in the bright lights of public attention. Jack couldn't imagine anything less desirable.

Believing his career had been over had devastated him. Now he wasn't sure he wanted to go back to work for the West Company. Marissa was under his skin and in his head and that type of work would keep them apart. Never mind that she would be on his mind.

He got off the plane. The walk down the long, quiet corridors of the airport gave him time to think. Though dozens of people milled around the baggage claim, his eyes fell on Marissa. Wearing dark sunglasses and a brown fedora hat and a trench coat, she was waiting for him. Though not the oddest outfit among the other travelers, her tall, slender build drew attention. Even with her face and hair covered, people watched.

Happiness surged inside him and he approached, scarcely aware of the ground moving beneath his feet. "Hey, stranger."

She lightly punched his shoulder. "You didn't call. Just the one text. I was worried. I wasn't sure if you were coming back." She looked at him from over her sunglasses.

Guilt assailed him. "I should have called. A few of the locations had bad cell reception and when I was finished, I wanted to get home." To her. To be with her. To catch up and talk about his trip and see how she was doing. Having that conversation over the phone meant missing something, something he needed.

She set her hand on the side of his face. "I'll forgive you. This time. But next time, more than one text message with the time of your flight, okay?"

She kissed his cheek. The softness of her lips and the scent of her made his blood run hot.

"I'm sorry. Won't happen again." There would be a next time. In the future, they would be together. He hadn't worked through the details, but he wanted her and he had a long track record of going after what he wanted.

"Tell me how it went," she said.

The truth gave him pause. "I'm cleared for duty."

She broke into a huge smile. "That's great. Why aren't you more excited?"

Mixed emotions about it, grateful his injury had healed, but not eager to start another mission. "Getting my head around it."

"While you get your head around it, I have a surprise for you. I booked a room at the five-star hotel a three-minute cab ride from here. Waiting for us are champagne and chocolates to celebrate."

She had anticipated he would pass. "What if I hadn't been cleared for duty?" Jack asked.

"Then it would have been a sympathy gift and I'd have let you eat all the chocolate," Marissa said. She slid her hands to rest on his chest.

"That's thoughtful of you," Jack said. He couldn't recall the last time someone had made a personal, kind gesture like this. "I didn't expect you to pick me up."

"I know. I wanted to," Marissa said. "I have another surprise for you, too."

"What's that?" Jack asked. He was unable to keep his voice completely steady.

Marissa brought her mouth close to his ear. "I'm wearing only a thong under this."

He could think of nothing else, except what she might look like without the jacket. He saw his backpack slide onto the luggage carousel. Darting to it, he snagged it, then took her hand and together, they raced out of the airport.

Marissa's soft hair was spread across his chest and his pillow. Jack touched the ends, enjoying the silkiness between his fingers and her delicate skin against his. Her even breathing calmed him.

The hotel room she had booked had dark gray walls and light gray wood floors. The bedspread was light blue and the curtains white, giving the room a hazy, lazy feel. It was smaller than the other hotel rooms they had stayed in and he liked the coziness. He hadn't slept well the past few nights and this felt like a much-needed escape.

He was reclined against the headboard, fluffy pillows behind his back and he hated to move and disturb her. Closing his eyes, a sensation akin to happiness washed over him.

"Will you return to working overseas?" Marissa asked.

He had thought she was asleep. The question was on his mind, too. Working for the West Company was a natural progression of his career. Military, special ops, a short stint at the CIA and then working for the most secretive, clandestine organization in America. While he had long thought about being a farmer like his father and grandfather, it was an about-face that he wasn't sure he was ready to make. His siblings had stuck with the family business and at times, he missed them. He missed birthday parties and big holidays and spending Sundays together. Farming was what he would return to doing one day.

Having Marissa in his life put his choices into a different perspective. And that scared him. To make a big step now, his life would change dramatically. He didn't want to make the decision because of her, but she was an important factor in his life.

"I haven't decided what I'll do next," Jack said.

"I'd miss you. Do you think you could only take jobs during the week? Or maybe only travel to cities with direct flights to New York?"

Secret operations didn't work that way. His work often took him to places barely accessible by foot and he couldn't work Monday through Friday and be home in time for breakfast Saturday morning. "Not likely."

"You could take more assignments like this one." She rolled over and traced her hand along his side.

"The company I work for doesn't have assignments like this one. This was a favor to Griffin and the assistance from the West Company has been a courtesy to me."

Her lower lip extended in a pout. "Then you'll be gone months at a time."

He was becoming more averse to the idea, too. "Sometimes."

"Do you see me being a part of your life?" she asked.

A heavy question, but one he was ready to answer. "Yes." In what capacity, he couldn't say. She would be bored by his constant absence. If he made a career change and returned to his roots, would she want to be a Missouri farmer's wife?

His thoughts stopped on a dime. Wife? A wife? He hadn't considered being married in many years and he hadn't known Marissa long enough to make that jump with her.

Being a farmer in Springfield meant a lower-profile nightlife, no movie openings or Broadway plays. The more he thought about it, the more appealing it was to him. Spring festivals, local school fairs, community college plays and church picnics. Getting to know the people around him, becoming part of the fabric of the town and being a neighbor with Marissa at his side.

The change was so dramatic, he needed to catch his breath.

"I know you and being in your life is good. I'll take it for now," Marissa said, adjusting her pillow and moving her body to rest close to his.

She had no idea where his thoughts had gone. If she had, she might run from the room and not look back. What she had in mind couldn't be anything like what was in his.

Jack woke at seven in the morning to Marissa shaking his shoulder. "Jack, get up! Luke called. He and Zoe Ann are getting married today at the courthouse."

Jack sat up. The muscles in the back of his legs were tight. His thoughts jolted. "We haven't secured the courthouse."

"Don't worry about that. It's a last-minute plan. We need to hurry." Marissa was on her way to the shower. She looked over her shoulder and frowned at him. "Stop looking so worried. It's a courthouse. It's secure. And no one knows about this. Luke and Zoe Ann only called everyone this morning."

Jack rolled to his feet.

"I need to stop home to pick out something to wear," Marissa said.

Jack snagged his phone from the night stand and typed a message to the West Company and the security team. They had a limited amount of time to get into gear.

Two hours later, Jack and Marissa were waiting in a hallway at the courthouse with a few of Luke and Zoe Ann's closest friends. Kit and Griffin couldn't make the wedding in time and Luke and Zoe Ann didn't want to postpone. Lenore was on her cell phone, arranging for a reception after the event at a nearby restaurant.

Father Franklin came around the corner. The smile dropped from his face. Lenore abruptly stopped speaking and her and Father Franklin's eyes met and held.

Jack watched the exchange, not sure what he was seeing. He would have guessed bad blood, but animosity didn't seem to burn between them.

Lenore looked away first and continued to talk on her phone.

"Did you see that?" Jack asked.

Marissa was looking at her mother. "That weird exchange with Father Franklin? I saw it."

"Something going on between them?" Jack asked.

Marissa slid her arm around his. "Father indicated at one point, he wished there was. But I saw something in that look from my mom, too. Maybe it's not as one-sided as Father believes."

A clerk opened a brown wood door and stepped into the hallway. "Walker? Luke Walker? You're next."

They filed into the small chapel and took their seats.

Marissa and Jack walked home from the restaurant hand in hand. The wedding, the fantastic dinner after and the champagne had her in a great mood.

"They seem really happy. I think it will work," Marissa said.

"Luke and Zoe Ann?" Jack asked.

"She's music and poems and painting and he's numbers and suits and spreadsheets. But they're really cute together and she makes him happy," Marissa said. She had seen her brother with girlfriends who were similar to him and they hadn't made him smile the way Zoe Ann did. Like her and Jack: different but good. Or was she naïve to believe that they could find common ground?

"You have a strange look on your face," Jack said.

"I've been thinking," Marissa said. "About us. About your job. Luke and Zoe Ann are completely different people. They have almost nothing in common."

"I was surprised they decided to get married. They don't have jobs or a place to live and the baby will be a lot of stress," Jack said.

He was quick to point out the negatives. "They are embarking on the adventure together," Marissa said.

"That's one way to think about it," Jack said.

What Jack thought of Luke and Zoe Ann wasn't her primary concern. "How do you think about us?"

Jack stopped walking. Marissa met his gaze. She prepared herself for a bomb to drop. For him to say that he didn't think about them. That they were not good together.

"I've been waiting for the right time to talk to you about this. When I was away, I missed you. I wanted you with me."

Marissa threw herself into his arms and kissed him. They were the words she'd needed to hear.

"Wait, as much as I appreciate your enthusiasm there's more."

She dropped to her feet.

"I think this could be something for real. But I want us to take it slow. I want us to spend time together."

She waited to give him time if he had more to say. After a long beat, she hugged him. Time together was what she wanted, too.

Ambrose's latest set was outrageously fabulous. For this shoot, he had brought in live alligators. Two gators and their troop of handlers.

"How will we get close to the gators?" Marissa asked.

Ambrose laughed. "Two photo shoots. Their trainers will work with the gators and I'll work with the models and we'll edit the photos together."

A measure of relief struck her. "This is pretty cool. Another designer may have used stock photos."

Ambrose clasped his hands together. "My new line is absolutely over-the-top and I want the campaign to be that way, too."

Avery sprang to mind. She would love a set like

this. The more daring, dramatic and adventurous the better. "Avery would love this."

Ambrose's eyes went cold and flat. "I miss her, too."

"I can't believe the police haven't found her killer. They had so many pictures from the show. Someone has to know something."

Ambrose set his hand on his hip. "Why do you bring this up every time I see you? Do you think I had something to do with Avery's death? That I'm the one covering things up?"

"Ambrose, no, you're just someone who understands how much I cared for Avery and how awful this is. The police aren't making any progress and I don't understand why."

Ambrose narrowed his eyes. "Avery and I were friends. I didn't accuse you of trying to harm her, even though you and she had a falling out. I would appreciate you not making insinuations."

"No insinuations." Had Ambrose snapped under the stress? He was getting entirely too upset about her comments, which weren't intended to be critical of him. He was taking them like a personal affront.

Ambrose looked away, his jaw tight. "I don't know anything. If I did, I would have told the police one of the many, many times they've questioned me. And now you're questioning me."

"I didn't mean to upset you. I'm trying to get to the bottom of this."

"You should do your job and let the police handle Avery's murder investigation," Ambrose said.

He stalked away and regret carved into her. She should not have brought up Avery. Ambrose must find talking about her death deeply upsetting. This was a big day for Ambrose, the beginning of a new collection, and she was ruining it with her questions.

Marissa strode to Jack, guilt and annoyance pinging at her. "I was talking to Ambrose and I upset him. It was almost like he felt guilty about Avery. Which makes no sense. He isn't any more responsible than me."

Jack folded his arms. "You think Ambrose knows something he hasn't told the police."

Ambrose had been overly defensive and perhaps Jack's questions were getting to her and making her question herself. "I'm starting to think he knows something and feels bad about it." The words tumbled from her mouth and she was caught off guard at how true they were. Her instincts were telling her that Ambrose knew something about Avery's death. "It's not what he said that makes me wonder, it was how he said it. He was so upset."

Marissa's name was called. She looked over her shoulder. "I have to go. We'll talk about this more later." A squeeze of his hand and she hurried onto the set.

Jack hadn't put together the pieces, but Ambrose was involved with Avery's death. He knew who had killed her, or maybe he had a suspicion. Now that Marissa had spoken to him, he would be on edge. Would he unknowingly or intentionally tell the killer that Marissa was suspicious? If he did, it could bring another round of attacks against Marissa.

The killer was in their circle: either their social circle or their professional one.

Half the set was being used to photograph the models and the other half was set up for the gators. Jack could hear the gators moving in their steel cages. They sounded angry. He would be, too. The handlers were working with one of the gators, trying to move it into position and under the lights.

It wasn't a great idea to work with the gators in this setting. Shots of them in the wild would be more practical and safer at a distance.

Ambrose was watching the photo shoot, standing behind the photographer's lights. His shoulders were tight and he tapped his foot impatiently. Abruptly, he turned and left the set.

Jack followed him, staying out of sight.

Ambrose was talking on his cell phone, but Jack couldn't hear what he was saying. The man paced in a small circle, irritation wafting off him. After several minutes, he tucked his phone into his pants pocket and strode toward the area with the gators. Alarm zipped through Jack.

Jack jogged toward the cages. Ambrose was standing on top of one, a determined expression on his face. One of the gators slithered out of the cage and began running in Marissa's direction.

The screams of alarm were second to the sound of things smashing and breaking as the gator charged wildly, his tail hitting everything in his path. Lights on stands, the set, props and tables, tossed and overturned.

Jack saw a dart gun attached to the side of the cage. Ambrose had disappeared. Jack picked up the dart gun. He had never used one before. Was it as accurate as a gun? He could hit someone else. No time to waver, he aimed at the gator and shot three times. The gator made a rumbling sound and whipped its tail, smashing chairs and a half empty rack of clothing to pieces. Two of the gator's caregivers had realized what had occurred and approached with nets and wire, trying to subdue the reptile.

Jack didn't see Marissa. Most of the staff and models had fled.

He sprinted to her dressing room. It was empty. Where had she gone? Ambrose was also missing.

"Marissa!" Jack called.

The gator's handlers were working with it to bring it back to its cage. The other gators were beating their tails, agitated about the situation.

Jack's feet were moving before he realized his destination.

Ambrose was holding Marissa with one hand, trying to force her against the gator cage. The gator was slamming his jaws against the metal, desperate to escape.

"Ambrose!" Jack said.

Ambrose looked up and the distraction cost him. Marissa broke free and rushed to Jack. Jack put her behind him. "What are you doing?" Jack asked.

Ambrose was sweating. He wiped his forehead. "She tried to kill me. Like she tried to kill Avery."

"I saw you release the gator. Give it up, Ambrose, and step away from the gators," Jack said.

Ambrose was panting. "It won't end this way. I can't go to prison." He unlatched the gator's cage.

Jack reached for his gun, expecting the gator to rush forward.

Instead, it turned on Ambrose and attacked. Marissa turned her head away. One of the gator handlers shot the gator with a dart.

Jack led Marissa away, trying to block out the sound of Ambrose's screams.

At the police station, after giving their statements, Jack had compared the drawing from Avery's closet and the drawing the police had seized from Ambrose's house as evidence against him. Though the designs were different, the creator was one and the same. A student in Ambrose's fashion design class had drawn both. When Avery figured out that Ambrose was stealing designs from his students, she demanded he give credit to his students.

He'd killed her for it. Ambrose had wanted the success and fame. He wasn't about to share the spotlight, or the financial windfall.

Avery's death had been a crime of passion. Ambrose believed that Marissa had witnessed something backstage connecting him to Avery's murder and he had hired professionals to silence her. Clarice had made the connections between the designs as well and had confronted Ambrose.

Ambrose had been willing to kill again and again to protect his empire.

His lies had cost him; he'd lost big, too. The gator attack has caused the loss of his leg. When he was released from the hospital, he would be charged with Avery and Clarice's murders and with the attempted murder of Marissa Walker.

Another of the security guards had driven Marissa home. With Ambrose under arrest and in the hospital, Jack wasn't needed. Marissa would be safe without him.

The idea struck him hard.

His phone beeped with a message from Abby. Rob had been discharged from the hospital. He was recovering in a rehabilitation facility for his drug and gambling addictions.

Jack parked in Marissa's garage and entered the house. He found Marissa sitting on the balcony outside her kitchen. She held a glass of wine in her hand as she stared at the moon.

She glanced up when he opened the door. "Room for one more?"

"Always. Come on out," she said.

Jack stepped onto the wood balcony. "My boss called. Wanted to know when I'll have this wrapped up. He has another assignment in mind for me."

Marissa swirled her wineglass. "What did you tell him?"

"That I need to see about a few things. Like if you would consider being a farmer's wife."

Marissa inclined her head. "A farmer's wife?"

"I want to move back to Missouri. I want to work on my family's farm and for you to live with me. We could travel when you had a job, but home wouldn't be New York City. I love you, Marissa, and I can't pretend that going back to work as an operative will make me happy. You make me happy. Being with you makes me happy."

"A slower life?" Marissa asked.

Jack nodded. It was hard to read her. Was she into the idea? Thinking of a way to reject him?

"With time to paint?" she asked.

He nodded a second time and knelt on the wood next to her.

She broke into a million-dollar smile. “The next stage of my life with the man I love? I love you, Jack. I’m ready for my next adventure with you.”

* * * * *

Don’t miss these other suspenseful stories by C.J. Miller:

SPECIAL FORCES SEDUCTION
DELTA FORCE DESIRE
GUARDING HIS ROYAL BRIDE
THE SECRET KING
TRAITOROUS ATTRACTION

Available now from Harlequin Romantic Suspense!

Edith Beaulieu is supposed to be getting the Coltons' former estate ready for its mysterious new owners when a series of accidents puts her in harm's way—and pushes her into ex-marine River Colton's arms!

Read on for a sneak preview of THE COLTON MARINE by Lisa Childs, *the next thrilling installment of* ***THE COLTONS OF SHADOW CREEK.***

"You overheard enough to realize that he'd make me fire you."

"Oh, I know that," he heartily agreed. "What I don't know is why you wouldn't want to fire me." Was it possible—Could she be as attracted to him as he was to her? He'd caught her glances whenever he went without a shirt. Had he just imagined her interest?

"So do you want me to fire you?" she asked.

"No." And it wasn't just because he still wanted to search for those rooms. It was because of her—because he wanted to keep spending his days with her. "I told you that I need this job."

"You don't need this job," she said, as her dark eyes narrowed slightly with suspicion. "With your skills, you can do anything you want to do."

"Really?" he asked.

"Yes," she said. "Your injury is not holding you back at all."

It was, though. If he didn't have the scars and the missing eye, he might have done what he wanted to do sooner. "So you really think I can do anything I want?"

She sighed slightly, as if she was getting annoyed with him. "Yes, I do."

So he reached up and slid one arm around her waist to draw her tightly against him. Then he cupped the back of her head in his free hand and lowered her face to his.

And he kissed her.

Her lips were as silky as her skin and her hair. He brushed his softly across them.

She gasped, and her breath whispered across his skin. With her palms against his chest, she pushed him back but not completely away. His arm was still looped around her waist. "What are you doing?" she asked.

"You told me I can do anything I want," he reminded her, and his voice was gruff with the desire overwhelming him. "This is what I want to do—what I've wanted to do for a long time." Ever since that first night he'd heard her scream and found her in the basement with her pepper spray and indomitable spirit.

Her lips curved into a slight smile. "I didn't mean this…"

But she didn't protest when he tugged her back against him and kissed her again. Instead she kissed him, too, her lips moving against his, parting as her tongue slipped out and into his mouth.

HRSEXP0617

Love the Harlequin book you just read?

Your opinion matters.

Review this book on your favorite book site, review site, blog or your own social media properties and share your opinion with other readers!